Praise for V. M. Burns and *The Plot Is Murder*

"A promising debut with a satisfying conclusion."

—*Publishers Weekly*

"Cozy mystery readers and historical novel aficionados will adore this warm-hearted, cleverly plotted new series."

—*Kings River Life*

"V. M. Burns is off to a fantastic start."

—*Escape with Dollycas*

"This debut cleverly integrates a historical cozy within a contemporary mystery. In both story lines, the elder characters shine; they are refreshingly witty and robust, with formidable connections and investigative skills."

—*Library Journal* (starred review)

Books by V. M. Burns

Mystery Bookshop Mysteries

THE PLOT IS MURDER

READ HERRING HUNT

THE NOVEL ART OF MURDER

WED, READ & DEAD

Dog Club Mysteries

IN THE DOG HOUSE

THE PUPPY WHO KNEW TOO MUCH

BARK IF IT'S MURDER

Published by Kensington Publishing Corporation

Wed, Read & Dead

V. M. BURNS

KENSINGTON BOOKS
www.kensingtonbooks.com

KENSINGTON BOOKS are published by

Kensington Publishing Corp.
119 West 40th Street
New York, NY 10018

All Kensington titles, imprints, and distributed lines are available at special quantity discounts for bulk purchases for sales promotion, premiums, fund-raising, educational, or institutional use.

Special book excerpts or customized printings can also be created to fit specific needs. For details, write or phone the office of the Kensington Sales Manager: Kensington Publishing Corp., 119 West 40th Street, New York, NY 10018. Attn. Sales Department. Phone: 1-800-221-2647.

Kensington and the K logo Reg. U.S. Pat. & TM Off.

ISBN-13: 978-1-4967-1830-3 (ebook)
ISBN-10: 1-4967-1830-5 (ebook)
Kensington Electronic Edition: May 2019

ISBN-13: 978-1-4967-1829-7
ISBN-10: 1-4967-1829-1
First Kensington Trade Paperback Edition: May 2019

10 9 8 7 6 5 4 3 2 1

Printed in the United States of America

Acknowledgments

Special thanks to my agent, Dawn Dowdle, at Blue Ridge Literary Agency, and my editor, John Scognamiglio, and to all of the wonderful people at Kensington.

Thanks to the Cozy Mystery Crew and Unicorns for the support and encouragement. Thanks, love, and appreciation to my family, Benjamin Burns; Jackie, Christopher, and Jillian Rucker. I'm grateful for my work family, Chuck, Jill, Lindsey, and Tim, and our fearless leader, Sandy. I also need to thank my wonderful team (Amber, Derrick, Eric, Robin, Jennifer, and Jonathan) and the best trainers and greatest supporters ever (Tena, Jamie, Grace, and Deborah). Once a trainer, always a trainer.

Special thanks to friends Cassandra Morgan, Sophia Muckerson, and Shelitha Mckee for all of the help, encouragement, prayers, and straight talk.

As always, thanks to the Tribe. Thankfully, no dinosaurs or meteors were needed.

Chapter 1

"If you don't get your fanny out of that dressing room in the next thirty seconds, I'll come in and drag you out."

I recognized the tone in my grandmother's voice well enough to realize she meant business. Three hours of trying on every bubble-gum-pink bridesmaid dress in South Harbor's one and only wedding shop had left all of us in a foul mood. I took one last look at my reflection in the mirror and resigned myself to my fate. The hoopskirt under my ballroom gown was so large I had to turn sideways and wiggle to get through the dressing room door, but given this was the seventh or eighth dress I'd tried on, I had mastered the technique fairly well.

In the main viewing area at the back of the large store, I walked up the two stairs and stood atop the platform designed to look like a wedding cake to showcase the dresses to loved ones. I stood atop the platform of shame and waited for the laughter I knew was inevitable.

My timing was impeccable. Three other brides and their guests had just walked to the back of the store, so my audience had tripled since my last humiliation. I heard snickers and one guffaw from the store personnel. Initially, the sales consultants had contained their reaction much the same as the queen's guard outside of Buckingham Palace, not showing one iota of a smile. However, three dresses ago that all changed. Now, they smiled and snickered openly.

My grandmother, Nana Jo, and my mother, the impending bride and source of my current embarrassment, sat on a comfy sofa sipping champagne. Nana Jo had just taken a sip when she looked up and saw my latest ensemble.

Nana Jo snorted and champagne squirted from her nose. "You look like a giant pink piñata."

I turned and stomped down the stairs and headed back to my dressing room.

In between the laughter, my mom said in a confused voice, "I don't understand it. It looked so cute on the hanger."

I squeezed back into the dressing room, caring little if this satin and tulle monstrosity got snagged or not. My sales consultant helped me get out of the dress while she avoided making eye contact. I suspected a few of the chuckles I'd heard had come from her, although I couldn't be sure.

"Your mom has a very distinct taste." She picked the pink piñata off the floor and made sure it was returned to its protective plastic.

"You can say that again." I took a drink from the glass of champagne she'd snagged for me after I'd walked out in a hot pink version of the velvet draperies Scarlett O'Hara had fashioned into a ball gown in *Gone with the Wind*. "How many more?"

I should have been suspicious when she didn't respond and quickly turned away, but I was too busy texting my missing sister, Jenna, who'd managed to back out of today's humiliation by declaring she had an important legal brief to write. Her day would come and revenge would be sweet. When I turned around and saw the next fluffy pink concoction, I nearly spit *my* champagne. Instead, I grabbed the champagne bottle and took a long swig.

The eighth, *or was it ninth,* dress was a tight-fitting mermaid-style gown with a super tight sequined gold bodice layered to look like scales that went down my hips to my knees and then the fluffy tulle skirt expanded in waves into a long train of pink, which puddled at my feet. I didn't even bother looking in the mirror. One look at the sales consultant's face told me everything I needed to know. From her raised eyebrows to the twitching lips, I knew I looked absolutely ridiculous. I contemplated taking it off and refusing to wear it out of the dressing room, but it was the last one. I might as well get it over with.

Mermaid dresses looked great on tall women, but I was only about five feet three, so the tight part of the dress fell lower on me. The sequined upper part of the gown was so tight I couldn't open my legs to walk and had to shuffle out of the dressing room. Climbing the stairs to get atop the platform required the help of two sales consultants and a great deal of tilting on my part.

Nana Jo laughed so hard and so long, she started gasping for breath and tears rolled from her face. My mom just stared at me as though I truly had just crawled out of the sea.

"Look, we've been at this for over three hours. I'm tired and hungry and my patience has waned," I announced to anyone listening.

I was about to turn and shuffle back to the dressing room when I looked up and saw my mom's fiancé, Harold Robertson, and my friend-who-is-more-than-a-friend, Frank Patterson, gawking at me from behind my mom's chair.

"You're just hungry, dear. I'm sure you'll feel better after you eat something. That's why I invited Harold and Frank to meet us for lunch." Mom smiled.

I stared openmouthed into Frank's eyes and saw the look

of shock and mirth he tried to hide reflected back at me. I'd endured ridicule and degradation from my family and complete strangers, however, Frank Patterson was different. It had taken quite a while after my husband Leon's death before I was even ready to entertain the idea of a male friend, let alone a romantic relationship. So, I wasn't quite ready for Frank to see me in all of my mermaid glory.

I took a step backward in my haste to find a place to hide and tumbled off the back of the platform. My only consolation was if I'd still been wearing a ball gown with a *Gone with the Wind* hoopskirt, when I fell on my rear, my dress would have lifted like the rear hatch of my SUV. Instead, the long flowing train got wrapped around my feet and I lay trapped on my back like a mummy.

I didn't believe Nana Jo could have laughed harder, but she managed. After my first few seconds of stunned embarrassment, where I flopped and wiggled around on the floor like a fish out of water, Frank's arms went around my waist as he lifted me to my feet.

Once I was upright, I made the mistake of trying to walk and realized my legs were still trapped and nearly toppled over again. Thankfully, Frank was still there and grabbed me before I fell again. His soft brown eyes sparkled and his lips twitched as though a laugh was just seconds away.

"Laugh and you're a dead man," I whispered and gave him a look that had once brought a two-hundred-pound football player to tears when I taught in the public high schools.

The look worked, and Frank wiped the mirth off his face and helped the sales consultants untangle the fabric binding my feet. Once I was free, I turned and stomped, well, shuffled, back to the dressing room with as much dignity as I could muster. Oh, yes, my sister, Jenna, would pay dearly for leaving me to suffer alone.

Dressed, and in my own clothes, I marched out of the

dressing room to find my audience had dwindled down to a party of one, Frank Patterson.

"Where'd they go?" I looked around.

Frank opened his arms and engulfed me in a warm hug. "You look like you could use a hug."

I sighed and snuggled closely. I took a deep breath and released the tension that had built up in the past few hours. Frank owned a restaurant a few doors down from my North Harbor bookstore and he always smelled of coffee, bacon, herbal Irish soap, and red wine. I took a large sniff and felt the ripple of laughter rise up inside him.

"Let me guess, I smell like bacon and coffee?"

I took a big whiff. "Don't forget the Irish soap and red wine."

He laughed. "It's a good thing I don't serve liver."

My stomach growled. "I'm so hungry I'd probably eat it if you did. Where'd they go?"

He pulled away. "I told them we'd meet them at the Avenue."

I raised an eyebrow. "Let me guess, that was Harold's idea?"

"Actually, I think Grace suggested it. Your mom wants you to taste some pastries or cake or something."

I sighed. "I thought when they said they wanted a small wedding, it would be simple."

We walked to the front of the store and Frank held the door. "Small doesn't necessarily mean simple."

I should have known my mother well enough to know better. She'd always had *grand* taste. Nana Jo blamed my grandfather. He'd always referred to my mom as his little princess and she'd spent her entire life living up to it. My father had been equally guilty of perpetuating the princess mind-set. He'd done everything for her. When he died, she couldn't write a check or pump her own gas and she had never paid a single bill. Jenna and I spent quite a bit of time arranging her finances so her rent and utilities were automatically withdrawn. Jenna took away her credit cards and arranged for Mom to have a weekly allowance, which was the only way she seemed to grasp the concept of budgeting. Now, she'd met and fallen for Harold Robertson, one of the wealthiest families in Southwestern Michigan. Harold was a widower who seemed content to continue the princess legacy.

Frank drove us the short distance to the Avenue hotel, one of the finest hotels in South Harbor. The Avenue was an older building that sat atop the bluffs and looked out over the Lake Michigan shoreline. From a distance, the hotel looked grand and imposing. Up close and personal, the wear and tear of chipped paint, cracked marble floor tiles, and wallpaper that had once been white but was now yellow showed. The bones were there, but the building needed an update. Despite these shortfalls, the grand staircase that greeted guests at the entry was still quite impressive.

Guests entering the building from the semicircular driveway found themselves on the landing and could ascend to the lobby or descend to the dining area. We spotted Mom and Nana Jo and followed the downward path to the restaurant. Waiters hovered around in red livery with gold braids and black pants. Frankly, it seemed a bit much for lunch, in my opinion, but my mom loved it and smiled brightly at the young freckle-faced youth who brought her iced tea.

"Are you sure you're warm enough, Grace?" Harold took my mother's hand and stared into her eyes.

Mom shivered and looked into Harold's eyes like a lost fawn in a vast forest. "It is rather chilly, but I don't like to be a bother."

Harold hopped up and removed his jacket. With a flourish, he draped his suit coat around her shoulders. Then he turned and got the attention of a passing waiter. "Can you please see the heat is turned up?"

The waiter practically snapped to attention and hurried off to see the heat was increased.

Before Harold was settled back into his seat, the manager came to the table, apologized for the inconvenience, and offered a complementary hotel blanket to go over her lap, and another log was added to a nearby fireplace.

I felt drenched just watching all of the activity.

Nana Jo picked up a menu and fanned herself. "Grace it's an oven in here. Your hormones must be out of whack. You need the patch."

Mom ignored her mother, a skill she'd honed over the decades, and I removed my cardigan and drank a half glass of ice water to help lower my core temperature.

Ignoring Nana Jo wasn't an easy task. She was tall, loud, and very opinionated. Few people would recognize Grace Hamilton as a relative, let alone the only child of Josephine Thomas. Nana Jo was tall, while my mom was petite, barely five feet tall. Nana Jo was about a hundred fifty pounds heavier than Mom, who weighed an even one hundred pounds. However, the two women were alike in their ability to annoy and aggravate their children.

Lunch itself was uneventful, apart from seeing the attention the hotel and restaurant waitstaff dedicated to Harold and consequently to Harold's guests. Harold Robertson was a tall, white-haired, bearded man who was one of the only people I had ever met I would describe as *jolly*. He had been a successful aeronautical engineer with NASA for over forty years. However, his brain power wasn't the reason the waitstaff were falling over themselves to ensure his every wish was fulfilled. Harold's claim to fame in Southwestern Michigan was that he had the good sense to be born into one of the wealthiest families in either North or South Harbor. Robertson's Department Store had been the premiere store in this area for over one hundred years. The store catered to the lakeshore elite. As a child, I remembered the grand building with its high ceilings, crystal chandeliers, and marble columns. Even though we couldn't afford to shop on the upper floors, I remembered the red-coated doormen and elevator operators. My excursions to Robertson's were limited to the bargain basement. The store had weathered the economic downturn of North Harbor better than most and had only closed its doors completely about ten years ago. In fact, I went to the liquidation sale, expecting to finally buy things like furs and jeweled evening gowns like the ones I'd dreamt about as a child. Unfortunately, the old building had lost its charm. I was underwhelmed and depressed by the yellowed, peeling wallpaper, the threadbare carpets, and the smell of mothballs that assaulted my senses when I stepped through the door. The world had changed, but Robertson's had failed to adapt. The old cage-styled elevators were a fallback to a time that no longer existed.

Harold inherited the store and the family fortune, but he had pursued his dreams by becoming an engineer with NASA. He'd only returned after his wife became ill and he wanted to be close to family. He nursed her until she took her last breath. He now seemed dedicated to caring for my mom in much the same way.

I couldn't help but smile as I watched the way he catered to her every whim. No detail was too small.

Nana Jo leaned close and whispered in my ear, "I wonder how she manages to find men who fall over themselves to make her happy."

I shrugged. "Luck, I guess."

Nana Jo snorted. "Luck, my big toe. More like a curse, if you ask me." She shuddered. "Who wants that kind of attention?"

I agreed with Nana Jo. Harold's constant attention, no matter how well-meaning, would drive me batty. However, my mother was a different breed.

"I prefer a man with more spunk, someone you can argue with." She laughed. "You should have seen some of the fights your grandpa and I had." She gazed off into the distance. "Makes a marriage stronger." She tsked. "Of course, then you get the fun of making up." She guffawed.

"Nana Jo, I don't want that image in my brain." I shook my head as if trying to erase an Etch A Sketch.

She laughed.

Lunch was tasty. Good food and a glass of wine restored my humor. After lunch, we ate cake. In fact, cake was the main reason Mom wanted us to eat at The Avenue. The pastry chef presented us with samples from three different cakes as possible choices for the reception.

The pastry chef was a tiny little woman with electric-blue hair. She presented the first sample. "This is a chocolate almond cake with raspberry mousse filling topped with chocolate ganache." She watched our faces as we tasted.

"This is delicious. Chocolate cake is my favorite." Harold's eyes sparkled, but then he turned to my mother. "What do you think, Grace?"

Mom took a small bite and then washed it down with a long drink of water. "It's very good, and I know a lot of people like chocolate, but . . . well, I was hoping for something a little more . . . well, unique."

Harold promptly nodded in agreement. "Of course, you're right. It's delicious, but you can eat chocolate cake anywhere. A wedding is a special occasion." He gazed at my mother as though she was the first person to entertain the idea the earth was round.

For the second tasting, we were presented with a white cake. "This is a traditional white cake with vanilla mousse filling and white fondant topping."

I'd never quite understood if you're supposed to eat fondant. It made the cake look nice and smooth, but it wasn't the tastiest topping I'd ever had. This one was no exception.

Based on the look on my mom's face, she wasn't a fan of this one either. "White is definitely traditional, but not very unique, is it?"

I agreed with her on that one.

The third tasting was presented. "This is a pink champagne cake with a filling of rum-infused custard and whipped cream frosting."

"Hmm. That's good stuff." Nana Jo licked her fork.

Harold turned to see my mom's reaction so he could know what his opinion should be.

Mom took a bite and smiled. "I really like the pink, don't you, Harold? It will go with the color scheme."

The cake wasn't the bubble gum color my mom seemed to like best, but it was definitely pink. Regardless of the cake's color, it was by far the tastiest of the selections. The chef explained she used champagne in place of water for the cake. I struggled to think of anything that wouldn't taste good if it was doused in champagne.

Cake choice made, we moved on to the ballroom, which was massive. The crystal chandeliers and marble columns, with views of Lake Michigan from nearly every window, would be an ideal space for a large wedding.

"Grace, I thought you wanted a small wedding? You could hog-tie cattle in this room," Nana Jo said.

Mom fluttered her hands around. "Well, we want to make sure the guests have room to dance, but maybe you're right."

"Our library can accommodate up to thirty-six guests comfortably and the patio could be used for cocktails," the manager continued his sales pitch.

"Well, this room isn't big enough to cuss a cat," Nana Jo said.

Frank whispered in my ear, "How much space does it take to cuss a cat?"

I shrugged. "Beats me. None of us have one."

"What do you think, Sam?" Mom asked.

"I agree with Nana Jo."

The manager looked as though he was about to provide all of the sales features for the library, but I'd beat him to the punch.

"The ballroom is too big. The library is too small. The—"

"If you say, there's a room that's just right, I'll gag." Nana Jo stuck her finger in her mouth but thankfully didn't actually gag.

"Actually, I was going to say the library is too small for the reception, but it might make a nice place for a family breakfast."

"Oh, what a wonderful idea," Mom said with such amazement the compliment made me question when was the last time I'd had a wonderful idea.

I mumbled, "I do get good ideas every decade or so."

Frank chuckled until he saw the look my mom shot my way and then coughed to cover up his laughter.

We reserved the library for a family breakfast and avoided the manager's sales pressure to reserve the ballroom to ensure it would be available. His "I'm only looking out for your best interest" suggestion would require a nonrefundable thousand-dollar deposit, which Harold was glad to pay, but Nana Jo's Midwestern frugal nature refused to concede.

"I have to get back to work," I said.

"I'd better go with you." Nana Jo grabbed her purse.

"Well, if you must go." Mom fluttered and looked around in the "I'm so helpless" way she had.

However, Nana Jo and I were immune.

"Yep, we gotta go. See you tonight at Frank's place for the family dinner. We'll talk then." Nana Jo gave mom a kiss on the cheek and hurried out of the door mumbling, "Once I've had a glass of whiskey to steady my nerves."

"Don't be late to dinner tonight," my mom yelled at our retreating backs as we made a quick exit out the door.

Despite my frustration with shopping for bridesmaid dresses, I wouldn't have missed tonight's *family* dinner for all of the fish in Lake Michigan. Tonight, my mom and Harold were introducing the two families. I didn't know a lot of truly rich people. This would be my chance to see how the other half lived. Plus, it would allow me to be nosy and learn what I could about my mom's intended.

Frank drove us back to my car, and I drove the short distance over the bridge from South Harbor to North Harbor. All of the one-way streets downtown South Harbor made the drive about two miles total. However, the differences between North Harbor and South Harbor felt like the twin cities were separated by more than a bridge. The two cities shared the same Lake Michigan shoreline but were light-years apart. South Harbor was affluent and thriving, with cobblestone streets, a bustling downtown, and beachfront property both on the beach and on the bluffs above the Lake. In contrast, North Harbor had abandoned and burned-out buildings and boarded-up houses and downtown offered very little foot traffic. There was a small area of renovated buildings, bakeries, art galleries, and cafés, which were trying to revitalize the economy and bring people back downtown. My bookstore, Market Street Mysteries, was one of those. The brick brownstone stood on a corner lot with a parking lot shared with a church. There was an alley that ran behind the buildings, and I was fortunate to have a garage. The previous owner built a fence to connect the garage to the building, probably in an attempt to keep the homeless and late-night bar hoppers from trespassing. However, the result was it created a nice courtyard area where my dogs, Snickers and Oreo, loved to play. The garage had an upstairs studio apartment my assistant, Dawson Alexander, called home.

Nana Jo and I entered the store through the back. There was a glass door that led up a flight of stairs to the right. Snickers and Oreo must have heard us coming because they were waiting at the bottom of the stairs. The two chocolate toy poodles pounced and barked their greeting. I hurried to let them out to keep the noise down while Nana Jo went through to help Dawson take care of the Christmas crowds. This was my first Christmas season, and I'd been pleasantly surprised by the traffic we'd received so far.

December in Southwest Michigan was cold and snowy. Christmas was only a few weeks away, and the wind off Lake Michigan was harsh and bitterly cold. Snickers, the older of the two poodles, true to her nature, stepped over the threshold, squatted and took care of business quickly, and hurried back inside to heat and warmth. Despite the red and green Christmas sweater she wore, she didn't like the cold and would just as soon have taken care of her bio needs inside as out. Oreo, on the other hand, had a more carefree, frolicking nature. He leapt into the air and tried to catch snowflakes. He was halfway across the yard before he realized his paws and his underbelly were cold. He then hurried to the back door, expecting to be let back inside. After ten years of Michigan winters, you would expect him to have caught on that snow was cold. Unfortunately, he was a slow learner. Snickers and I coldheartedly stood our ground and watched him through the glass until he hurried to the corner of the fence, hiked his leg, and heeded the call of nature. Snickers looked up at me as though to say, *Remind me again why you wanted a second dog?* I shrugged and opened the door to admit him as he bounded inside. He shook, scattering wet snow around the room, and then pounced, getting my jeans wet. I pulled the towel I kept at the back door off its hook and cleaned as much snow from his underside and legs as I could before letting him down. The static from the towel made the hair on his ear flaps stand out, and I smiled. Oreo might not be the brightest member of our pack, but his zeal and energy always put a smile on my face.

I went upstairs to the area I'd converted into a loft where I now lived. I grabbed a couple of dog biscuits from the jar I kept on the counter and tossed them into the dogs' beds and then hurried downstairs to help.

Each time I went into my bookstore, I was overcome with joy. Owning my own mystery bookstore had been a dream my husband and I shared. After his untimely death just over a year ago, I fulfilled my promise to him to sell our house and take the insurance money and live out our dream. Death of a loved one helped to put things into perspective. For me, Leon's death reminded me life was too short not to be happy. So, I quit my job as an English teacher at the local high school, sold the house Leon and I had lived in, and bought the brownstone we'd walked by and dreamed of one day owning. It was bittersweet to live the dream without him by my side, but, over the past year, I'd found a host of friends and family who helped to fill the void.

The store was bustling and Nana Jo was running the cash register. My assistant, Dawson Alexander, was stocking a shelf. Dawson was the quarterback for the Michigan Southwest University Tigers, or MISS YOU as the locals called it. He was tall and slender; the MISU trainers asked him to "bulk up." So, he'd gained over twenty pounds of pure muscle, which was helpful on the football field and also came in very handy for hoisting boxes of books. The fact Dawson loved to bake, and was exceptionally good at it, provided the conduit for some of the weight gain. Unfortunately, I suspected I too had gained a good ten pounds since he started working here and baking all sorts of sweet, delicious items.

Market Street Mysteries wasn't on the same level as big-box stores, but business was steady and that was enough to keep the lights on. My staff consisted of my grandmother, Nana Jo, who refused to accept a salary; Dawson, who rented the studio apartment above my garage and I paid a small salary, which he more than earned by providing baked goods; and my twin nephews, Christopher and Zaq, when they were on break from college, which thankfully, would be in a few days.

Dawson, Nana Jo, and I worked steadily for the remainder of the afternoon. When my older sister, Jenna, walked in, I looked at the time and realized we'd been working nonstop for four hours. It was time to close shop and it wasn't until I sat down that I realized how tired I was.

"You owe me big-time." I glared at my sister, who stared innocently and fluttered her eyelashes.

"I have no idea what you mean."

I pulled out my cell phone and swiped until I came to the selfies I'd snapped before I gave up and delegated the task to my sales consultant.

Jenna looked at the pictures and tried to keep from laughing but failed and eventually gave up and laughed long and hard.

Nana Jo and Dawson looked over her shoulder. Nana Jo had seen the originals but still laughed at the shots as much as Dawson and Jenna.

"Great. Laugh, but I won't be alone in those pink concoctions. Just remember that." I pointed at my sister.

"*Your mother* is crazy if she thinks I'm wearing any of these clown dresses." Jenna handed back my cell phone. It was always *your mother* when Mom was being demanding or irritating.

"I don't understand how she thinks she's going to plan a wedding in three weeks." I hoisted myself out of the chair and went to the back and got the broom. After sitting for just a few minutes, my joints felt tired. I knew if I continued sitting, I'd never get the store cleaned and ready for tomorrow.

Christmas was just three weeks away, and my mother was getting married on Christmas Eve. I tried not to stress out about all of the things that needed to happen in the next three weeks. Bubble-gum-pink-piñata-gone-with-the-wind-mermaid dresses were just the tip of the iceberg. Unlike most brides, who spent over a year planning the perfect wedding, my mother told us just two weeks ago she was getting married on Christmas Eve. Thinking about everything that needed to happen made me want to scream. I must have looked like a crazy woman.

"Don't worry about cleaning, Mrs. W. We'll take care of that." Dawson took the broom from my hands and held out a chair.

I stared. "Who's we?"

The bell that chimed whenever someone entered the store jingled and Jillian Clark and Emma Lee entered the store.

"Hello, Mrs. Washington," both girls said.

Emma Lee gave Jenna a hug. "We knew you'd be tired after wedding shopping." She took off her coat and placed it over the bar at the back of the store.

Emma was a petite Southern belle with long, dark hair and almond-shaped eyes that showcased her Asian heritage. Emma was a student at MISU and was dating my nephew, Zaq. At about five feet tall and one hundred pounds, Emma was often dwarfed by my nephew's six-feet frame. When the two were together, he towered over her, but the two didn't seem to notice or care.

"We would have been here earlier, but I had a rehearsal." Jillian placed her coat on the bar next to Emma's and went to the back to get a duster.

Dawson followed her, and I couldn't help but smile. He and Jillian were a couple, and he followed her so they could have a few moments alone.

Jillian was the granddaughter of one of Nana Jo's friends,

Dorothy Clark. She had a tall, slender body and walked with the grace that only a ballerina possessed. She had dark eyes and dark, frizzy hair, which she'd tried to tame by braiding and pinning to her head tonight. However, several curly tendrils refused to be contained and created lovely curls on the sides of her head.

When Jillian and Dawson returned, she was wearing an apron and proceeded to dust. "Now, you better go upstairs and get dressed or you'll be late for the party."

I looked at my watch. "You're right."

"Shake a leg." Nana Jo hurried to the steps. For a woman in her seventies, who was a couple inches under six feet and well over two hundred fifty pounds, my grandmother was still pretty spry. It probably had something to do with her yoga and aikido classes. She was a brown belt.

I followed at a slower pace. This was the first opportunity any of us, my mother included, had had to meet Harold's family. I knew she was nervous and, despite the humiliation she planned for me in a pink bridesmaid gown, I wanted to make a good impression.

I showered and dressed in a vintage print A-line, high-waist dress. The top was navy with three-quarter-length sleeves and a scoop neck, while the skirt had a bold navy and white floral imprint. Since I'd started writing historic British cozy mysteries, I'd found myself drawn to clothes from the late 1930s and early 1940s, the period I wrote about. The dress had a vintage feel, without being too kitschy. I had a pair of navy heels that matched the outfit perfectly. The dinner was only a few blocks away, which was the only reason I dared wear the shoes in the middle of winter in Michigan. Plus, Frank promised to make sure the sidewalk from my store to his restaurant was not only free of ice and snow but was well salted.

When I came out to the main living space, Jenna and her husband, Tony, were sitting at the large dining room table with their sons, Christopher and Zaq. The twins were dressed in dark jeans with white shirts and jackets. Despite the fact that the twins were dressed in similar items of clothing, their personal style showed through, distinguishing each boy. Christopher was serious with a preppy style, while Zaq was the techie and tended to be nerdier in the way he dressed. Tonight, that was obvious from the tweed jacket and bow tie Zaq wore. Christopher looked dapper with a solid-color suit jacket and tie. Only when I got close enough to hug him and took a good look at the tie, did I realize what I had initially mistaken for a paisley print was actually a skull and crossbones.

I hugged my nephew. "Nice tie."

"Thanks, Aunt Sammy." Christopher bent down to hug me.

"Don't encourage him," Jenna said.

Tony shook his head. He was a man of few words.

I looked around. "Where's Dawson?"

Jenna tore a page from a catalog.

"What are you doing?" I walked over and picked up the page.

"You'll thank me." She smiled and ripped another page from the catalog I'd just recognized was one of my favorite stores.

"Not likely. I just got that catalog today and I haven't even had a chance to look at it." I picked up the other pages she'd ripped out and scattered across the table. "What are these?"

"Potential bridesmaid dresses." She smiled. "I'm not wearing that pink crap you tried on today." She cocked her head to the side and looked at another picture but must have decided against it and flipped to the next page. "Besides, we don't have time to get any of those dresses altered and delivered in three weeks. We're going to order nice dresses or suits that we won't be ashamed to be seen in public with and can wear for more than a few hours."

I picked up the pages again. "I'm sold, but how are you going to convince *your* mother?"

"Simple. I'll just tell her I saw it in a fancy magazine and it's the latest thing for the twenty-first century." She folded the pulled pages and put them in her purse. "The boys will need interview suits, so they'll be fine." She looked at her sons.

Nana Jo came out of her bedroom dressed in a royal-blue pantsuit with rhinestones around the neck and cuffs. Her statuesque build and auburn hair looked stunning.

The boys whistled. "Looking good, Nana Jo."

"Thank you. Thank you." She twirled. "Now, let's go so we can get this party started before your mother has a cow. She's texted me at least four times reminding me not to be late."

I realized I'd left my cell phone in the bedroom and hurried to get it. Sure enough, I had several messages from Mom too.

We bundled up for the short walk down the street. Dawson looked as though he'd rather have a root canal but helped Jillian with her coat.

"Dawson, can I talk to you for a minute?" I stood back to allow the others to pass. "You all go on ahead. We'll catch up."

Jillian smiled and hurried downstairs with the others. Dawson lingered back, head down.

"Is anything bothering you?" I asked.

He shook his head but avoided looking at me.

I waited. Years as an English teacher in public schools taught me the power of silence and it didn't fail me this time either.

"I just feel awkward. I mean, this is a family dinner and I'm not family. You've all been really kind to me, but I was thinking your mom might not want me there."

I suspected this was the problem. Leon and I had never been blessed with children but, in the months since Dawson moved into the garage loft, I'd come to view him as the son I'd never had. He'd never known his mother, and his father was, last I heard, in prison. When Alex Alexander wasn't in jail, he was an abusive alcoholic. I prayed for the right words to say. I looked at Snickers and Oreo, who'd been fed, let out to take care of business, and were waiting for me to leave and drop their dog treats on the floor, a ritual whenever I left. "Family is about more than blood and shared DNA." I picked up Snickers. "I've had this dog since she was six weeks old. She's twelve and has a bad heart, but she's still my baby. If anyone tried to hurt her, I'd . . ." I swallowed the lump that rose in my throat. "I don't know what I'd do, but she's my baby." I looked up. "I may not have given birth to you, but I've come to look at you like a son. I care about you just as much as I care about Christopher and Zaq." I looked at Dawson and saw his eyes fill with tears. "We consider you a part of our family. Families aren't finite. When Jenna married Tony, he became a part of our family. When my mother marries Harold, our family will expand again, and each time someone special enters one of our lives, we expand and make room in our hearts. My mom invited you because she looks upon you as family. I can't force you to come, but you are welcome."

Tears streamed down his face, and I reached up and hugged him. We stood that way for several minutes until Snickers squirmed her way up and started to lick away Dawson's tears. He made the mistake of laughing. When he opened his mouth, she stuck her tongue in.

"Eww, plagh, ick. She got me." He tried to wipe the dog kiss out of his mouth.

I put Snickers down and reached in my purse for the bottle of Listerine spray I kept for just such situations as this.

He sprayed his tongue and Snickers made a deliberate maneuver to sit with her back to Dawson. He laughed. "I think I hurt her feelings." He picked her up and gave her a hug, careful to keep his mouth well out of reach of her tongue.

For several seconds, she turned her head and refused his friendly overtures. Eventually, he found the right spot on her stomach and scratched while she closed her eyes and leaned back against his chest.

"Do you two need a moment alone?" Jillian joked from the bottom of the stairs.

Dawson put Snickers down and gave Oreo, who had been waiting patiently by the biscuit jar, a pat. He then reached into the jar and pulled out a couple of dog biscuits and tossed them down for the poodles. I picked up the remote and turned on the jazz station so they would have something to listen to while we were out, and we all made our exits while they were distracted with treats.

North Harbor Café was just down the street from my bookstore and the cold December night meant we wouldn't linger to look in store windows along the way. Frank's restaurant had a reputation for good food and drinks and business had been doing very well since he'd opened. The crowds standing and waiting for seats were a testament to its popularity with the locals.

We waved at the hostess as we passed on our way to the back of the restaurant and walked up the stairs. I glanced back at the looks we received from some of those waiting. While the upstairs of my building had long ago been converted into a loft apartment, Frank's restaurant was not. One day, he planned to open the upstairs for dining, but for now, it was closed off and only opened for private parties.

The rumble from a multitude of conversations and televisions mingled with laughter and the clang of plates and glasses followed us through the restaurant and wafted up the stairs. As we climbed, the noise from below grew fainter. The first-floor ceiling was high, so we had to climb quite a few steps to make it to the second floor. I'd accounted for the walk in heels from my store but had neglected to account for the trek up Mount Everest. In tennis shoes or flats, I could have made the climb like a pro. In three-inch heels it was an adventure. At the top of the stairs, I stopped to get my breath. I expected to be assaulted by the same noise level I'd encountered on the first floor. However, the silence hit me like a ton of bricks. The contrast between the noisy lower level and the funerary silence upstairs was jarring, and I felt disoriented. I looked around to get my bearings and reorient myself.

There were less than twenty people milling around. After less than a minute, it was clear there were two distinct camps. The Robertsons huddled on one side of the room. The Hamilton clan was on the other.

Dawson leaned close and whispered a quote from *The Lord of the Rings: The Two Towers,* one of my favorite movies, in my ear, " 'You'll find more cheer in a graveyard.' "

Frank Patterson walked up to me and handed me a glass of champagne and kissed me on the cheek. "I think you're going to need this."

I made eye contact with Jenna and looked the question, *What's going on?* She shrugged and inclined her head toward Nana Jo.

I walked over to my grandmother. Nana Jo was certainly no wallflower and could talk to anyone about anything. I was shocked she hadn't extended an olive branch and crossed the chasm that separated the two families. "What's going on?"

She sipped her champagne. "I used to believe I could talk to anyone, but those tight-lipped, hoity-toity aristocratic wannabes can kiss my grits." She tossed back the champagne and sauntered over to the drink table and picked up another glass.

I was so shocked I didn't hear Emma's approach until she

spoke. "Boy, you guys missed the sparks. I thought Nana Jo was going to drop-kick Harold's sister-in-law." She inclined her head slightly, and we glanced in that direction.

A middle-aged woman with dark eyes and dark hair in a black suit, with a matching fur coat and more jewelry than I'd seen on one person, stood near the window. She looked as though she was afraid to touch anything. Next to her stood a short, bald man with glasses. He was one of those nondescript men who blended in with their environment so well people never noticed them.

"I don't think I've ever seen that much jewelry before," Dawson said.

"Check out the fur coat," Jillian whispered.

"Full-length sable." Emma nodded knowingly. "My great-aunt Vivian Anne has one. Although if I didn't know better, I'd say this one is fake."

"She probably needs it to cover up that stick up her—"

"Nana Jo!" I turned and stared at my grandmother, who merely shrugged. "What on earth happened?"

There was silence for several minutes and then Nana Jo reluctantly explained. "I waltzed over to the Ice Princess over there and held out my hand and introduced myself." She took a sip of her champagne.

I waited for the rest.

"Frosty looks down her nose, sniffs, and refuses to shake my hand."

"Really?" I asked.

Emma and Nana Jo both nodded.

I stared openmouthed. "Maybe she . . ."

"Maybe she's deaf, dumb, blind, and was raised in a barn?" Nana Jo added.

I shook my head. "I can't think of any good reason for bad manners."

"There are no excuses for bad manners." Nana Jo finished

her champagne and exchanged her empty glass for mine and took a sip. "She looked down at me like Mr. Darcy looked at Mr. Collins in that movie you like to watch."

"*Pride and Prejudice,*" Emma, Jillian, and I all said together.

"Whatever." Nana Jo sipped my champagne. "I was madder than a wet hen and about to give that stuck-up ninny a piece of my mind when Harold and Grace strolled over. Harold was so excited and wanted to introduce Grace to his sister-in-law, Margaret." She stared daggers at Margaret across the room. "That uppity witch had the nerve to sneer at Grace as though she'd just pooped on her best shoes."

I was shocked by bad manners and poor breeding until I learned she'd snubbed my mom. "Really?" I could feel my eye start to twitch.

Jenna and the others had joined the group while Nana Jo was talking.

Jenna nodded. "That's not all. So, Harold introduces Mom and Margaret stares down and says, 'I thought you worked here,' as though Mom was a servant or something."

I raised an eyebrow, cocked my head to the side, and stared openly at the enemy. It was one thing for Jenna and me to mock our mother. We were entitled, but how dare this pretentious upstart think she was going to do anything to ruin my mother's happiness.

"Who's the man?" I asked.

"What man?" Nana Jo didn't even bother to look. "The marshmallow is Harold's brother, Oscar."

I turned to Frank. "Would you get me another glass of champagne, please."

He looked warily at me.

My brother-in-law, Tony, patted him on the back. "I've seen that look before. When a Hamilton woman gives you the look Sam just gave you, it's best to walk away. Do not pass Go. Do not collect two hundred dollars. Just walk away."

Frank started to speak, but Tony shook his head. "It's best not to know. Plausible deniability."

Frank nodded knowingly. Christopher and Zaq nodded and the four men walked away.

I glanced at my mom, who was standing near the center of the room. She looked as though she would burst into tears at any moment. Harold too looked as though he would weep. He petted and attended to my mother.

Jenna leaned close. "Okay, what's the plan?"

I looked at my sister. "What do you mean?"

"Don't give me that. I know my sister. When you start enunciating each and every syllable and you get that look in your eye, I know something's up and you have a plan. Now, spill it."

I shrugged. "No plan. Not yet anyway." I sighed. "Let's just provide as much support to Mom as we possibly can and get through this."

Everyone nodded, and we walked over to where my mom and Harold were to provide a wall of love and support.

Jenna held back and whispered in my ear, "So, we wait until it's over and then we slash her tires, right?"

I shook my head. "Nope. We wait until it's over and then we let Nana Jo shoot her. She can claim she thought it was a bear."

I walked over to the Ice Princess and introduced myself. "Hello, I understand you're Harold's sister-*in-law*." I emphasized the in-law. She looked as though she didn't appreciate the reminder she wasn't a direct descendent of the wealthy Robertson family. Score one for our side.

She stared down her nose at me, but I stood tall and straight and stared back. "Since we're going to be related, albeit by marriage, I wanted to introduce myself. My name is Samantha Washington. Grace Hamilton is my mother." I turned to my sister. "This is my sister, Jenna Rutherford."

Frank, Tony, and the twins walked over. Frank handed me a glass of champagne.

I took a sip. "And this is her husband, Tony. They're both attorneys." I didn't bother to wait for her to acknowledge them but continued on with my introductions. "These are Jenna and Tony's sons, Christopher and Zaq."

The boys bowed.

"We're so proud of them. They're both on the dean's list at Jesus and Mary University."

JAMU was to the Midwest what Harvard and Yale were to the East Coast. In fact, in some polls, JAMU actually ranked higher than the two prestigious Ivy League schools.

I turned to Dawson. "This is Dawson Alexander, he's the quarterback for the MISU football team and like a son to me."

Dawson bowed respectfully.

"Frank Patterson is the owner of this establishment and a very good friend." I noticed, with each introduction, my words became more clipped and my tone dropped. Unlike most people, when I was angry, I tended to get very quiet and enunciated more.

Frank inclined his head. "My pleasure."

"I think you've already met my grandmother, Josephine Thomas."

Nana Jo glared.

"Nana Jo recently returned from a performance in New York." I leaned forward and whispered conspiratorially, "She's a bit of a local celebrity."

Margaret's expression became shocked as she nodded to Nana Jo.

I looked around. "I can't forget our dear friends, Jillian Clark and Emma Lee. Jillian is a student at MISU. She sings, dances, and was just offered an internship with the Bolshoi Ballet for the summer."

Jillian blushed but stood tall and straight.

"And Emma Lee is a brilliant premed student at MISU. She comes from a long line of doctors." I turned to Emma. "Did you say there's been a doctor in every generation of your family for two hundred years or three hundred?"

Emma smiled. "Actually, it's four hundred."

"Of course, she can trace her family lineage back to the Mayflower." I looked around. "I think that's everyone." I stared at Oscar. "It's obvious you're Harold's brother. I can see the family resemblance."

He smiled and nodded but didn't say anything.

I turned to Margaret. "And you are?"

She hesitated and a flush rose up Margaret's neck and left her skin blotchy.

"I've heard so much about Southern charm. You are from the South, aren't you?" I added.

She gave a false nasally laugh. "Well, yes. Yes, I am. I'm from a small town in Virginia. I doubt you've heard of it. Few people have."

"Try me," I said.

She hesitated a few seconds.

"Sam used to be a teacher before she retired to start her own business," Jenna said.

Margaret plastered on a fake smile. "Lexington. I'm from Lexington."

"Lexington is where Washington and Lee University is. My uncle's the president of the university," Emma said with enthusiasm.

I smiled. "Emma *Lee,* you know, descendant of General Robert E. Lee . . . Washington and *Lee.*"

Emma laughed. "Well, we don't talk about that much, other than to mention how grateful we are he wasn't successful."

Harold walked over to our group. "Aren't you a relative of General Robert E. Lee too?"

Margaret laughed deprecatingly and fanned herself. "A distant relative . . . a very distant relative."

Harold muttered, "I could have sworn you said you were a descendant." He waited for an explanation, but none came.

Eventually, dinner arrived and we sat down to eat. Margaret barely said a word throughout the entire meal. However, we kept up a steady stream of conversation and ignored her. Mom no longer looked as though she would burst into tears at any moment, and we were on cruise mode. Engagement cake and coffee and we could get out of here. I breathed a sigh of relief too soon.

Margaret looked at her watch and leaned across the table. "What plans have you made for the wedding?"

Mom fluttered her hands. "Well, we haven't exactly nailed down our exact plans yet."

Margaret gasped. "Not nailed down your plans? But, I thought I understood you are getting married on Christmas Eve."

"We are getting married on Christmas Eve." Harold patted Mom's hand. "There are a lot of decisions to be made, but we've picked the cake and are close to picking the venue."

"Dear me." Margaret tsked. "I was afraid of this. The longer you wait, the less likely you are to get the *best* venues." She glanced around the room as though to say this was clearly not the best, and I had reached my fill when it came to swallowing my words.

"Are you implying there's something wrong with North Harbor Café?" I folded my napkin and stared at her. "Because if you are, I'm about two seconds from—"

No one got to hear what I was two seconds away from doing because, at that moment, a whirlwind came up the stairs wearing three-inch heels and a white suit with a white mink coat and matching hat. When she reached the top step, she stood for dramatic effect, shrugged out of her coat, tossed it over the railing, and announced, "No fear, Lydia Lighthouse is here."

We stared at the figure, but before we could figure out what on earth a Lydia Lighthouse was, Margaret hopped up from her seat. "Lydia, darling." She hurried over to the woman and the two air-kissed. Then Margaret turned to face the group. "When I heard my brother-in-law was planning to get married in a few weeks, I knew I'd find the perfect wedding present." She turned to the white-clad figure. "Lydia Lighthouse is the wedding planner for the elite. She's traveled all over the world and will be able to insure all of the *right* people are invited and the wedding will be in the society pages and best magazines." She paused as though waiting for applause. None came.

Lydia Lighthouse was my mom's height, slightly over five feet, but not by much. She was as thin as a rail and looked to be in her early fifties.

Nana Jo leaned close to me. "She's got on more makeup than a five-dollar hooker."

Lydia Lighthouse definitely wore a great deal of makeup and her false eyelashes were so long, it looked as though she had caterpillars on her eyelids. She had blue eyes, fair, pale skin, and her hair was bright red; she wore it pulled back under her mink cap. Lydia Lighthouse waltzed across the room, placed a white clutch handbag on the table, and pulled out a long cigarette holder and gold lighter.

"Is that a real cigarette?" I was stunned. It had been such a long time since I'd been around anyone who smoked a real cigarette, let alone inside a restaurant.

"Sure is." Nana Jo grinned.

Frank walked over to Lydia Lighthouse. He discretely whispered, but he might as well have saved his breath.

Lydia stared at him as though he'd just landed from an alien spaceship. "What do you mean I can't smoke inside? What kind of establishment is this?"

Frank gritted his teeth. "It's actually illegal to smoke inside of restaurants in this state."

Lydia made an elaborate motion of flinging her lighter down. She huffed and then collected herself and plastered on a smile. "Oh, well, when in Rome." She smiled. "Would you please get me a glass of champagne," she ordered rather than asked.

Frank hesitated for a moment but smiled and gestured to one of the waitstaff, who promptly brought the whirlwind a drink.

Unlit cigarette dangling from one hand and glass of champagne in the other, the whirlwind stood at the head of the table. "A toast."

Everyone stood and raised their glasses.

"To the happy couple, may they enjoy many years of wedded bliss." Lydia raised her glass.

We all raised our glasses and toasted Mom and Harold.

Lydia sipped her champagne.

"Who the hell are you?" Nana Jo asked the question that was dancing around inside all of our heads.

Lydia looked up in surprise. "I thought I'd introduced myself." She smiled and spoke loud and very slowly as though Nana Jo was hard of hearing and losing her faculties. "I'm Lydia Lighthouse."

Nana Jo narrowed her eyes and stared. "I heard you the first time you gave that ridiculous name. What I mean is *why* are you here? This is a private party. Who invited you?"

Lydia's smile froze and her icy-blue eyes grew as cold as Lake Michigan right before a storm.

Margaret must have noticed the temperature drop and a quick headcount had to tell her she was drastically outnumbered if a brawl started. She hurried to intervene. "I was just explaining that Lydia Lighthouse is the premiere wedding planner in the country and she's agreed to help plan Grace and Harold's wedding."

You could have heard a cricket chirp in the silence that followed.

"Now, who is the bride?" Lydia looked around the room. Her gaze rested on Emma and Zaq and her brow furrowed. "I always tell my couples how important breeding and pedigree are."

Emma colored and Zaq started to stand, but Emma restrained him. His eyes were stormy and he looked ready to explode.

I could see Jenna bristling. However, Lydia continued, oblivious to how close she was to being tossed out on her ear. "I breed Yorkies. You have to be really careful of the bitch because you never know what you'll get in the end." She laughed.

Nana Jo stood. "What in the name of God are you talking about and you'd best be careful because you're pretty close to getting stabbed." Nana Jo fingered her knife.

Lydia looked at Nana Jo, puzzled. "I was talking about the importance of breeding. Weddings are a union. What you put into this union will determine what you get out of it." She stared at Margaret, who looked embarrassed and blushed. "For example, my entire family is full of blue-eyed redheads with a fiery temper. Me, my brother, my husband, my parents, my grandparents—nothing but redheads. So, you always know what you're getting." She laughed, but when no one joined in, she sighed. "However, when you combine a loving, generous man and a sweet, caring woman, you will have a union that overflows with love and is able to survive anything."

Nana Jo sat down and muttered something that sounded like "crazy witch."

"Who's the bride?" Lydia looked around.

Mom raised a tentative hand. "I am."

Lydia waltzed over to my mother. "You just leave everything to Lydia. I'll make sure your wedding is the event North Harbor Michigan will never forget."

Chapter 2

"I'm not wearing that!" Jenna's voice took on the tone she used when she went into full-blown lawyer mode. Watching her was akin to watching an old-fashioned percolator when the coffee was ready, or the pressure cooker Nana Jo had many moons ago. It bubbled and bounced right before the lid blew off and exploded a chicken all over the kitchen.

"It will be perfect for a Christmas Eve wedding." Lydia ignored the rumble in Jenna's voice that signaled danger.

Nana Jo leaned close and whispered, " 'Danger, Will Robinson.' "

I raised an eyebrow and nodded. We both scooted forward in our chairs and made ourselves comfortable.

Lydia Lighthouse looked from Jenna to my mom. "What do you think, Grace? It's your wedding. You're the bride after all."

Mom looked like a deer caught in the headlights of a car. "I don't know . . . I think Jenna might have a point. I mean, tartan plaid does seem a bit . . . well, a bit too much like a theme wedding," she said softly.

"Theme?" Lydia huffed. "Excuse me. I was only trying to provide the best wedding I could on a shoestring budget and with zero timeline." She flung the tartan plaid monstrosity at her assistant, April.

"Five bucks says she puts on the waterworks next," Nana Jo whispered in my ear.

I nodded my acceptance of the bet.

Lydia pulled a handkerchief from her sleeve and turned her back. "I'm sorry if you don't like any of my ideas. I was just trying to make this wedding something the people of North Harbor would talk about for the next twenty years."

I reached in my pocket and pulled out a five-dollar bill and handed it to Nana Jo, who folded it and stuffed it down the front of her shirt.

"Lydia, I'm sorry. I didn't mean to upset you," Mom pleaded. "You're doing a fantastic job." She turned to Jenna. "Now, Jenna, maybe you could at least try it on. You may feel differently once you—"

"I will not. I refuse to try on that tablecloth, and I definitely will not be wearing anything that remotely resembles a tartan tablecloth. So, if that's what you want, then you'd better get Sam to wear it. I'll sit this one out," Jenna said with granite in her voice.

"Oh, no you don't." I sat up straight. "If Jenna isn't wearing the tablecloth, then I certainly won't be wearing it either."

"Girls, really. It's not a tablecloth." Mom walked over to April and took the dress and held it up.

Jenna paced, with her hands behind her back, twice around the area in the back of my store, where we were sitting, and then suddenly spun around and faced Nana Jo. "Do you or do you not have a tartan tablecloth."

Nana Jo nodded. "I do. I pull it out every Christmas."

Jenna turned and glanced from Mom to Lydia and then sat down. "I rest my case."

I had to stop myself from applauding. It was very Perry Mason–esque.

Lydia folded her arms across her chest. Her eyes were narrow slits and she practically fumed. She reminded me a great deal of Smaug, the dinosaur from *The Hobbit*.

Nana Jo leaned across and whispered, "You can just about see the steam coming out of her nostrils, can't you?"

Mom's gaze went from Jenna to Lydia Lighthouse, as if she were watching a tennis match. She must have decided blood was thicker than water. She looked at the dress. "It does bear a resemblance to Mom's Christmas tablecloth." She looked around in a confused state. Straddling the fence wasn't easy.

"Looks exactly like the tablecloth I've used for Christmas dinners for the past thirty years. I've got matching napkins too," Nana Jo said with pride. "Maybe you'd like to use them as hats for the girls?"

Lydia sputtered and huffed, then took a deep breath. "Fine. Forget the dress." Lydia Lighthouse snatched the dress out of Mom's hands and tossed it to the floor. She paced back and forth. Her six-inch heels clicked hard with each step. "If you think you can do better with two weeks until the wedding, fine." She clicked and clacked across the floor like a Clydesdale horse and then turned to her minion. "Make a note to have the photographers from *Great Lakes Bridal, Wedded Bliss,* and *Midwest Bride Magazine* all omit pictures of the wedding party and focus only on the bride and groom."

Lydia Lighthouse's assistant, a mousy woman with mousy brown hair, bushy eyebrows, thick glasses, and an overbite, which a dentist could use as the poster child to induce parents to spring for braces, scribbled furiously on the tablet she kept with her constantly.

If Lydia thought being excluded from photographs was a punishment, she obviously didn't know our family very well. Jenna reached over and we high-fived, which caused the wedding planner to huff again, roll her eyes, and click-clack harder across the floor.

"That woman needs to switch to decaf," Nana Jo whispered loud enough for *that woman* to overhear.

Lydia turned quickly and glared at Nana Jo, which was a waste of energy.

Nana Jo stuck her thumbs in her ears and wiggled her fingers as she stuck out her tongue. Yep, nothing but class in our family.

Lydia rolled her eyes and turned away.

I almost felt sorry for her. In fact, I was about two seconds away from agreeing to wear the dreaded tablecloth when she turned around and snapped her fingers. The mouse rushed over to the table and picked up the second of the garment bags she'd lugged into the store. She scurried back to Lydia and handed her the bag.

Lydia looked at her as though she were gum she'd scraped off the bottom of her shoe.

The assistant's face flushed red. She mumbled an apology and unzipped the bag and removed a gold lamé lace tablecloth on a hanger.

Lydia turned to my mom. "Now, Grace, I know you're a woman of taste." She sneered at Jenna and me before she turned back to Mom. "This is the latest creation from Paris. Gold is in this year, and everything is about lace."

Mom stared at the dress with a face that I'd once used as Lady Macbeth in a middle school rendition of *Macbeth*. Mom's "Out, damned spot!" face put my acting to shame. She looked at Lydia. "It's lovely. Is it for the bridal table?"

Lydia's face cracked and her smile slid to the floor. "Of course not. Your family is obsessed with tablecloths." She took a deep breath and plastered her smile back in place. "It's your wedding dress. Isn't it lovely?"

Mom's eyes grew large and she stared at the lace garment. "It's . . . lovely, but I've already picked out my wedding dress," she whispered.

Lydia flipped her hand in the air. "Oh, that rag might have been okay for a wedding in a hovel, but I could never permit one of my brides to be seen dead wearing something off the rack. Lydia Lighthouse's brides wear only the finest gowns from the best designers." She was so busy smiling, she hadn't noticed the crestfallen look that flitted across my mom's face. Instead, she continued plowing forward like a steamroller. "Gold is the trend for weddings this season. Gold and lace are big. I was ecstatic when I found a gown that married the two items together so well." She smiled at her pun. "All this loveliness for a quarter mil, I practically stole it."

Nana Jo must have been swallowing when she spoke because she began to choke, and I had to pat her back a few times before she was able to speak. "A quarter MILLION WHAT?"

Lydia smiled. "Dollars, of course. Harold told me money wasn't an object as long as Grace was happy, so . . ."

"So, you decided to milk the poor man like a cow?" Nana Jo practically screamed.

A flush rose up Lydia's face. "Harold told me he was paying for the wedding, therefore I assumed *he* was my client. My job is to please my client. He wanted 'a wedding.'" She used air quotes. "That would show off his beloved bride to all the world. He did not tell me that, in addition to pulling a rabbit out of a hat and producing an elegant and beautiful wedding in less than one month, I would have to answer to an overbearing, tasteless, argumentative, quarrelsome cat and two ungrateful, spoiled brats who care more about their own needs than those of their mother." She clicked and clacked as she ranted.

"Whoa, Nellie. You might want to back that cart up a pace or two before I roll you over with it." Nana Jo rose to her feet and stood, towering down like a tree.

Tears formed in Mom's eyes.

I rose from my chair. No one made my mom cry and got

away with it. I glared at Lydia. I was so intent on figuring out what kind of knot was in Lydia's scarf so I could use it to strangle her that I didn't hear the bell indicating someone had entered the shop.

"What's going on here?" Harold's normally low voice boomed.

I turned to see Harold and almost didn't recognize him. The normally jovial, ever-patient Harold looked furious. "What have you done to Grace?"

In all of the chaos, I'd lost sight of Mom. At Harold's words, I turned and looked at my mom, who was sitting in a chair with tears streaming down her face.

Jenna and I walked over to her and tried to comfort her.

"Well?" Harold bellowed.

We pointed at Lydia.

Harold glared at Lydia. "Did you do this?"

Lydia screeched, "Me? You think I've done this?" She took several deep breaths and then burst into tears. "All I've done has been to try to provide an elegant Lydia Lighthouse wedding, and I've been thwarted at every turn."

Harold stared from Lydia to Mom and then to Jenna, Nana Jo, and me. He walked to Mom and squatted down in front of her. "Grace, dear, please don't cry. Let me take you home."

Mom rose and permitted herself to be led out.

At the door, Harold stopped and turned and faced Lydia. "I'll deal with you later." Then he and Mom walked out of the store.

Chapter 3

Later, I made myself a cup of tea. Ever the glutton for punishment, I replayed the scene over and over again in my head. Lydia Lighthouse had poor taste, but that didn't necessarily make her a bad person. Perhaps, with more time to plan and prepare, she would have created a wedding any bride would be proud to have. I wasn't exactly an expert on weddings. Leon and I had gone to the courthouse and gotten married over our lunch hour. I think I wore blue jeans and a Mickey Mouse sweatshirt. Jenna and Tony had gotten married in the living room of their first apartment. They'd both just graduated from law school and were more concerned with saving the world than planning a large, elaborate wedding. Neither of us had provided my mom with the opportunity to plan the elaborate weddings she'd dreamed of for her daughters. Maybe Lydia was right. Maybe we were being selfish. If wearing a green tablecloth would make my mom happy, what difference did it make? It was one day. Honestly, as ugly as the tablecloth was, it was better than any of the dresses I'd tried on at the bridal shop.

Decision made, I took my tea and went to my upstairs office and sat down at my laptop. Owning a mystery bookstore had been a dream my husband, Leon, and I shared, but my dreams went beyond merely selling books. I also dreamed of writing them. After Leon died, I realized how short life was and sat down and started writing a British historic cozy mystery. It had taken a while for me to feel comfortable sharing the fact I'd written a book with anyone except my family and closest friends. In fact, I didn't even have the courage to send my manuscript out to agents. It was Nana Jo who sent my manuscript to the second cousin of one of her friends, Pamela Porter, who also just happened to be a literary agent. Pamela loved my book and was preparing to send it to an editor at one of the New York publishing houses. I tried not to think too much about that because my stomach contracted and I started feeling lightheaded. Instead, I focused on Pamela's last email, which had said to keep writing. So, I fired up my laptop and prepared to do just that.

✒

Wickfield Lodge, English country home of
Lord William Marsh—December 1938

"Daphne, you can't be serious? There's no way you can plan a wedding in three weeks." Lady Penelope Carlston, formerly Marsh, stared at her sister.

"Well, that's exactly what I'm going to do." Daphne lifted her chin in the determined way she had.

Lady Elizabeth looked from one of her nieces to the other. Casual observers might not have realized Lady Penelope and Lady Daphne Marsh were sisters. The two young women were as different as night and day. Lady Daphne Marsh was a blond-haired, blue-eyed beauty with creamy skin and a perfect figure. Lady Penelope Marsh was a raven-haired, dark-eyed woman, with a sharp mind and athletic physique. However, the two sisters shared the same determined streak, which was reflected in Daphne's eyes.

"But why?" Lady Elizabeth sat on the sofa of the comfortable drawing room and knitted. "Why the rush, dear?"

"James has to go abroad in January, and I have every intention of going with him."

James FitzAndrew Browning, 15th duke of Kingfordshire, Daphne's intended, leaned against the fireplace and smoked. "I told her it was a crazy idea." He looked around the room. "I hoped all of you would talk her out of it."

Lord William read his newspaper and smoked his pipe from a cozy chair with one leg propped atop an ottoman. "Dashed inconvenient timing. No way to get a proper wedding in that amount of time, especially with everything going on in the world. There's a killer on the loose in Halifax, the Halifax Slasher." He puffed.

Lady Elizabeth knitted. "I don't believe there is a Halifax Slasher. It's just some trick to sell newspapers."

"Besides, even if it were true, Halifax is a long way away." Lady Penelope smiled.

Lord William leaned forward. "It's not just this slasher business." He tapped his newspaper. "Jews are having to ship their children out of Germany and Poland to England to protect them, and Britain's instituted the national register for war." He shook his head.

Lady Penelope's and Lady Elizabeth's gazes locked. In that glance, a resolution was established and acknowledged by a nod so subtle and brief, it was barely visible.

"Christmas Eve is less than three weeks away." Lord William huffed on his pipe. "No way to plan a proper wedding in that amount of time."

"Proper or improper, I don't care." Daphne jutted out her chin even farther. "I intend to be married one way or another by Christmas Eve."

Lady Elizabeth stared lovingly at her niece. She and Lord William had never been blessed with children of their own, but when Lord William's younger brother, Peregrine, and his wife, Henrietta, were killed in an automobile accident, Lady Elizabeth and Lord William raised the two girls as their own.

Lady Elizabeth set her knitting aside. "Then we better get busy. We've got a wedding to plan and a very short time in which to do it."

Chapter 4

Sunday was the day I spent time with my mom. That generally meant church, brunch and shopping, movies, or time just spent hanging out. I used to call Sundays my therapy day; not because time spent with my mother was therapeutic, but because it created my need for therapy. Despite being in my mid-thirties, time spent with my mother still left me as confused as it had when I was in my teens. However, when I finished writing last night, I lay in bed and obsessively replayed the scene with Lydia Lighthouse over and over in my head. Despite the replays, every version ended the same way, with my mother in tears.

I got up and dressed without checking my cell phone. Showered and dressed, I grabbed the phone off my nightstand as I woke Snickers and released Oreo from his crate. That was when I noticed I had a missed call. I checked for messages while the poodles stretched as though they'd worked all night. For Oreo, that probably included chasing squirrels and birds in his sleep, but for Snickers, her activity was more cerebral than physical. Based on her success record, I suspected she spent a great deal of time plotting ways to trip me while I carried food so it would end up on the floor, which was her domain. Plotting food mishaps must have been exhausting because she spent a great deal of time stretching. When the morning stretching was completed, we went downstairs to tend to the call of nature.

While the poodles took care of business, I listened to the voice mail message I'd missed earlier this morning. It was from my mom. She didn't feel up to church today and would talk to me later. I stared at the phone in shock. This couldn't be happening. I listened to the message twice more before calling my sister.

"Something's wrong with Mom."

"What? Did she have a stroke? Is she in the hospital?"

"I don't know, but she left a strange message."

"What did the message say?"

I repeated the message verbatim. After listening to it the fourth time, I had it down pat. There was silence on the line. "Jenna, are you still there?"

"You called me at . . . eight in the morning because Mom left a message saying she didn't feel like going to church today?"

"Exactly. There's got to be something wrong."

Silence.

"Jenna, listen. I can count on one hand the number of times Mom has missed church over the past thirty years. This is the same woman who went into labor with me on Sunday morning but refused to go to the hospital until after church finished because she didn't want to start my life off on the wrong foot." I paused for breath. "Next, there was simply the message and nothing else. No guilt. No implication I was somehow to blame that she would now spend eternity in hell because she was missing church. Now, you know that's suspicious."

"You've been reading and writing too many mysteries. Everything isn't a clue. Sometimes a message is just a message."

"I can't believe you're not worried."

"Believe it."

I heard the silence and knew she'd hung up on me. "Jenna?" When she didn't respond, I called Nana Jo.

"Sam, I love you, but you better have a darned good reason for waking me up at this ungodly hour on a Sunday morning," Nana Jo whispered in the phone.

"I think something's wrong with Mom."

That got her attention. I couldn't see her, but I knew she was sitting up and wide-awake. "Why? What's wrong? Did she have a stroke?"

My dad and grandfather both died of strokes, and it must have been in the back of all of our minds since it was the first question both my sister and my grandmother asked when contemplating something was wrong with Mom. "Not that I know of, but she called and left a message that she didn't feel like going to church."

Nana Jo was quiet, but I could hear her breathing and knew she hadn't hung up. "I'll be ready in fifteen minutes." She hung up.

It only took five minutes to get the dogs inside and upstairs with treats before I headed out. One of the cool features on my new-to-me Ford Escape was the remote start, which I loved during the winter months. I could lift the garage door and turn on the remote start to let the car warm up so, by the time the poodles finished their business, I had heat. I almost wished I didn't have a garage so I could allow the defrost to take care of the snow and ice on the windshields. Scraping snow off the windshield each morning was one of the things I hated about life in Michigan during the winter. Now that I had a garage, scraping was a thing of the past, at least for overnight snows.

Dawson came downstairs from his studio over the garage just as I was backing out. He had a large bag of laundry and a book bag strapped to his back, along with the bowl he often used for bread under his arm. Like a running back protecting a football, he held onto the bowl as though his life depended on it. Considering he was wearing flip-flops and a sweat suit in, I glanced at the outside temperature on the dashboard, five-degree weather, his life very well could be in jeopardy. At least his extremities were in danger of frostbite. I knew he didn't have far to travel, but the motherly part of me wanted to send him back upstairs for a coat and boots. The fact that I wasn't his mother was irrelevant. However, by the time I got the window down, he was already inside the building and heading upstairs. Next time, I'd remind him, again, that you lose over 70 percent of your body heat through your head. He needed to wear shoes and a hat when he went outside, even if it was only for a few seconds.

I drove the short distance to Shady Acres Retirement Village, where my grandmother owned a villa. I slowed down and picked up Nana Jo, who was waiting for me. If Dawson was underdressed for the cold weather, Nana Jo was the polar opposite. She had a heavy full-length down coat that swished whenever she made the slightest movement, a faux fur cap that covered her ears, boots, leather gloves, and a scarf her friend Ruby Mae knitted for her. Her eyes were the only part of her body left uncovered as she pulled the scarf up to cover her mouth and her nose.

"Turn that tushy warmer up to full blast," Nana Jo ordered.

If the remote start was my favorite accessory on my car, heated seats had to be Nana Jo's favorite. Heated seats or *tushy warmers,* as Nana Jo called them, enabled her to remove a couple of layers of outerwear almost instantly, something she rarely did in my old Honda CRV. I still missed the CRV. It had been a great vehicle with few problems, but it was old and didn't have the latest gadgets. The newer models all had so many features. It was a wonder the cars still needed humans to drive them. However, I'd found my used red Ford Escape a month ago and fallen instantly in love.

"Coffee." Nana Jo pointed at the Java Joe's drive-thru and I happily obliged.

Caffeinated and warm, I sped to my mom's South Harbor villa. I replayed the voice mail message Mom had left on my cell this morning and Nana Jo agreed it sounded fishy. By the time I arrived at my mom's house, I noticed my brother-in-law Tony's car already parked in front. I smiled. My sister wasn't as heartless as she sometimes wanted people to believe. Obviously, she'd sent Tony to make sure Mom was okay.

Nana Jo and I got out and rang the bell. Tony answered.

"How is she?" I hurried inside.

I didn't wait for a response as I pushed past my brother-in-law and entered the foyer. Despite my internal conflict and concern for my mom's well-being, years of training forced me to stop and remove my wet boots before I tracked snow and water onto the carpet. Although, I'd rarely actually stepped foot on the carpet in my mom's house. There were plastic runners that extended from the front door to the kitchen and down the hall. However, I could say from personal experience, I'd stepped on quite a large amount of water puddled on the plastic.

Tony provided a hand for Nana Jo as she removed her boots, and I followed the plastic to the kitchen. I found my mom sitting at the kitchen table. She was wearing a pink bathrobe and sipping a cup of tea.

"Mom, are you okay?"

She sipped her tea. "Of course, dear. Would you like a cup of tea?" She rose as if to get a cup, but I waved her back.

"I had coffee."

She sat back down but said nothing. Another sure sign something was wrong.

"What's the matter? Are you feeling okay?" I asked.

Nana Jo came in and stood over her daughter. "You okay?"

She put the back of her hand on Mom's forehead and checked her temperature. "You don't feel feverish."

"I'm fine. I just didn't feel . . . up to going to church today, that's all." She sipped her tea. "I don't understand what all of the fuss is about."

I stole a glance at Nana Jo, whose eyes were narrowed. She placed a hand on her hip. "Grace Ellen, you tell me what's wrong this minute, or, so help me, I'll put you over my knee and give you the spanking you deserve."

Tony hurried out of the room, but not before I saw he looked as though he would burst into laughter.

Mom sat for several seconds as though she didn't know what on earth Nana Jo meant. However, one look at her mother must have been enough to assure her Nana Jo would have no qualms about spanking her sixty-year-old daughter. She sighed. "It's just this wedding."

"What about it?" Nana Jo asked impatiently.

"Being around Harold's family and Lydia Lighthouse, well, it's made me wonder if . . ."

"Made you wonder what?" She tapped her foot.

Mom flushed slightly. "It's made me wonder if I'm the right person for him. I mean, he's such a wonderful man. He's kind and sensitive and just . . . so thoughtful; but, well . . ."

Nana Jo stared. "Spit it out. He's kind and thoughtful, that's great, but do you love him?"

"Oh, yes. I do."

"Then what's the problem?" Nana Jo sat down.

"Well, Lydia Lighthouse and his sister-in-law, Margaret, have made me feel like I'm not the right person for him. I'm not rich. I'm not smart and someone with his background has expectations."

"Pshaw." Nana Jo rolled her eyes. "What kind of expectations? At your age you certainly know about sex. He doesn't want you to do anything too kinky, does he?"

I nearly laughed out loud but caught myself and coughed instead. However, I heard laughter from the hall and knew Tony hadn't gone far.

"No, there's nothing like that."

"Well, darn it. Maybe you can teach him some things." Nana Jo slapped her hand on the table and laughed.

"Mother, I'm serious."

"Okay, okay. What kind of expectations?"

Mom stared into her coffee cup. "He's wealthy and comes from a very prominent family. People in his social class have responsibilities. I thought a simple but elegant wedding in South Harbor would be enough. I've always wanted a real wedding. I never got to plan one. Robert and I got married at the base military chapel." She looked at me. "Your father had to leave for basic training and we wanted to be married before he left." She smiled at the memory, but the smile quickly evaporated. She sighed. "I was only thinking about myself, not about Harold's family and his responsibilities."

"Mom, I don't think I fully understand what responsibilities you're referring to. Harold is a retired engineer from NASA."

"Yes, but his family is very prominent. They owned Robertson's Department Store and were pillars of society. People will expect him to have a grand wedding. Important people like the mayor and maybe even the governor will expect to be invited."

She said the governor in such a hushed, reverential tone in the same way peopled talked about the pope.

"Well, if Harold wants to invite the mayor or the governor, what's stopping him?" Nana Jo leaned forward. "Grace, I don't understand why you're so upset."

Mom stared into her cup. "Can't you see? I don't want to embarrass Harold with tacky, low-class dresses and floral arrangements. He deserves someone who will be an asset to him. I would never be able to forgive myself if people . . . laughed at him because of me."

We had been so intent on listening to Mom, we hadn't heard Harold enter the room. He stepped into the room and walked to my mom's chair. "Grace."

She looked up surprised. "Harold, I didn't hear you come in."

He took her hands. "My dearest darling, I don't know who's been filling your head with this nonsense, but you could never embarrass me. I love you with my entire heart." He clutched her hands to his heart and stared lovingly into her eyes. "I'm the one who is honored someone like you would consider marriage. Nothing you could ever do would be considered tacky or low class. You are the finest woman I have ever known."

"Oh, Harold." Mom stood and the two kissed.

I wiped away a tear.

Nana Jo's voice cracked. "All right, now that's settled, I want to know who's been filling your head with this nonsense."

Mom and Harold embraced and then he helped her back down into her seat. He took out a handkerchief and wiped his eyes and then sat down in a chair near my mom, where he could continue to hold her hand.

Mom fluttered the hand Harold wasn't holding. "Well, I don't know anyone specifically said those exact words, but I couldn't help but feel my choices weren't exactly classy enough." She looked down. "Given your family's position, people will expect haute couture and fine cuisine."

Harold slapped the table, rattling Mom's tea. I jumped.

"I knew it. It's that Lydia Lighthouse who's put those crazy ideas in your head." Harold stood. "I'll strangle that woman if it's the last thing I do." He turned and marched out of the house.

We sat in silence for several seconds, but eventually Mom

got up and went to the kitchen, opened a drawer, and pulled out a large box. She dumped the contents of the box onto the table.

"What's all this?" Nana Jo fingered the items.

"Well, this is actually something I've thought about doing for some time." She looked down but lifted her head and pushed out her chin. "I've wanted to do a family genealogy for a long time. I actually sent away for these kits months ago." She blushed. "I wanted to do one of those DNA searches. I hear you can learn all about where your family originated." She looked from me to Nana Jo. "So, I was hoping you would all agree to a DNA sample."

I stared from the test tubes to my mother and then my grandmother and waited for the explosion that never happened.

Nana Jo shrugged. "I've seen those same commercials and, to be completely honest, I've been curious myself." She picked up one of the test tubes. "I'm curious, but gosh darned if I want to legitimize anything that crazy Lydia Lighthouse says. However, I'm not going to keep from doing it simply because of her either." She picked up the instructions. "What do I have to do?"

Mom smiled. "All you have to do is spit in the test tube. They all have barcodes. You go online and register the barcode so they know the saliva in the tube belongs to you and mail it back." She handed each of us a test tube and an envelope. "I bought four kits so we could all do it."

The entire process took less than two minutes. I couldn't help looking at my mom with a certain level of respect and awe. She always seemed so fragile and helpless, yet here she was researching her family tree. "I'm pretty amazed you've been working on a family genealogy."

"It's pretty fascinating. They had a speaker come to the senior center a month or two ago and she showed how to go to different websites and find information. I've had Zaq and Christopher helping me, and we've already found some interesting things." She looked at Nana Jo. "I didn't know Dad's grandmother was full-blooded Cherokee Indian."

Nana Jo nodded. "She died not long after your father and I got married. Boy was she a hard egg." She shook her head. "Used to scare the living daylights out of your father."

"How?" I asked.

"Apparently, she claimed to be some kind of medicine woman and used to go out in the middle of the night looking for herbs and brewing up all kinds of crazy concoctions." She laughed. "Your dad told me about how one year there was a real bad drought and most of the farmers' crops were destroyed. Well, his grandmother stripped down butt naked and went outside and danced around in the moonlight." She laughed. "A few days later it rained."

"I never heard that story before." I smiled.

"I'd completely forgotten about it until your mom mentioned her." She smiled.

Since we were all assembled, we decided brunch was in order.

"Can we go to Tippecanoe Place?" Mom asked.

I wasn't thrilled about driving to River Bend, Indiana, on a cold, snowy December morning, but it had put a spark in my mom's eyes. That was worth the drive. I nodded.

Tony declined on the pretext of having work to do. So, Mom, Nana Jo, and I headed out. Nana Jo pulled out her phone and made reservations so, by the time I pulled up to the semicircular driveway of the former Studebaker Mansion, our table was ready.

I parked and hurried inside. We were seated in the former library, which still had the family's books on the bookshelf. One wall of the room had three floor-to-ceiling windows.

The walls were a rich mahogany with a coffered ceiling and built-in bookshelves on the opposite wall surrounding a doorway. There was a corner fireplace with a large mirror overhead. The mantle was decorated for the Christmas season with ribbons, pine sprays, candles, and a wreath. The décor was lovely, but my attention was captured by the books. Something about sitting in a room filled with books caused my pulse to race, and I kept staring over at the leather-bound spines and squinting to read the titles.

"You're going to strain your eyes if you keep squinting like that. Why don't you get up and read the titles," Nana Jo said.

I didn't need a second invitation. I hopped up and hurried over to the nearest bookshelf and took a deep breath. The musty book scent was still there, underneath the wonderful aroma of vanilla from the nearby waffle bar. One of the things I liked about Tippecanoe Place was the fact it was a museum as well as a restaurant. The Studebaker family's furniture, pictures, and memorabilia were not only on display for viewing but could be touched and handled. There were some items that were delicate and placed behind glass out of reach or cordoned off, but practically everything else was out and available to be handled. And handle them I did. When it came to books, I was definitely a hands-on person. I picked up a leather-bound book from a table and ran my hand over the embossed, gold leaf title. I opened the book and heard the familiar crack of the spine. I leafed through the pages and allowed my mind to drift. I wondered when was the last time a member of the family had read the book.

"Fascinating book, don't you think?"

I was so engrossed I'd forgotten I wasn't alone. I nearly jumped out of my skin.

A short, thin man with a pencil-thin moustache and hair slicked back in the style popular in the roaring twenties smiled. "Sorry, I didn't mean to startle you."

"I didn't hear you come up." I placed my hand over my heart to slow it down.

He chuckled. "I'm David Miller." He extended his hand and we shook.

"I'm the manager and tour guide. I saw you looking at the books and couldn't resist."

I placed the book in his hand. "I'm sorry. I'd always heard it was okay to touch the . . ."

He waved away my protest. "It's perfectly okay." He flipped the book open and scanned the page and then passed the book back to me. "I merely wanted to share something unique about this particular book."

I glanced at the passage. "Is that German?"

"Pennsylvania German. Clement Studebaker was the president of the Studebaker Corporation, which in 1884 was the largest manufacturer of wagons in the world." He smiled. "He built the Studebaker Mansion because he needed a house that reflected his position in the world." He smiled. "What most people don't know about Clem Studebaker is that he was a Dunkard."

"Excuse me?"

David smiled. "I said *Dunkard*." He enunciated. "Clem Studebaker was a member of the Dunkard Brethern, a small group of Schwarzenau Brethern."

I smiled. "What is the Schwarzenau Brethren?"

"The Schwarzenau Brethern were a conservative group that withdrew from the Church of the Brethren around 1926. *Dunkard* is German and comes from the word *tunken,* meaning 'to dip.' This indicates the method of baptism. The Dunkard Brethern believed in immersion three times during baptism, once for the father, once for the son, and once for the Holy Spirit."

"What else did the Dunkards believe?"

"Well, they were ultraconservative. Women dressed very

plainly and wore white caps, similar to Mennonites. Some of their beliefs included greeting with the 'holy kiss' and they practiced feet washing. The Dunkard Brethern did not swear oaths, drink, or smoke tobacco and divorce was strictly prohibited."

"Interesting. Are there still Dunkards?"

David nodded. "Oh, yes. They're still around."

"Sam, I'm sure this is very interesting, but are you going to eat?" Nana Jo asked.

I nodded. "I'll be right there." I turned back to David. "This is very interesting and I'd like to learn more. Would it be okay if I came back another time when I didn't have so many distractions?" I inclined my head toward Nana Jo and Mom.

He nodded. "Certainly. Here's my card." He handed me a small business card with his name and telephone number and the hours he was available for tours.

"Thank you." I handed him the book and hurried back to the table. An idea had started to form in my brain while talking to David Miller, and I couldn't wait to get home so I could jot down some of the information he'd shared about Clem Studebaker and the Dunkards. A little research would be needed on my part, but I was certain a Dunkard might come in handy in 1938 England. Perhaps Tippecanoe Place could provide some ideas for Daphne and James's upcoming nuptials.

Brunch was excellent, but I was slightly distracted. My brain was thinking about Dunkards and Schwarzenau Brethern and I wasn't paying careful attention to the conversation at my own table.

"Earth to Sam," Nana Jo said. "That's the third time you've wandered off."

"I'm sorry. What were you saying?"

Nana Jo nodded toward Mom.

"I was thinking this might make a good place for the wedding." She looked timid. "What do you think?"

I looked around. "Actually, I think it would be a beautiful place to have a wedding. I know they host weddings here all the time, but . . ."

"But what?" Mom asked.

"Well, I just don't know if you would be able to book something on such short notice."

Mom's face fell.

"It never hurts to ask." I tried to sound enthusiastic. "Did you talk to Lydia about it?"

"I tried, but she said it was too small. Actually, she's already booked the River Bend Auditorium."

Unfortunately, I'd chosen that moment to take a sip of coffee. I nearly choked. "River Bend Auditorium? Are you serious? That place is huge."

"I know. She said we'll need the space for all of Harold's family connections."

"Wait. Did you say she's booked it?"

She nodded.

"Wow. Does Harold know?" Nana Jo asked.

"I haven't had a chance to tell him yet."

Nana Jo whistled. "I thought he was angry earlier. He's going to be ready to strangle Lydia Lighthouse or whatever her name is."

"What do you mean?" Mom looked surprised.

"You don't honestly believe that's her real name, do you?" She stared at her daughter and shook her head. "Lydia Lighthouse is as phony as that Southern belle accent she uses. Why, the characters in Sam's books are more real."

I wasn't sure if I should be insulted or flattered, but I decided to go with flattered.

River Bend, Indiana, was thirty miles south of North Harbor, Michigan, and was the closest big city to us. With a population greater than a hundred thousand, River Bend was huge compared to North Harbor. North and South Harbor residents traveled to River Bend for shopping, big-box bookstores, and concerts. For news, Southwestern Michigan residents could choose from Chicago or River Bend. Most North and South Harbor folks chose River Bend. River Bend might have been in a completely different state, but there was a tremendous difference in the news reported for the Windy City's three million inhabitants and news reported for sleepy North Harbor's population of ten thousand. Even when it came to weather, River Bend was closer to North and South Harbor. Apparently, it made a big difference when it came to which side of Lake Michigan you were on when forecasting.

Since we were already in River Bend, we drove by the auditorium. It was only about one mile from Tippecanoe Place toward downtown. I'd been to a ton of events there over the years. One of my friends worked for a CPA firm that always had their company Christmas party there. I'd accompanied her one year and was thoroughly impressed. From the street, the building looked like every other downtown office building, with lots of concrete and beige. However, once inside, you noticed the ceiling and entire back of the building was glass and it butted up to the St. Thomas River. Massive amounts of light flooded the building and illuminated the spectacular view of the St. Thomas rapids. From the top entrance, you walked back toward the thirty-foot floor-to-ceiling wall of windows. The Great Hall was more than sixteen thousand square feet. It was where the Christmas party I'd attended was held, and it was decorated for the holiday season. It was spectacular.

Once inside, we stood at the top of the massive floating staircase that led to the lower level and admired the view of the river.

"Lydia envisioned I'd walk down these stairs." Mom motioned with her arms.

"That's a really big space," I said. "How many people are you planning to invite?"

Mom shrugged and fluttered her hands. "Lydia was going to send out a lot more invitations. She thinks we should plan for five hundred."

"Five hundred people?" I stared. "Do you even know five hundred people to invite?"

Mom shrugged again. "With the magazines, newspapers, and the VIPs . . ."

I wasn't sure what would be worse, to have a wedding with five hundred guests or to plan for a wedding and not have five hundred guests show up. I would be terrified to be the center of attention in an event where I had to walk down the stairs in front of so many people, but it would be worse to plan for a large turnout and not have people show up.

"That's a lot of stairs." Nana Jo leaned over the glass railing.

We walked down the stairs to the lower level. The room was beautiful and would make an excellent venue for a large wedding.

"Ah, Grace, imagine running into you."

We turned. Lydia Lighthouse trudged toward us like a steam-roller, while her assistant trailed behind with a tablet taking notes. In addition to the mouse, three other people trailed Lydia, like rats following the Pied Piper. One was a young man with dark hair pulled back into a ponytail and a five-o'clock shadow that made him look artistic. He wore a white double-breasted chef's jacket but omitted the traditional hat. The other was a tall African American with smooth, dark skin, a moustache, and a bald head that reminded me of Lou Gossett Jr. He was dressed in jeans and a white T-shirt, which made him look quite dapper. The third was a frumpish older woman with frizzy red hair.

We walked up to the party and Lydia air-kissed my mom and ignored both Nana Jo and me.

"This is my bride, Grace Hamilton." She turned to the man with the ponytail. "Grace, meet the caterer, Rudy Blakemore."

Rudy shook hands with my mom and nodded to Nana Jo and me.

"Here is the ice sculptor, Maxwell Dubois."

Max Dubois bowed.

"Ice sculptor?" Nana Jo asked. "Are you kidding?"

Lydia ignored Nana Jo and moved on to her third follower. "This is the florist, Felicity Abrams of Felicity's Florals." She turned to Felicity. "Best florist in the Great Lakes area." Lydia pulled Mom away from the group slightly. "I've just negotiated a tremendous discount on the flowers. She's only going to charge one hundred thousand dollars to do all of the flowers, including the table arrangements, corsages, bridal bouquets, and boutonnieres."

Felicity frowned.

"One hundred thousand dollars?" Nana Jo nearly screamed. "Are you off your rocker?"

Lydia huffed. "Look around." She waved her arm. "This place will need to be decorated from floor to ceiling. Flowers in December for a room this large should be three times what you're paying."

I stared at the space and had to admit, the room was massive. She was right. Flowers could be expensive, and Lydia wouldn't be looking at inexpensive flowers. Nothing would be in season in Michigan in December, except pine trees. Any flowers used would need to be shipped in from a warmer climate.

I stared at Felicity, who looked as though she wanted to bite the head off nails. In fact, the only one of the group who looked happy was Lydia, who had the smug expression of a cat who'd just eaten the last cream.

Nana Jo leaned close. "Why do I get the impression Harold

isn't the only one who'd like to get their hands around Lydia Lighthouse's neck?"

"You know Harold and I haven't completely agreed we want to have the wedding here," Mom said meekly.

Lydia Lighthouse was a freight train and she ran forward just as forcefully. "Grace, we talked about this and I thought we agreed you wanted the best for Harold. Someone in his social position will want to make an impression." She walked and talked rapidly, clicking and clacking her heels on the marble floors as she gestured. "There's really no other place in the area that can accommodate a wedding of distinction, especially on such short notice. In fact, the only reason we were able to get this place was due to a last-minute cancellation."

Mom looked flustered and confused.

"Besides, it's really too late. I've already booked it and placed a five-thousand-dollar nonrefundable deposit." She stopped pacing to stare at Mom, who looked as though she would cry. Thankfully, Mom's cell phone rang.

"Harold, we were just talking about you."

Lydia looked as though she had been sucking on lemons, but when she caught my eye, she immediately plastered a fake smile on her face and became overly interested in a piece of lint on her skirt.

"Yes, dear, I'm with Lydia now. We're at the River Bend Auditorium with the caterer, ice sculptor, and florist. I—"

"No, dear, I said *ice* sculptor." A flush slowly rose from her neck. "Well, I'll do my best." She ended the call and turned to Lydia. "Harold wants to talk to you. He said he'll be here in thirty minutes."

Lydia looked at her watch. "Certainly, a groom should have a say in the arrangements. After all, it's his wedding too," she said brightly.

Nana Jo and I exchanged looks. If Harold was still as angry as he was this morning, I was sure he'd have a lot to say.

It took forty-five minutes for Harold to arrive, but wild horses couldn't have dragged us out of that building. By the time he came down the stairs, the building event planner had brought out a 3-D model of the building and was showing various configurations for breaking the space up to best suit our needs. The current configuration included an area for cocktails, the dining area, and a nightclub section for dancing.

Rudy, Maxwell, and Felicity were discussing the best placement, design restrictions, and access for loading and unloading. Apparently, ice sculptures were quite heavy and, not surprisingly, needed to be kept in a refrigerated area to prevent melting.

Harold marched over to the table. "What do you think you're doing?"

Mom tugged on his sleeve. "Dear, this isn't the right time."

For the first time since I'd known him, Harold ignored my mother's wishes. "Not the right time? I can't think of a better time." He turned back to Lydia. "How dare you insult the woman I love. Grace Hamilton is intelligent, beautiful, sophisticated, and sensitive."

"Mr. Robertson, I have no idea what you're talking about." Lydia smiled.

"You brought this poor woman to tears with your implications she was somehow not good enough for me or outside of my social class. Well, I'll have you know she *is* outside of my social class. She's far too good of a woman for me."

Mom practically swooned.

Nana Jo looked as though she would gag.

"This is Grace's wedding, and she is to have whatever *she* wants. By golly, if she wants to get married on elephants in the middle of a circus, then that's where we'll get married, and anyone who doesn't like it can take a flying leap right into the St. Thomas River." He glared. "That includes the mayor, the governor, or the president of the United States."

Lydia tried to get a word in but was halted by Harold. "The next person that makes my fiancée shed one more tear will answer to me." He glared at each person, including Nana Jo and me.

Mom threw herself into Harold's arms. "Oh, Harold."

He glared at Lydia for a half second and then focused all of his attention on my mother. "I'm sorry you had to hear that, dear. Let's go home." He escorted Mom out of the building.

We stared at the couple as they climbed the stairs and then watched as Harold held the door and assisted Mom into his car, which he'd left at the front door.

"I pity the fool who gets on the wrong side of him," Nana Jo said.

"I've never seen him that angry before," I said. "He looked ready to strangle someone."

Lydia sniffed and flung her white scarf around her neck.

When the police found her later, that scarf was still around her neck, but they had to cut it off.

Chapter 5

Wickfield Lodge, Servants Hall—December 1938

"How can you even think about a wedding when there's a madman on the loose?" Millie shivered.

Millie was a day maid. She was young and a bit silly.

"What are you on about now?" Mrs. McDuffy asked.

"The Halifax Slasher." The maid stared at the housekeeper in wonder. "It's all over the papers. He's killing people just like the Ripper."

"You 'ush!" Mrs. McDuffy didn't have time or patience for nonsense. "That's just a lot of nonsense to sell papers, and, if it weren't, Halifax is a long way from Wickfield Lodge." She folded her arms across her chest.

The chastened housemaid dropped her head and fell silent.

"Lady Daphne will make such a lovely bride." Flossie sighed.

The Marsh family servants assembled in the servants' hall while Thompkins informed the servants of the arrangements he'd recently discussed with Lady Elizabeth. The solid, uptight, and straitlaced butler took his duty to the family seriously. He would insure Lady Daphne had the wedding of her dreams. If hard work and determination could do it, then the butler was well equipped. He'd make sure the young woman he'd watched grow from a bouncing baby to a beautiful debutante had exactly what she wanted.

"Of course she will, but three weeks isn't much time," Mrs. McDuffy, the housekeeper said with a bit of trepidation. "There'll be washing and ironing and airing out of all the bedrooms." The middle-aged housekeeper was stout with freckles and fluffy red hair. She was a bit coarse, with a bad habit of dropping her *H*s when she spoke, but she was as committed to the Marsh family, and especially Lady Elizabeth, as the butler. She'd make sure the house was ready and glanced at the three housemaids under her charge, who'd have to work night and day to get everything into shape.

"Regardless of the time, we will do what must be done to uphold the honor of his lordship and the Marsh family." Thompkins delivered his reprimand with a straight back and his head held high.

"I never said no different. I've never shirked my responsibilities to 'er ladyship and I ain't about to start now." She folded her arms across her chest and huffed. "My girls'll make sure this 'ouse is in tip-top shape. You just wait and see."

Thompkins nodded. He knew Mrs. McDuffy would work tirelessly to make sure all was ready.

"Mr. Thompkins, sir." Gladys, the housemaid,

timidly raised a hand. "Do we know how many guests to expect?"

"Not yet, but I'd say we better plan for at least a hundred."

"Do you think the King will come?" Flossie looked dreamily at the butler. "Them being cousins and all."

"I don't know. His Majesty has always been very fond of Lady Daphne." Thompkins stood straighter. "Nevertheless, we will need to make sure everything is spotless and each of us are at our best. You never can tell."

"Oh, lawd." Flossie looked as though she would pass out.

"Now, don't you go getting no crazy notions in that silly 'ead of yours. Just you mind what you're doing. It's going to be 'ard enough without you mooning about the king," Mrs. McDuffy said.

"I wouldn't hold out much hope if I was you," Jim, a footman, teased. "The king didn't go to his own brother's wedding. I can't rightly see him coming down here for a mere cousin."

Flossie's smiled dropped away.

Frank McTavish, a footman and son of the groundskeeper, kicked Jim under the table. "Don't you fret none. There'll be plenty of aristocrats even if the king doesn't come."

"You think so?" Flossie asked.

"Just you wait and see." Frank winked.

"Three weeks is all good for the rest of you, but that's hardly enough time to get all of the cookin' and bakin' done for a party that size. When do you suppose we'll be gettin' a menu?" Mrs. Anderson, the cook asked.

Thompkins bristled. "Her ladyship will address

the staff first thing tomorrow. I'm sure she will provide everything you need then."

Mrs. Anderson turned to her daughter, Agnes. "We better get started on some things first thing tomorrow. We'll be busy with the weddin' menu and with guests in the house, and there won't be time to breathe if we don't get started early."

Mrs. McDuffy used the table to help hoist her large frame out of the chair. "We best get busy. There'll be plenty of scrubbing and washing that we can do."

Thompkins coughed. "One more thing." He frowned at the housekeeper, who reluctantly returned to her seat. "Due to the short time frame, Lady Daphne and His Grace have decided to hire someone to help with some of the arrangements."

Mrs. McDuffy's eyes narrowed. "'Ired someone? Who?"

"I believe they called him a wedding planner." Thompkins looked around at the servants.

Mrs. McDuffy snorted.

The rest of the group whispered.

Gladys raised a timid hand. "I'm sorry, Mr. Thompkins, sir, but what exactly is a wedding planner?"

Thompkins knew he intimidated the young housemaid, but he wasn't exactly sure what a wedding planner was himself and didn't want to look foolish in front of the staff. "I believe it's someone who helps plan weddings."

"Well, I bloody well figured that much out just by the name," Mrs. McDuffy said.

The butler bristled. "Mrs. McDuffy, I'll remind you to watch your language."

Mrs. McDuffy rolled her eyes.

"I saw it in a flick." Flossie's eyes grew big. "This family hired a real artistic bloke to help plan their wedding. You should have seen all of the beautiful flowers and things and the dresses. There was silk and satin everywhere. And, the food looked amazing," she gushed.

"Well, I don't care who they hire. I'll not have anyone interferin' in me kitchen." Mrs. Anderson smacked her hand on the table and stared at the butler.

"You mark my words. No good will come of 'iring some ruddy person from outside of the family," Mrs. McDuffy said.

⌒⌒⌒⌒⌒

My phone rang early. I opened one eye and stared at the time. It was still dark outside and not even Snickers was ready to be up quite this early. "Hell—"

Mom's voice was two decibels louder and two octaves higher than normal, which was almost at the point only dogs could hear.

"Calm down. I can't understand you." I sat up in bed and put the phone on speaker to save my eardrums.

Between her sobs, I could only make out every other word. "Who's dead?"

I stared at the phone because staring increased your hearing. At least it seemed reasonable at the time. "Did you say, Lydia Lighthouse?"

I got out of bed and hunted around for shoes. "I'll be there as soon as I get dressed," I replied to my mom's order to come at once. "I might have to get someone to watch the . . . Hello?"

She'd hung up.

I looked at the clock. It was barely six on Monday morning. Of all the ways to start a week, a frantic call from my mom before sunrise and coffee would probably top my list for worst starts ever. To be honest, I wasn't fond of Lydia Lighthouse. She was loud, brassy, bossy, overbearing, and snooty. If I analyzed my feelings, I was embarrassed to say the only surprise was that someone hadn't killed her earlier. Planning a wedding was stressful enough without dealing with Lydia. Nope, my stress was for the purely selfish reason that without Lydia, someone, and I mentally inserted my name, would have to help coordinate the wedding. I shook my head to clear images of myself in a green tartan tablecloth.

I hurried to dress and raised my hand to Nana Jo's bedroom door but thought better of it. Instead, I went into the kitchen and quickly made coffee. The single cup coffeemaker was quick and, just a few minutes later, I was back at her door. This time I followed through and pounded on the bedroom door.

There were several bumps and a crash that sounded as though a pile of books hit the floor, which was quickly followed by a few well-chosen oaths. The door swung open. "Someone better be dead, or they soon will be."

"Lydia Lighthouse."

Nana Jo stared at me as though I'd lost my senses. "What?"

I shoved the coffee mug at her. "Lydia Lighthouse was murdered. Mom just called. We've got to get over to her place before she has a stroke."

I turned and walked away with Nana Jo still standing at her door.

Snickers wasn't thrilled about getting up two hours earlier than normal, but she did her business and hurried back upstairs. Oreo spent five minutes stretching and then found a mound of snow that wasn't yellowed from previous visits and took care of his business.

By the time the poodles were taken care of, Nana Jo was dressed. She pulled a knit cap over her head. "I'm going to need a lot more coffee and a sausage biscuit before I can face your mother."

"Agreed." I followed her downstairs.

It was too early for what constituted South Harbor's rush hour traffic. The sun hadn't yet risen, so it was dark and cold. The drive to Mom's South Harbor villa was delayed by a stop at a fast-food drive-thru. Nana Jo finished a sausage biscuit and a hash brown patty that smelled fantastic in the confines of my car before we pulled up to Mom's house. I focused on sipping my coffee without spilling it, which was a skill I had yet to master.

When we arrived, the front door to my mom's house flew open and she stood at the door, waiting for us to enter.

I hurried inside, juggling a coffee, my purse, and a greasy bag of food, with a newspaper stuffed under my arm.

"What took you so long?"

"Good morning to you too," I said as brightly as possible, but the sarcasm was wasted on my mother.

I walked into the house and looked for someplace to set my coffee and bag so I could remove my boots. Having finished her food in the car, Nana Jo was less encumbered and was able to deboot faster. She held out her hand. "Here, let me help you."

I breathed a sigh of relief and handed over my precious cargo. The last thing I needed on top of my mom's hysteria was to spill coffee or track wet snow through the house. Those sins would not be easily forgiven.

At the table, I sat down and reached for my coffee. Unfortunately, my mother took that opportunity to shove the newspaper at me, which caused me to spill my coffee.

My mom sighed and went to the kitchen to get a towel. "It's a good thing I took Grandma Sarah's tablecloth to the cleaners."

"It's just coffee, Grace. Calm down," Nana Jo ordered.

Few people had the power to stop my mother in the middle of a hysterical fit, but Nana Jo had the gift.

Mom sat at the table.

"We rushed over as fast as we could." She sat across from Mom. "Now, how did you find out about the murder?"

Mom pointed to the newspaper.

Nana Jo unfolded it and read while I ate my sausage biscuit and the now-cold hash browns.

Lydia Lighthouse's murder was on the front page of the newspaper. One advantage to a small town was murders don't happen every day. Domestic disputes, drunken brawls, or weather-related accidents that were exacerbated by alcohol were prominent. Murder, not so much. So, a great deal of space was allocated for a real murder. According to the newspaper, she was found facedown on the drawbridge that crossed over the St. Thomas River. An early morning bridge worker saw what he thought was a heap of clothes on the bridge. Closer inspection showed the heap to be a person. Thinking it was a homeless person, he went to ask the woman to move. I mentally translated that to *he went to force her to find another place to sleep*. It wasn't until he was directly over the body that he realized the heap of clothes was a dead woman.

"I can't say I'm going to miss her." Nana Jo folded the newspaper.

"What am I going to do?" Mom burst into tears.

Nana Jo and I exchanged a glance. "Grace, pull yourself together." Nana Jo passed Mom a handkerchief. "I know you weren't any crazier about Lydia Lighthouse than the rest of us."

She shook her head.

"You've only known the woman for a week. She was a snob who treated you like dirt. Frankly, I don't understand why you're so upset she's dead."

Mom looked up. "I'm not upset she's dead." She sniffed.

"Then what's with the waterworks?" Nana Jo asked.

"I'm upset because they're going to arrest Harold for her murder."

Chapter 6

By the time Nana Jo and I had picked our jaws up off the ground and Mom was able to talk coherently, Harold hadn't been arrested for the murder; not yet anyway. However, Mom was certain it would just be a matter of time before the police arrested him.

"But why would they arrest Harold?" I asked.

"You saw him yesterday. I've never known him to get that angry at anyone. When we went home and I told him about the hundred thousand dollars' worth of flowers and the five thousand to reserve the room, well, he was really angry."

"I don't blame him for being angry. Anyone would be," Nana Jo argued. "She was taking advantage of him and spending his money like water."

"Wait. I thought Lydia Lighthouse's services were free. Margaret said she was her wedding present." I stared at Mom.

"Actually, I thought that too, but Lydia explained Margaret was only paying for labor. The actual expenses were up to Harold."

"Holy cow. Did Harold know that?"

Mom colored. "Well, not at first. At first, he was under the same impression as the rest of us. However, last night I had to tell him Lydia had asked for a check for one million dollars to cover expenses, so I gave it to her."

My mom's timing was incredible. I had just taken a sip of coffee and what didn't try to go down my windpipe ended up on the table.

Mom rose and got a paper towel while Nana Jo pounded me on the back to bring up any coffee still lingering in my windpipe.

After a minute, I was finally able to stop coughing. "Did you say one *million* dollars?" I croaked.

Mom nodded. "Well, yes, that's what she said she needed."

"But where on earth did you get a million dollars?" Nana Jo asked the question that had been floating around my head.

"Well, I don't have that kind of money, but when Harold and I got engaged, he added me to his bank account."

"Holy mackerel." I stared at my mom. "I knew Harold was well off, but I had no idea he was *that* well off."

Nana Jo was so quiet, I wondered what was going through her mind. "What's the matter?"

"If Lydia Lighthouse had taken one million dollars of my money, I'd strangle her too."

"You can't seriously believe Harold killed her?" I asked.

Nana Jo shrugged. "It really doesn't matter what I believe."

"What do you mean?"

"Let's face it, Sam. Lydia Lighthouse was a stranger. She was only here for your mother's wedding. Harold argued with her. He threatened her. And, he had one million reasons to want her dead. Even Stinky Pitt could get a conviction with that."

Stinky Pitt was Detective Bradley Pitt of the North Harbor Police Department. He wasn't the sharpest knife in the drawer. We'd encountered him several other times when he'd jumped to the erroneous conclusion that I, Dawson, and even Nana Jo had committed murder.

Nana Jo and I exchanged glances.

"There's only one thing to do." Nana Jo looked at me. "You're going to have to figure out who murdered that woman, or your mother will be getting married in the North Harbor Jail."

Chapter 7

We made it back to the bookstore before opening, but just barely. Thankfully, Dawson was there to help. I worked on autopilot during the morning, not thinking about Harold or my mother or trying to solve another murder. My body went through all of the motions. I helped customers, smiled, sold, shelved, and reshelved books. At one, Nana Jo suggested I go to Frank's and grab lunch for both of us.

I bundled up for the short walk. It was snowing and the view looked like a postcard. Big, fluffy white flakes of snow blanketed the street. Wreaths hung from the streetlights and green garland was wound around the poles, giving the brick streets and brownstone storefronts a seasonal vibe.

My thoughts refused to acknowledge the Christmas spirit. In fact, I glanced at a reflection of my face in the window of one of the shops and realized my facial expression would have made Ebenezer Scrooge feel downright jolly. Nevertheless, rather than make adjustments, I stuck out my tongue and muttered, " 'Bah Humbug.' "

By the time I walked into North Harbor Café, I was covered in a light dusting of snow. I took a minute and shook myself, Oreo-style, and stamped my feet, leaving a small mound of snow at the door.

I walked over to the bar and hopped up on a barstool, then removed my coat.

Frank was behind the bar. He smiled. "Hey, beautiful."

I scowled. "Hey, can I get two soups and two chicken salad sandwiches to go?"

He walked over and placed a pitcher of ice water with lemon and a glass of ice in front of me. "What's wrong?"

"Nothing."

"Right." He leaned across the bar so his face was inches from my ear. "No warm greeting. No smile. No kiss. A guy might think you didn't like him anymore." His breath was warm on my earlobe and heat rose up my neck. I breathed in his scent of bacon, red wine, and herbal Irish soap.

"I'm sorry." I turned my head and kissed him lightly.

"Now, that's better." He smiled and pulled back so he could look me in the face. "Now, I'm going to get your order placed in the kitchen and then I'll be back, and you can tell me what's bothering you."

He left and went to the kitchen, and I took several deep breaths. I was very fortunate to have met Frank Patterson and just because I was in a bad mood was no reason to take it out on him. He was kind, thoughtful, and very caring. He was also a great cook and deserved to be treated better. I felt ashamed. When he returned, I was close to tears.

"I'm so sorry for being grumpy earlier, I don't—"

"It's okay. I just look forward to seeing you, so when you're in a bad mood, well, I just want to help."

One of his waitresses came out of the kitchen and placed a plate of warm salted caramel chocolate chip and pecan cookies in front of me with a tall glass of milk.

I stared in surprise, but Frank merely smiled. "I got the recipe from Dawson."

I took a bite and allowed the chocolate to melt on my tongue. I closed my eyes and I must have moaned because when I opened my eyes, Frank was smiling. "Do you need a moment?"

I nodded and took a sip of milk.

"Now, what's wrong?"

I ate my cookie and told Frank about Lydia Lighthouse and my mother's fears that Harold would be arrested for her murder. "I can't even let my mind focus on the fact Christmas is less than two weeks away. Which means my mom's wedding is less than two weeks away and the woman hired to plan the wedding is dead." I whispered the last words and looked around to make sure no one was listening. "Nana Jo says I have to figure out who murdered Lydia before the wedding."

Frank dried glasses while he listened. "Well, you could leave it up to the police. It is their job to figure out who killed her."

I stopped with the cookie midway to my mouth and stared. "Are you kidding? I can't leave this up to Stinky Pitt. He couldn't detect his way out of a paper bag." I popped the last chocolatey morsels into my mouth and swallowed the last of the milk.

Frank smiled. "So, I guess the decision is easy."

"You're right. I have to help." I released a heavy sigh. "Or at least try to help."

"You'll figure it out. You always have in the past." He took my hand and caressed the inside of my wrist. "Plus, you won't be alone. You'll have Nana Jo and the girls. And me."

My breathing was becoming labored and I felt like I was drowning in his gaze. Thankfully, the waitress came with my order and broke the spell. Frank swore and I smiled.

"Thank you." I grabbed my order and leaned across and gave him a kiss. "Thank you for everything." I hopped off the seat, put on my coat, and hurried out the door.

Dawson had declined lunch because he had to be on campus in a couple of hours for class and football training. The rush of customers had died down, and Nana Jo and I were able to sit down at one of the bistro tables in the back and eat lunch.

"I sent a message to the girls and they're going to meet us here after we close," Nana Jo said.

"Great. I think we need to call Jenna too. After all, she is an attorney."

Nana Jo smiled. "I already did."

"What are we going to do about the wedding? I don't know the first thing about caterers, photographers, florist, music." My throat was getting tight and my heart started to race. "I'm not wearing a tablecloth if Jenna doesn't have to wear one."

"Calm down. I talked to Dawson and we have a plan." She smiled.

"Dawson? Are you joking?"

She shook her head. "Nope. He wants to help."

I started to protest, but Nana Jo held up two fingers. "We've got two weeks. I don't think we can afford to turn down help from anyone."

"You're right."

"Good, so tonight's meeting will have a few more people than usual, but don't worry. We'll figure everything out."

A few extra people she said. The stream of people piling into my back room felt like a small army. In addition to the normal Sleuthing Seniors book club members, Ruby Mae Stevenson, Dorothy Clark, Nana Jo, and Irma Starczewski, there were a host of others. Dawson, Jillian, and Emma were there representing the MISU front. Christopher and Zaq represented both the family and the Jesus and Mary University (JAMU) contingent. Also representing the home front was my sister, Jenna, and Mom. I struggled to classify where Frank Patterson fell in all this. He took off his winter coat. He was wearing a Market Street Mysteries T-shirt, and I fought back a smile. He declared his allegiance without saying a word. The room was extremely tight when you added in the people, plus all their winter weather wear—boots, hats, scarves, and overcoats. Without being asked, Jillian and Emma took everyone's outerwear and put them in my office.

I mouthed a thank-you as they passed.

Dawson brought folding chairs up from the basement. It was a cozy fit, but we made it work.

Nana Jo pulled out her iPad. "Let's get this party started." She looked around. "Now—"

Harold Robertson walked in and stood for a few seconds and looked around. "Josephine, would you mind if I say a few words?"

"Of course." Nana Jo sat back down and waited.

Harold stood facing everyone, hat in hand. "Josephine told me you would all be meeting here tonight and I asked if it would be okay if I said a few words."

Harold was a tall man with white hair and a white beard. In all of my previous interactions with him, he had been full of life. Tonight, the light had been snuffed out. He looked old and haggard.

He cleared his throat. "You all know I was angry with that Lydia Lighthouse woman. She was a deceitful, conniving thief. She lied and stole and . . . well, she was rude to the sweetest, kindest, most gentle woman in the world." He looked at my mom with goo-goo eyes.

Mom looked teary and dabbed at her eyes.

"Mr. Robertson, as a lawyer, I want to caution you to be careful what you say." Jenna looked around. "Everyone here is a friend, but they could be subpoenaed and forced to reveal anything you say."

"Pshaw," Nana Jo snorted. "Harold, you're among friends here. Friends and family, and family sticks together, subpoena or no subpoena."

"Here. Here." Dorothy smacked the table.

"No court will make me talk. I'll be d—"

"Irma!" everyone shouted.

Irma broke into a coughing fit.

"Am I the only law-abiding citizen in this entire group?" Jenna looked serious, but her lips twitched.

Harold forced a smile. "Thank you. Thank you all, but I don't have anything to hide. I've told the police everything I'm telling you."

Jenna rolled her eyes. "Ugh. I wish you hadn't done that."

"But I'm innocent."

"That may be, but the prisons in this country are full of innocent men and women," Nana Jo said.

"Well, they're full of men and women who *claim* to be innocent," Jenna said. "But, you really should have legal counsel."

"Couldn't you represent him?" Mom asked.

"Well, I—"

Harold held up a hand. "I couldn't ask that of you. I don't want to tarnish your good name. In fact, I came here, primarily, to tell you all I think it would be best if I separated myself a bit . . ." He glanced at my mom. "It won't be good to be associated with someone accused of murder."

"Are you joking?" Nana Jo laughed. "Buddy, where have you been for the past six months?"

"That was different. You were all protecting your family." Harold shuffled his feet.

"Not all family is related by blood." Dawson smiled.

Harold shook his head. "I could never ask . . ."

Jenna smiled. "You didn't ask. I'm volunteering. That is, if you want me."

Harold bowed. "I would be honored."

Jenna walked over to Harold and gave him a hug. "It's what families do."

I wiped away tears, and I wasn't the only one.

Nana Jo stood. "All right, all right, enough of that. Now, we need to get this meeting started because I have a date." She sat down and pulled out her iPad. "We have a lot of things that need to be taken care of. So, let's get some of those things out of the way first."

Harold sat down next to my mom and they gazed in each other's eyes and held hands like giddy schoolchildren.

"First, we have a wedding happening in less than two weeks." She looked at Jenna.

"Nana Jo asked me to find out what arrangements were confirmed and which ones were left." She pulled out a notepad and put on a pair of reading glasses. "I called the River Bend Auditorium, and, while Lydia Lighthouse called to reserve the facility, she never actually paid the deposit."

"What? She told us she gave them a five-thousand-dollar deposit," I said.

"Yep. Lydia promised a lot of things. I talked to the florist, the ice sculptor, the caterer and none of them had been paid."

"But I gave her the money," Mom whispered.

"I know, and she cashed the check. She just never got around to making the deposits."

"So, what does that mean?" Mom asked.

"It means she stole our money." Harold looked red-faced and furious.

"That sums it up pretty well." Jenna removed her glasses. "I'll try to recover the money, but that will take time."

"No use crying over spilled milk." Nana Jo looked around the table. "That's why I invited Jillian and Emma. Jenna will be representing Harold and handling any legal problems. Sam and I will need to focus all of our time and attention on figuring out who killed Lydia Lighthouse. We're not going to have time to coordinate a wedding too. Jillian and Emma just started winter break and have generously agreed to delay their trips home and to help coordinate a *small* wedding."

Everyone turned to stare at Jillian and Emma. Both had an air of excitement.

Emma turned to Mom. "That is, if it's okay with you?"

Mom nodded. "Of course, dear. Thank you both so much." She hugged them.

"Great. Also, Dawson, baker extraordinaire, has agreed to create your wedding cake."

Dawson leaned over to Mom. "I'll understand if you'd rather have a professional do the cake. It's just that all of the bakeries I called said they'd need more than two weeks to do a wedding cake. They're booked up for the holidays. You'd have to get a plain cake, nothing custom." He looked genuinely concerned. "I know you had your heart set on a cake from the Avenue, but the pastry chef there said you would have had to put your order in a week ago."

Mom got up and hugged Dawson. "I would love to have you make my wedding cake. I'm sure it will be delicious."

Dawson blushed.

"I called Reverend Timmons and he will, of course, officiate the wedding at the church. So, now, we just need a venue for the reception." Nana Jo looked pointedly at Frank.

He stood up. "I'd like to volunteer my restaurant. It's not fancy and can only hold about two hundred people comfortably between both levels, but if we close the restaurant for a private party and rearrange the tables, I think it'll work." He smiled. "Of course, I will cater the food and alcohol."

I rushed over and kissed him. When we came up for air, I whispered, "Thank you."

"Wow. If I'd known this was the way to your heart, I'd have volunteered a lot sooner."

"Thank you, Frank." Harold stood and offered his hand. "I can't possibly allow you to do all of that for free."

Frank shook his head, and Harold persisted.

"You two can work out the details later. We have a lot to get to." Nana Jo looked at her iPad.

The two men shook again, and I took the opportunity to return to my seat.

Dorothy Clark pulled out her cell phone and started texting. She was uncharacteristically distracted.

"Now, I think that takes care of most of the wedding arrangements, but if you have questions, please see Jillian or Emma." She looked around the table. Her gaze landed on Christopher and Zaq. "Christopher and Zaq have agreed to help out during Christmas break at the store so Sam and I are free to investigate."

I walked over and hugged my nephews. Neither were huge mystery fans, although they'd spent quite a bit of time helping out in the bookstore and were each finding authors they enjoyed. Christopher really enjoyed reading *Dark Reservations* by John Fortunato. Zaq, a technology guru, was actually enjoying John Sandford's Kidd books, which featured a computer whiz-for-hire. I would need to get them something special for Christmas. When the twins were small, shopping for birthdays and Christmas was easy. I took their lists to the nearest toy store. As they got older, their toys became more expensive and revolved around electronics and video games. At twenty, they weren't willing to wear clothes selected by any of the women in their lives and were most satisfied with money or gift cards. Maybe I could see if Emma could help me identify something for Zaq. Christopher was in between girlfriends, so I might have to use some of my own detective skills to find out something he would like.

Nana Jo interrupted my daydreams. "Sam, are you listening?"

Clearly, I wasn't, because I was still standing, staring vacantly, but I sat down and turned my attention to the meeting.

Nana Jo looked at everyone. "It's only been a few hours

since we learned of Lydia Lighthouse's murder, so I don't know if anyone has had time to get their sources working to find out any information or not. I'm having dinner with Freddie in . . ." She looked at her watch. "In an hour. He's got his son, Mark, looking into whatever the state police can find and I hope to have more to report tomorrow." She swiped her iPad. "I did a little research on Lydia Lighthouse on the Internet."

"Anything useful?" I asked.

"Her website is pure BS. She presents herself as a Southern belle who has dedicated her life to making brides' dreams come true. Pure fiction. However, the good stuff is what I found on one of those service review sites."

"You mean like those sites where you rate service companies?" Dorothy asked.

Nana Jo nodded. "Yep. Lydia Lighthouse has an average rating of two point one on Service Reviews R Us."

"Is that bad?" I asked.

"It is when it's on a scale of one to ten," Nana Jo said.

Frank whistled.

"One reviewer compared Lydia Lighthouse to Hitler." Nana Jo scrolled down until she found the entry. " 'Obviously, Lydia Lighthouse learned her social skills from *Mein Kampf*. She and Hitler share a lot of the same personality traits. I heard from a friend Lydia Lighthouse had a reputation as a pit bull. However, as the bride, I never expected the dog would attack me. Nothing I wanted was considered. Not only did I not get the flowers, cake, photographer, or venue I wanted, I didn't even get to wear the dress I wanted. My fiancé and I are simple people, and we wanted a simple wedding. Barbecue and cowboy hats with sunflowers were my dream. Lydia's response when I told her my ideas: *just because you're common trailer trash doesn't mean you have to let the world know it.*' "

"Wow!" Christopher said. "Why didn't they fire her?"

Nana Jo scrolled down. "Oh, she tells us." She scrolled

until she found the selection. " 'Why didn't I fire her you ask? Because Lydia Lighthouse requires you to sign a contract agreeing to pay her whether you have the wedding or not. The wedding was beautiful, but it wasn't what I wanted, and I felt like a guest at my own wedding. Given a choice between working with Lydia Lighthouse and spending the night in a rat-infested cellar, I'll take the rats.' "

"That's exactly what she did to us." Mom looked at Harold, who patted her hand.

Ruby Mae Stevenson put aside the pink fluffy baby blanket she was knitting and raised her hand. "Can you give us the names of some of the other people associated with Lydia? If we can't find out anything on her, maybe we can find out something about the others."

Nana Jo nodded. "Good idea." She looked at me. "Sam, do you remember the names of the other people we met yesterday?"

I shook my head.

However, Mom surprised me by raising her hand tentatively. "I know their names." She looked around like a timid bird about to fly out of its cage. "I wrote them down so I could tell Harold." She opened her purse and pulled out a napkin. "I didn't have any paper, so I used this napkin. The caterer's name was Rudy Blakemore."

"He runs a restaurant called Rudy's Place," Frank said.

"Do you know him?" Nana Jo asked.

Frank winked. "Not yet, but I think Sam and I should go check them out."

"Good." Nana Jo typed into her iPad. "Who else?"

"The ice sculptor was Maxwell Dubois."

"I've heard of him," Ruby Mae said. "He's in a band."

"The florist was Felicity Abrams of Felicity's Florals," Mom said.

"Felicity Abrams has a shop near my sister's art gallery." Dorothy typed on her phone. "I'll tackle her tomorrow. Oh, and I was texting my sister and I think I've found a photographer for the wedding. He's great. He just had a showing at her gallery last week." She texted like one of the high school students I used to teach. "He's free and . . . yes. He can do the pictures." She texted and then looked up from her phone with a smile.

"Thank you." Mom smiled and looked as though she would cry.

"No, thank you." Dorothy winked. "Now we can discuss the details over dinner and drinks. He's a real hottie."

"Is that everyone?" Nana Jo looked at my mom, who nodded.

"What about her assistant?" I asked.

"Yeah, mousy girl. Now, what was her name?" Nana Jo tapped the table. "April . . . Jones." She typed on her iPad.

We wrote the name down.

"Anything else?" Nana Jo looked around.

I raised my hand. "I think we need to consider everyone." I looked at Harold.

My mother gasped. "Sam, you can't honestly believe Harold . . ."

Harold colored and he looked choked up, but he held up a hand. "It's okay. I agree with Sam. You shouldn't rule anyone out."

"That's not what I mean. I certainly don't believe you killed Lydia."

"Well, I should hope not." Mom dabbed at her eyes.

"What *are* you getting at, Sam?" Nana Jo asked.

"It's just that no one here really knew Lydia except . . ."

Harold nodded. "Except my brother and sister-in-law, you mean?"

I nodded.

"Sam's right. If it weren't for them, she wouldn't have ever darkened our door." Nana Jo looked at Harold. "I'm afraid we'll have to put them on the list."

"I certainly understand." He swallowed hard and nodded. "Oscar and Margaret Robertson."

We all wrote the names down.

"Anything else?" Nana Jo looked at me.

I shook my head.

"Good. I need to get ready for my date. Let's get busy sleuthing."

Chapter 8

"I'm hungry. Let's stop and get something to eat on the way home." Zaq helped Emma on with her coat.

"Perhaps you would permit Harold and me to take you all out to dinner. We could discuss arrangements," Mom generously offered.

"Certainly, I have a few ideas I'd love to discuss with you," Jillian said.

Emma opened her book bag. "I have tons of bridal magazines. Maybe we can get some ideas about the things you'd like."

Mom nodded enthusiastically. "I'd love that."

"I have to get back to the restaurant, but if you're interested in eating at the café, I can get your ideas for food while I work." Frank looked at me. "Wanna join us?"

I shook my head. "As exciting as planning my mom's wedding sounds, I think I'll pass."

I hugged Emma and Jillian. "Whatever you do, please steer her away from bubble gum pink and tartan plaid."

They looked confused but crossed their hearts.

The wedding planners all left. Jenna promised to drop the

girls off at the retirement village and Freddie arrived and whisked Nana Jo away, just as I finished taking the dogs out. The building was quiet at last. A light snow was falling outside, and my loft felt warm and cozy. The conditions were perfect for a trip to the British countryside.

⁓

"Mrs. Baker, what an unexpected pleasure." Lady Elizabeth leaned forward so she could yell. The vicar's wife was a lovely woman, but was also slightly deaf in her right ear. "And who do we have here?"

Mrs. Baker turned to the three frightened children she brought with her. "The boys are Johan and Josiah. They're twins, so I don't know which is which. They're twelve." She turned to a small girl one of the brothers was struggling to carry. "This is their sister." She pulled out a piece of paper. "Rivka. She's two."

Lady Elizabeth extended her hand to the boys, who merely stood mute and stared. They were tall for their age but extremely thin. Their clothes were ragged. Pants too short, which exposed their ankles, and jackets that were too tight but bore a distinctive yellow Star of David. The boys had dark hair. Their eyes were dark and sunken in, making the twins look older than their years. The girl was small, too small for her age. She had dark, curly ringlets that framed her face and a pale complexion. She placed her head on her brother's shoulder. However, when Lady Elizabeth smiled at her, she returned the smile.

The ladies sat and Lady Elizabeth rang the buzzer for tea. The children stood awkwardly.

"Would you like to sit?" Lady Elizabeth extended a hand toward the sofa.

The boys looked at each other and then stared at Lady Elizabeth, who nodded. The boys moved in front of the sofa and hesitated.

Lady Elizabeth smiled and nodded again and they sat.

"Your ladyship, I'm at my wits end." Mrs. Baker perched on the edge of her chair.

"Oh dear, please tell me what's happened."

Mrs. Baker clutched her purse in her lap. "As you know, last Friday, the first Kindertransport arrived in England with over two hundred Jewish children from Germany and Austria."

"Yes. I signed up as a foster home, but I was told all of the children had been placed."

"Well, that was true. Unfortunately, Lady Amelia Dallyripple has just informed me she has to make a trip to the Riviera and can no longer keep the children."

Thompkins arrived with a tea cart. He rolled the cart into the room and placed it in front of Lady Elizabeth.

Lady Elizabeth noticed only two cups and a small number of scones. She stared up at the butler.

Thompkins coughed. "If your ladyship doesn't mind, I thought the children might prefer something more substantial. Mrs. Anderson has soup, sandwiches, and, of course, cake for your young guests."

Lady Elizabeth smiled. "Excellent. Children, would you please follow Thompkins?" She motioned for them to follow the butler, who relaxed his normally stiff posture and extended an arm to direct the children.

Tentatively, the children rose and followed the butler.

Lady Elizabeth noticed they stared hungrily back at the tea cart as they left. After they left, she sighed, turned to her guest, and smiled. "Thompkins and Mrs. McDuffy will see they are well fed." She poured tea and handed the cup to Mrs. Baker. "Now, what's happened?"

Mrs. Baker took a sip of tea. "Lady Dallyripple has backed out and says she can no longer take the children." The woman spoke quickly. "It's just a few weeks until Christmas and several of the other families who'd originally signed up as foster homes are out of town for the holidays and can't be reached. The vicar and I have taken two, which will be challenging enough, but if we can't find another foster home, then we'll have five children, and I just don't know that I can handle five children at once. With the language barrier and all, it's got me beside myself." She looked around like a frightened bird.

Lady Elizabeth hesitated a half moment but smiled broadly. "We'll be glad to take the children."

Mrs. Baker sighed. "Oh, thank you. Your ladyship has no idea what a relief it is."

Lady Elizabeth waved her hand in a gesture indicating no thanks were needed. "Glad to help. From what I've read in the newspapers and what those missionaries who spoke at the Lady's Aid Society last month said, the situation in Germany is truly horrendous. It's certainly no place for children."

Mrs. Baker shook her head. "I'm afraid things may be worse than what we've heard."

"What do you mean?"

She leaned forward and whispered, "Most of the

children don't speak much English, but several of the
older ones have made comments about bombing and
family members taken out of their homes in the middle of the night. Stories are coming out about beat-
ings and brutal attacks."

Lady Elizabeth took several breaths to calm her
anger. "That's horrible. Something must be done."

Mrs. Baker nodded. "Indeed, now that England has
started the national registry, I suspect it's just a matter
of time."

Lady Elizabeth stared at the vicar's wife. "I suspect you're right."

Downstairs in the servants' hall, Mrs. McDuffy
stood with her hands on her hips and an angry look in
her eyes that would not bode well if she ever got her
hands on Mr. Hitler. "'Ow any 'uman bein' what calls
'imself a 'uman bein' can mistreat children . . . well,
'angin' ain't good enough."

Thompkins stood near enough to the housekeeper
to hear her rant.

The two servants watched the three children.
Confused that so much food was just for them, they
were reluctant at first, but after gestures to demon-
strate they were to eat as much as they wanted, the
children set upon the food like ravenous wolves.
Table manners, if they had any, were discarded and
the children used their hands to shove as much food
into their mouths as quickly as they could. They discarded spoons and drank their soup directly from the
bowl and used their sleeves to wipe their mouths.

The other servants stood by. Gladys and Flossie
wiped tears away. Gruff, Mrs. Anderson brought out

as many enticing items as she could find. So, the table was laden with everything from soup and sandwiches to scones, fruit, milk, eggs, cookies, and cake. It wasn't until she took a ham and placed it on the table did she see the youngsters stop. The boys' eyes got large and they immediately dropped the food they held in their hands.

Mrs. Anderson stared. "It's just good old-fashioned ham."

Thompkins stepped forward. "I believe pork is not allowed in the Jewish religion."

Mrs. Anderson looked stricken and quickly removed the ham. "I'm sorry. I had no idea."

The children watched the cook remove the ham and then resumed eating.

Mrs. McDuffy consoled the cook. "It's okay, dear. You wasn't to know." She looked around. "And the rest of you can stop gawking and get back to work. We've got plenty of work to do getting ready for the wedding and no time to stand around watching children eat."

Lady Elizabeth entered the servants' hall and everyone stood at attention. She took a minute and looked at the children and then turned to Thompkins. "Can I speak to you and Mrs. McDuffy, please?"

The two servants followed Lady Elizabeth into the small office the butler used for private conversations. Once inside, the servants waited until her ladyship sat.

"Please, sit." She indicated the two chairs, even though the butler would decline; she waited for Mrs. McDuffy to sit before she started. "I think you both know the conditions in Europe aren't very good at the moment."

Mrs. McDuffy sniffed. "'Umph. If the condition of those young children is any indication, I'd say things are gawd awful. Those poor children aren't much more than skin and bones."

Lady Elizabeth patted the housekeeper's hand. "I agree. Well, we may not be able to fix all of the problems in Europe, but we can at least make life easier for those three little ones."

"So, they'll be staying?" Mrs. McDuffy asked.

Lady Elizabeth nodded. "Yes. They were supposed to go to Lady Dallyripple, but she has to leave the country suddenly and can't keep them."

Mrs. McDuffy sniffed again. "The old cow didn't want 'em."

Thompkins bristled. "Whatever her reasons for not taking them, your ladyship can rest assured we will do our best to make sure they are well taken care of."

"I know, but I'm concerned with the plans for the wedding that it might be too much." Lady Elizabeth looked at her trusted servants.

"Fiddle sticks! Three small children won't be much more work," Mrs. McDuffy said.

Lady Elizabeth smiled. "Well, I appreciate your willingness; however, I think it would be best if we hired someone to help out. Mrs. Baker tells me the children don't speak English, so I think a governess, someone who spoke German, might be best."

Thompkins coughed. "Of course, your ladyship. I'll call the agency first thing."

"Thank you, Thompkins." She paused. "Perhaps, if they have someone who is either Jewish or at least somewhat familiar with Jewish culture, it might be helpful. However, I suppose that might be too much to hope for." She sighed.

"Good 'elp is 'ard to find these days. Not like in the old days when people lined up for jobs in service to a good family like this one." Mrs. McDuffy sniffed.

Lady Elizabeth smiled. "We have been fortunate to find good, honest, hardworking people, and I feel confident we'll find the perfect person to help in this situation too."

Thompkins coughed.

"Yes."

"I was just wondering what was known about the youngsters."

Lady Elizabeth sighed. "Unfortunately, not much. Mrs. Baker knows they're siblings. Johan and Josiah are twins and they're twelve. The little girl is named Rivka and she's two. She doesn't know their last names. She believes their parents were killed in Poland and they were staying with their grandparents in Berlin."

"The poor things." Mrs. McDuffy sniffed and dabbed at her eyes. "It's got to be very frightening for them, moving from Poland to Berlin and now to England."

"Exactly. That's why we've got to do everything we can to help them feel welcome and loved," Lady Elizabeth said.

Mrs. McDuffy hoisted herself up. "Well, your lady-ship can count on me and my girls to do our duty. Jews or Christian, it makes no difference. Children is children."

"Thank you, Mrs. McDuffy. I knew I could rely on you. Perhaps, you could have Lady Daphne's and Penelope's rooms upstairs in the nursery cleaned out and made ready. There should be room enough for the three of them and a governess."

"I'll see to it at once." Mrs. McDuffy turned to leave but stopped and turned back. "I'm sorry, is there anything else?"

"Oh, no. I just need to have a quick word with Thompkins."

"Right." Mrs. McDuffy nodded and then slipped out.

Thompkins stood at attention.

"Thompkins, would you please see the children all receive new clothes at once. Perhaps Frank or Jim could help with the boys. Normally, Daphne would be my choice for the little girl, but with the wedding . . . I hate to ask her."

"I understand completely. I think Gladys might be prevailed upon to help dress the little girl. She's a local girl, and isn't quite as flighty as other girls her age."

Lady Elizabeth nodded. "Perfect, but please check with Mrs. McDuffy first to make sure she can spare Gladys. I wouldn't want to offend her."

Thompkins nodded. "Of course." He paused. "Is there anything else?"

Lady Elizabeth took a deep breath. "I don't know how to say . . . I don't want to offend you in any way, but . . . I had heard that one of your daughters, Mary, I believe, married someone who is Jewish."

Thompkins nodded. "Yes, milady."

"I was just wondering if . . ."

"Darn it!" My cell phone vibrated. I looked at the time. It was almost two in the morning. I noticed Frank's picture before I swiped my phone. "Phone calls at two in the morning are never good. What's up?"

Frank sighed. "I'm glad you're up. Any chance you could come by the restaurant? I've got a problem."

"What kind of problem?"

"You'll see when you get here."

"I'll be right there."

Snickers and Oreo were asleep and didn't budge when I got up. So, I left them and put on my winter gear and hurried the few doors down to Frank's restaurant. All of the lights were on and he was waiting for me at the door.

He opened the door and I hurried inside. He locked the door behind me and shook off the snow that accumulated during my short trek.

"What's up?"

He put a finger over his lips and indicated I should follow him.

I followed quietly behind as he walked to the back of the restaurant. He motioned for me to follow and he led me through a door that opened into a narrow passage near the restrooms. There was a door that led to a back storage area, where food and boxes were stored. Curled up in the back corner was what I initially took for a bundle of clothes. Upon closer inspection, that was when I saw one of the bundles move. I jumped and would have turned and run if Frank hadn't reached out and grabbed my arm. I wasn't fond of dark cellars or basements; surely Frank wouldn't deliberately lead me here unless it was important. I took a deep breath and crept closer.

Frank pointed. I looked around him and noticed two sleeping figures stretched behind some large cartons of paper towels and toilet paper. On the floor was a blond-haired, chubby little boy, who looked to be three or four. The other was a girl with stringy, dark hair. She looked about twelve. The children's clothes were old-fashioned and, somehow, looked foreign.

I stared at Frank and mouthed, *Who? What?*

He shrugged. We tiptoed toward the door and farther away from the sleeping children.

Frank looked haggard. "I have no idea who they are or how they got here. Between taking care of the restaurant and talking to your mother and Harold about the menu for the wedding, I barely had a chance to breathe."

"But how?"

"No idea."

"Didn't anyone see two children come in? Surely, they wouldn't have just walked in without an adult. Someone had to have seen something."

"If they did, they never said anything to me. By the time I found them, all of the staff was gone."

"You don't suppose someone just abandoned them here, do you?"

He shook his head. "No idea."

We stared at each other.

"What do you think I should do?"

"You can't leave them there. You'll have to call the police."

At that moment, one of the bundles moved. The girl woke up. She opened her eyes and saw Frank and me watching her. She jumped to her feet. "*Destarsi.*" She reached down and shook the boy. "*Andiamo.*"

The little boy sat up and wiped his eyes.

"*FERMASI,*" Frank yelled.

The girl stopped and stared at Frank.

"What did you just say?" I whispered.

"I told her to stop."

I nodded. "What language was that?"

"Italian."

I was only slightly surprised Frank knew Italian. He knew several languages. In his past life, he'd been involved in secret government work, which he still didn't talk about. "Now what?"

Frank said several more things in Italian. I could tell from her eyes the young girl understood, but she merely stared.

"Do you think she understands?"

Frank nodded. "She does."

"What did you say?"

"I told her we weren't going to hurt her. I asked how she got here and where her parents were."

The two children stared at us, like frightened rabbits ready to bolt at the first opportunity.

"What do you think we should do?" I asked.

"I have no idea."

"Do they speak English?"

"Maybe we should call the police?"

The girl reached over and grabbed her brother by the coat and pulled him to his feet. She looked around until her gaze landed on a push mop in the corner. She ran to the mop and grabbed it like a sword. She slashed the air with the mop and walked forward.

I took a few steps backward as she advanced, to avoid getting hit by the mop. Frank didn't. Instead, he planted his feet and when she was about to bring the mop down on his head, he reached out and grabbed the mop with one hand and disarmed her. With the other hand, he grabbed her. He spun her around so she faced away from him.

The girl kicked and screamed, but Frank held on. He dropped the mop so he could use both arms and enveloped the girl in a bear hug. "Grab him."

I reached out to the young boy, who tried to sprint past

me. I wasn't as smooth as Frank, but I managed to grab and hold my small charge.

"Let me go!" She struggled and kicked.

"I guess that answers the question if they speak English or not." I glanced back at Frank.

He was bigger, stronger, and a lot more experienced, so holding onto his captive appeared pretty easy. He merely wrapped his arms around her and held on.

Eventually, she stopped struggling, probably a tactic to get him to relax his hold, but he was too smart to fall for that. When he didn't loosen his grip, she started flailing and kicking, but to no avail.

"Are you done?" Frank asked.

"I'll scream," she said.

"Go ahead. Maybe one of the neighbors will call the cops." Frank waited, but no screams came.

"You're hurting me."

"Actually, this technique restricts without causing pain, but I know other techniques that aren't as gentle." He looked over at me and winked.

"All right, all right. What do you want?"

"I want to talk to you," he said.

"That's it?" she asked.

"That's it."

"Okay."

Frank nodded to me. "Close the door and then let him go."

There was only one door into the room. I kicked it closed with my foot and then released the boy.

The boy promptly ran to Frank and started to kick and pommel him with his fists. Frank ignored him, and, once he saw the only escape route was blocked, he released the girl.

The girl turned to face Frank, her face red with rage. However, she was instantly engulfed by two small arms. When she looked down at him, her face softened and she hugged him to her. "It'll be okay, Angelo."

I stood guard in front of the door, with my arms folded across my chest.

"All right, mister, you got us. Now, whaddya want?"

"For starters, how about your names."

She hesitated, and I thought she wasn't going to answer, but eventually she responded. "My name is Lexi and this is my brother, Angelo."

"Nice to meet you. This is Sam and I'm Frank." He gave a quick look my way. "Now, what are you doing here?"

"We ain't steal nothing."

The English teacher in me cringed. "You didn't steal anything."

"Yeah, that's what I said, so you can just let us go." She took a step forward, but Frank halted her.

"Not so fast. If you didn't come to rob me, what're you doing here?"

"We just needed a place to sleep, that's all. It's cold outside."

"Have you eaten?" I asked.

She and Angelo answered simultaneously. She said, "Yeah," just as Angelo said, "No."

Frank sighed. "Look, I'm not going to hurt you, but if you promise not to run, I'll fix you something to eat. How about some soup?"

Angelo looked at his sister with big, dark, hungry eyes, which made my heart melt. It apparently had the same effect on Lexi, because she nodded.

I moved aside and opened the door. Frank walked out first. I waited for Lexi and Angelo, then followed and closed the door behind me.

"Take a seat." Frank indicated a booth at the back of the

restaurant. He went behind the bar and got two glasses and poured milk into them and set them on the table.

The two hesitated a split second and then sat and gulped down the milk so quickly, it was obvious they hadn't eaten in quite a while.

When their glasses were empty, he refilled them and placed the pitcher of milk on the table and went into the kitchen.

I sat down next to Angelo. "How old are you?"

He held up four fingers and looked at his sister, who nodded.

"And you?" I looked at Lexi.

She looked defiant but eventually said, "Eighteen."

I smiled. "You'll be eighteen in about six years, I'm guessing."

She rolled her eyes. "If you already know the answers, why bother asking questions?"

"It gives me something to do." I smiled

Frank came out with two bowls of chili on a tray with crackers. He placed the food in front of the children, along with napkins.

Angelo's eyes got big at the sight of his bowl of warm chili, and he immediately took his spoon and started to eat.

"Hang on. That's hot." Frank reached out to prevent Angelo from burning his mouth, but he grabbed the bowl and spoon and pulled it to his chest. Frank raised both hands. "I'm not going to take it away, I was just going to blow on it to cool it off."

"I'll do it." Lexi took a spoon of her chili and blew on it and then fed her brother. He took a bite and swallowed the chili without chewing.

Frank went to the bar and scooped ice from the large ice maker under the sink and came back and put a few ice cubes into each bowl.

We sat and waited while the children ate. They ate quickly.

Lexi put packets of crackers in her pocket when she thought no one was watching.

When they were finished, Frank asked, "I don't suppose you saved room for pie?"

Angelo bounced on his seat. "Pie? I got room. I got room."

Frank smiled and got up and went back to the kitchen. This time he came back with four plates of apple pie.

I smiled and we all sat and ate pie in silence.

"Wow. That was really good pie, mister," Angelo said. "You make it?"

"Thank you." Frank nodded. "I made the chili and the pie."

"Now what?" Lexi asked. "You fed us, so what happens now? You gonna turn us over to the police?"

"I don't know. Where're your parents?"

"Dead," Lexi said.

"Where do you live?" I asked.

She shrugged. "We was in a foster home, but we ain't going back there. So, if you call the police and they take us back, we'll just run away again."

"What do you think we should do?" Frank asked me.

"Why don't you just let us go?" Lexi asked.

"It's cold and snowing outside. It's too cold for you two to be outside. I guess you'll just have to come home with me." I reached for the dishes.

"Wait," Frank said. "Just leave those. I'll take care of it first thing tomorrow."

I'd never known Frank to leave dirty dishes, but I was too tired to argue.

"Do you think taking them into your home is a good idea?" he asked quietly.

"Probably not, but it's late and I'm tired."

"She's just going to run the first chance she gets." He looked at Lexi. "Or rob you blind."

"I ain't no thief."

I looked at Lexi. "You aren't a thief." Then I turned to Frank. "That's why you're coming too. You can guard my fine silver."

He stared for a few seconds and then sighed. "Okay, you heard the lady. Let's go."

Chapter 9

Frank grabbed his coat and locked up, and we made the short trip down the street to my building. The fastest path was through the bookstore, so I unlocked the door and turned off the alarm. Once everyone was inside, I locked the door and rearmed the system but left off the motion detector. I led the way to the stairs. Angelo's eyes had started to droop and Frank scooped him up and carried him upstairs.

I noticed Lexi's eyes lingering on the books. She walked slowly and touched the covers as she passed. "You own all these books?"

I nodded. "I guess. I own this bookstore and I sell the books. Do you like to read?"

She nodded. "I used to. My mom used to read to me a lot before . . . before she died."

"Did you ever read any mysteries?"

She shrugged. "Dunno."

"You don't know."

"That's what I said."

"Tomorrow, I'll let you pick out a book."

Her eyes brightened. "For real?"

I nodded. "But let's get some sleep."

If Nana Jo was home, she must have been asleep because her door was closed. I gave Lexi and Angelo my bed and grabbed blankets for Frank and me for the sofa. Angelo was asleep before his head hit the pillow. Lexi was enamored with Snickers, who woke up to see what was going on. When asked, I okayed Lexi letting Snickers sleep in the bed. Little did she know, Snickers didn't need my approval. When we turned out the light, Angelo was sound asleep and Lexi was snuggled up to Snickers.

Frank and I snuggled together on the sofa.

"Thank you for your help tonight. You didn't have to do this," he whispered in my ear, and the warmth of his breath sent a shiver down my spine.

"I couldn't just leave you to handle things by yourself." I breathed in his scent.

His arms engulfed me and made me feel warm and safe. My eyelids felt heavy and my muscles began to relax.

Before I took the last step into dreamland, I turned. "What are you going to do with them? Someone will be looking for them."

"I know." He yawned. "First, I'll try to find out their last names. Then I'll find out what's going on."

"How are you going to find out their last names?"

"Hopefully, they'll tell us, but if not, I've got their finger-prints on the glasses of milk. I'll have a friend run the prints and see if he can get a match."

I smiled. "That's why you told me to leave the dishes." I looked around at him and, even though it was dark, I could tell he was smiling. "I should have known. You never leave dirty dishes overnight."

"Dirty dishes attract creatures that aren't good for a restaurant."

"You know how to remove fingerprints from glasses?"

"I have a lot of skills." He nibbled my ear.

I giggled. "Don't distract me."

He sighed. "Yes, ma'am."

"Did you see the bruises?"

He nodded. "She's got bruises on her wrists and arms. I'm sure there are more, but she keeps them covered up."

"I suppose there could be a logical explanation, but I think they've been abused. When I was a teacher, we went to training seminars to help identify abused children. That's why I didn't insist they go back tonight. I have my phone on and there hasn't been an Amber alert about any missing children."

"Sometimes there are delays. Not all agencies are connected."

"I know, but it's two a.m. A few more hours probably won't hurt. They were starving and cold." I yawned.

Frank kissed me, and, within moments, I heard his even steady breathing.

The next thing I remembered was the smell of bacon and coffee and something sweet. I stretched and squinted at the light streaming through the floor-to-ceiling windows in my loft.

"Hmmm, is that pancakes?" Angelo asked.

"Yep, and if you want some, you're going to need to wash first," Nana Jo said.

I looked over the top of the sofa and saw Nana Jo, Angelo, and Lexi standing at the kitchen bar, while Dawson worked his magic on the stove.

"I ain't dirty. I ain't even been outside yet to get dirty." Angelo held up his hands.

"Not good enough. You're going to need a bath. You've got so much dirt on your belly, I saw a flower starting to grow out of your belly button."

Angelo pulled up his shirt and stared at his belly button. "I ain't got no flower in my belly button."

"Sure you do. It's just starting to grow, so it's pretty little right now, but I know belly button flowers when I see them. Now, scoot." She swatted the back of his pants and pushed him toward the bathroom. She passed Lexi and turned back. "You too."

"Look, I'm not a kid, and I ain't falling for that."

"Right. You're a young lady and too old to be walking around here like that." Nana Jo flung a bath towel at her. "So, you just go into that bathroom and take a shower and be sure to clean yourself thoroughly, or I'll be in there and see that you do." She put a hand on her hip.

Lexi looked as though she wanted to come back with a smart remark, but she must have thought better of it because she merely stomped off.

"And don't forget to wash your hair," Nana Jo yelled at the bathroom door. She looked around at me and I smiled. "And you can get up and run down to the drugstore on the corner and pick up some clean underwear and socks." She rolled up her sleeves and headed into my bathroom.

I looked over at Dawson. "How long has she been in that mood?"

He chuckled. "I don't know. I just came over to put some rolls in the oven, and I was told to get my butt over here and start making some pancakes." He walked over and handed me a steaming hot mug of coffee.

Frank must have left early this morning because I was alone and bundled up on the sofa. I quickly finished my coffee, got up, and looked for my shoes. "I guess I better get going."

I stopped at the bathroom downstairs in the bookstore to take care of the call of nature. I also took the opportunity to wash my face and brush my teeth, then hurried out to carry out my assignment.

The drugstore on the corner was an old-fashioned five-and-dime. Not only did they sell the normal items you would expect to find at a drugstore in the twenty-first century, but they also sold clothes, toys, hardware, and lawn and gardening supplies. At one point in the store's history, it had also sold ice cream, and the soda counter still remained. I forced myself not to go overboard and bought underwear and socks as ordered, but I also bought blue jeans and sweatshirts. I could wash their clothes, but this would give them some warm clothing. I rationalized the purchases by telling myself they could always take the clothes with them. My only splurge was to buy puzzles, coloring books, and crayons from the impulse shelf at the checkout counter.

I was back in plenty of time. I heard Angelo and Nana Jo in the bathroom. Apparently, he was still looking for his belly button flower. I opened the bathroom door and left the clean clothes on the counter and grabbed the dirty clothes discarded on the floor. I went to Nana Jo's bathroom and heard the shower. I knocked lightly and then opened the door and placed the clothes on the counter. I quickly grabbed the dirty clothes Lexi'd placed on the floor and left.

My washer and dryer were in a closet in between the kitchen and the bathroom. I sorted the kids' clothes, noting their undergarments weren't sparkling white. They were dingy and threadbare. I hurriedly grabbed the sheets from my bedroom and loaded my favorite appliance, a red high-efficiency front load washer with bleach, detergent, and fabric softener and tossed everything inside.

Laundry loaded and ready to go, I ate my breakfast of coffee, bacon, and pancakes. By the time I finished, a laughing Angelo ran into the kitchen.

Nana Jo helped him climb up on the barstool, and Dawson put a plate with pancakes and bacon on it in front of him and poured a glass of orange juice.

Snickers and Oreo sat by his chair and waited for food to drop so they could devour it.

Lexi joined us, wearing the new clothes I'd purchased,

which fit her surprisingly well. Her hair was still wet, but she looked clean and the bruises I'd seen on her arms were covered. She glared at Nana Jo, who merely pointed her to the empty barstool.

I took that moment to take advantage of an empty bathroom for a more thorough cleansing than I'd managed in the bookstore bathroom earlier. Thankfully, there was still plenty of hot water and the shower helped to not only cleanse my body but to stimulate my mind. Regardless of what Frank found out, I knew I had to call the police. Someone, somewhere, would be looking for these children.

Clean and ready to tackle my day, I emerged from the bathroom.

Nana Jo and Angelo were coloring at the kitchen table.

I looked around for Lexi but didn't see her. "Where's Lexi?"

"I sent her downstairs to find a book." Nana Jo looked at me. My face must have looked anxious, because she pointed to a corner where Lexi's and Angelo's shoes were lined up by the front door. She wouldn't get far in the middle of winter in Michigan without shoes. "Besides, Dawson's downstairs too."

I breathed a sigh of relief. "We need to talk."

Nana Jo nodded and got up from the table.

We walked over to the breakfast bar, close enough to still keep an eye on Angelo, but far enough away that he wouldn't be able to overhear our conversation. I filled Nana Jo in on how Lexi and Angelo came to spend the night.

She listened attentively. "That boy has bruises on his back and arms."

"I noticed some on Lexi's arms last night too."

"What are you going to do?"

"I was planning to go to the police station to talk to Stinky Pitt today anyway. Maybe he can help me find out where they belong and get word to their foster parents."

Nana Jo nodded. "I suppose that's the best thing to do."

I wasn't sure if it was the best thing or not, but I believed it was the right thing.

Christopher and Zaq opened the bookstore, and Dawson watched videos on the Internet of cake-decorating techniques while he experimented with various recipes. When I left, Lexi was sitting on the sofa wrapped in a blanket, reading.

I walked over to her. "What're you reading?"

She clutched the book to her chest. "That lady told me to pick out a book." She pointed to Nana Jo. "And you told me I could . . ."

I raised a hand to still the accusation. "It's okay. I was just curious which book you chose." I didn't have a large children's book section, but I'd purchased a few that I loved as a child, including Nancy Drew and Hardy Boys, along with Encyclopedia Brown. I'd decided to stock up on children's box sets for the Christmas season but had planned to reduce the section when the season was over.

She relaxed and turned the book so I could see the cover. "The old lady said I might like this one." She held up the book.

"*From the Mixed-Up Files of Mrs. Basil E. Frankweiler,* by E. L. Konigsburg, was one of my favorites." I smiled. "However, I don't recommend you keep calling Nana Jo an 'old lady,' or you're going to find yourself in bigger trouble than Claudia Kincaid." I tapped the book.

"Darn right!" Nana Jo said from the kitchen.

I winked at Lexi and noticed the first genuine smile in return.

"Will you two be okay here with Dawson while I run some errands?"

"Of course. We can take care of ourselves."

"Good. Frank will bring you lunch if I'm not back before

then, and if you're good, I'm sure Dawson will let you sample some of his delicacies."

"Hooray!" Angelo cheered.

North Harbor Police Station was on a small stretch of land on a street in between the two bridges that crossed the St. Thomas River, which separated North Harbor from South Harbor. The station was a large complex that served both towns and housed not only the police but also the court. In the past six months, I'd been to the police station so many times, the desk sergeant recognized me.

"You here for Detective Pitt?" The burly detective barely looked up from his computer.

I nodded and he indicated I should take a seat while he called.

I didn't have to wait long for Detective Bradley Pitt.

"Mrs. Washington, I've been expecting you," the detective said with the sarcasm I'd come to expect from him while he held the door for me to pass.

We walked in silence to the closet that had been converted to the detective's office.

Detective Bradley Pitt was short, fat, and balding, which he tried to hide by allowing the hair he did have to grow longer so he could comb it over his bald dome. He was extremely fond of polyester and every outfit I'd ever seen him wear was made of the fabric, including his shirts. In addition to missing the memo that comb-overs didn't hide baldness, he'd also missed learning he'd packed on pounds and his clothes were now too tight and too short.

I took a deep breath to stave off claustrophobia and fol-lowed the detective inside the closet and sat in the one guest chair. The space was so cramped I had to turn my legs side-ways so he could close the door.

Once the door closed, Detective Pitt sat in his chair and

leaned back. Unfortunately, the room wasn't large enough, and he hit his head on the back wall. He muttered an oath and then leaned forward. "I knew as soon as I heard Harold Robertson was planning to marry your mother it wouldn't be long before you'd be poking your nose into my case."

"Harold Robertson didn't kill Lydia Lighthouse, and, as a conscientious, law-abiding citizen, I would be remiss in my civic responsibility if I didn't try to help."

He made a sound as though he were sucking his teeth. "Yeah, right."

Detective Pitt considered me a nosy busybody, and I knew he resented my involvement. However, there was something in Detective Pitt's demeanor that told me he wasn't as loathe to see me as usual. He looked around and fidgeted.

I waited silently.

Detective Pitt shook his head. "I know I'm going to regret this, but . . ." He slid a file he had on his desk across to me.

I picked up the file and stared at the detective. I'd helped the detective a few other times in the past, but there was always more of a fight. He resented a *civilian,* nay an *amateur,* meddling in police business. In the past, I'd begged, pleaded, and cajoled to see the official police files. Sure, he'd eventually complied, but it was never this quick and never without great protest. Instead of opening the file, I merely stared.

My expression must have spoke the question my lips hadn't because he rolled his eyes. "All right, you've been right a couple of times and the last time you saved my bacon with the chief." He bowed his head and muttered, "Although he's still on me." He took a deep breath. "The truth of the matter is, I'm still in hot water with the chief and there are some around here that would love to see me fall on my . . . face. Plus, the Robertson family is big in this community. They're wealthy and influential. In fact, the chief's already heard from the mayor and a local congressman. They want a quick resolution and no mistakes. The chief wasn't even going to give me the case, but we're short staffed for the holidays. Detective Harrison broke his foot and has to have surgery." He dropped his head. "I figure you're going to find a way to prove Harold Robertson didn't kill that woman anyway, so I might as well get you working on my side right from the beginning."

I smiled. "Good. I'll be happy to help, but I'm going to need your help with something too."

His initial expression was shock, which was quickly followed by resignation. "Fine. What do you want, my kidney?" He reached in his desk drawer and pulled out a bottle of antacid and popped one in his mouth.

"All I want is some information." I quickly told the detective about Lexi and Angelo.

He turned his chair toward his computer and pecked for several moments. "No reports of missing children, but you'll need to call Child and Family Services to be certain."

"I was hoping you could call them for me and let them know the children are safe." I gave the detective my friendliest, most sincere smile.

He grunted and got up from his chair. I turned my knees sideways so he could open the door, and he left.

I read through the file on Lydia Lighthouse. There wasn't much there yet. The coroner hadn't completed the autopsy but suspected the cause of death was asphyxiation from the scarf tied around her neck. The only other noteworthy item was learning Lydia Lighthouse's real name was Lydia Jones.

By the time Detective Pitt returned, I had completed my review of the file.

"I called Child and Family Services. No foster children are missing. Are you sure the children don't have parents?"

I shrugged. "I'm not sure of anything. All I can tell you is what they said."

"Well, Mrs. Masterson said she can have someone pick them up tomorrow."

I bit my lip. "There's no hurry."

He looked at me. "You can tell her that when she comes to your bookstore." He looked at the file on his desk. "Got what you need?"

I nodded.

"Well, I'd like to wrap this up by Christmas, so don't drag your feet."

Back at the bookstore, Christopher and Zaq had everything under control. Upstairs, Lexi was still reading and Angelo was licking a large wooden spoon. Based on the batter around his mouth, I'd guess it was chocolate frosting.

I transferred the wet clothes to the dryer and put another load in, then went to my room. I sat at my laptop and tried to create a spreadsheet with a list of suspects, along with possible motives. My list was fairly empty. In fact, at the moment, Harold was the only suspect I had. However, I was certain that would change later today when everyone got busy investigating.

I tried to think about Lydia and imagine who had a strong enough motive to want her dead. She certainly was able to generate a lot of strong emotions. I searched the Internet for her and found the site Nana Jo read from with reviews. She had angered a great many people, but, as far as I could tell, none of them were in North Harbor, Michigan. Yet, I did notice there was definitely a consistent theme in the complaints against her. She had bossed the bride and overruled her requests. Most of the couples claimed they were overcharged. However, I wondered if these charges were valid. Weddings were expensive. I could easily see a bride and groom getting in over their heads and their bank accounts.

I searched weddings and found tons of sites dedicated to elegant weddings, beautiful weddings, and unique weddings. I found everything from butterflies and doves to hot-air-balloon limousines for shuttling guests. Before I knew it, I'd fallen down a rabbit hole and had been looking at wedding rings and dresses for over an hour.

"I need to clear my mind," I said to myself and opened my manuscript. I took a few minutes to remind myself what was happening when I stopped. "Oh, yeah, Lady Elizabeth was asking Thompkins if his son-in-law could help them."

⁓

"I was just wondering if perhaps your daughter, Mary, or your son-in-law might be able to help us, to understand some of the cultural and religious customs. I'd hate to do or say anything that might offend our guests. If they could recommend a book, I'd be happy to read up on Jewish culture, but I think if they wouldn't mind coming by, perhaps they could help all of us gain a better understanding more quickly."

Thompkins nodded. "I'm certain Joseph, my son-in-law, would be more than willing to help." He paused a split second. "They both will."

Lady Elizabeth smiled. "Thank you, Thompkins."

When Thompkins opened the door to the library later and announced a guest, Lady Elizabeth hoped it was his son-in-law. She tried hard to hide her disappointment when the butler announced another name.

"Philippe Claiborne." The butler turned and left.

Philippe Claiborne was a bright peacock of a man with dark hair and a pencil moustache. From his posture to the tilt of his head, his manner announced Philippe Claiborne was the center of the universe. The earth and all of the planets revolved around him. He walked with long, confident strides and made broad sweeping gestures with his arms, one of which held a long-stemmed cigarette holder, from which a cigarette dangled. He dropped ash with each sweeping gesture. His clothes were loud and trendy. He looked as though he'd just stepped off the silver screen.

"Lady Elizabeth." He bent low and kissed the hand she extended to him. "I am Philippe." He bowed again. "At your service."

Lady Elizabeth was caught by surprise and hesitated for a few seconds before she acknowledged the introduction. "Mr. Claiborne, it's my—"

Philippe Claiborne wagged his finger and tsked. "No. Excuse me, your ladyship, but Mr. Claiborne is my father. Please"—he stood very straight and cocked his head backward—"I am Philippe." He flourished his hand.

"Yes, forgive me. Mr. . . . ah . . . Philippe."

He grinned and strutted in a circle in front of the fireplace as he surveyed the room. He ran fingers across the mantle and examined a crystal ashtray.

"May I introduce my niece, Lady Daphne Marsh." Lady Elizabeth extended an arm toward her niece.

Daphne stepped forward and extended her hand. "Pleased to meet you, Philippe."

"Ah, but of course, you are the beautiful bride." He brought Daphne's hand to his lips and kissed it. When he stood, he looked at James. "And, this must be His Grace, James FitzAndrew Browning, the groom." He bowed to James.

James stepped forward. "Yes. Thank you for coming."

"Ah, but of course. Philippe is at your service, Your Grace."

James rubbed the back of his neck and stared. "Yes, well, please call me James. I don't go in for all that formal rot."

Philippe wagged his finger at James. "Yes, but the formal 'rot' as you call it, it must be observed. We must have order and protocol. It is what makes England great, is it not?"

Lady Elizabeth glanced at James. His ears were getting red and his brow furrowed. "Well, I'm sure we can sort that out later. Now, Mr. . . . excuse me, Philippe, I'm sure you have a lot of questions for the bride and groom and I'll—"

Philippe stood in the middle of the room with a broad smile and shook his head. "Excuse me, your ladyship, but Philippe has no questions."

"But I'm sure you'd like to discuss things like flowers and seating and . . ."

Philippe shook his head.

"I don't think I understand?" Lady Elizabeth stared.

"I beg your pardon, your ladyship, but Philippe has no need to discuss such things. Philippe never discusses such things." He walked around the room as an appraiser would look at a valuable painting. "That is not how Philippe works."

"It's not?" Lady Elizabeth stared.

"No. Philippe is a man of passion, of feelings. He must *feel* what belongs. He sees the house and he meets the bride." He bowed to Lady Daphne. "He meets the groom." He bowed to James. "And he knows what is the right flower." He walked up to Lady Daphne and extended a hand to her chin. He lifted her head slightly, as though examining a vase. "Exquisite. Delicate." He smiled. "Lilies."

Daphne gasped. "How did you know I like lilies?"

Philippe laughed. "It is obvious. No other flower would suit one with such delicate coloring." He grinned. "Yes, lilies but, given the timing of the wedding, I think perhaps we should include something more to show the contrast between the delicate beauty of the lily. Perhaps the red poinsettia?"

Lady Elizabeth glanced at her niece. Philippe Claiborne could not know that Lady Daphne abhorred poinsettias and had only that morning declared the fact to her aunt.

"Well, I've never been fond of poinsettias," Daphne said.

"Philippe understands completely, but your ladyship has perhaps not thought about how unlucky the lily is and the need to counteract that with something to bring luck, like the poinsettia." He looked at Daphne as if to say, *you poor child*. "Philippe would never permit such a beautiful woman to bring bad luck into her marriage by including more than just a small few lilies, the flower of death, often given at funerals."

Daphne's face grew pale. "I hadn't thought of that." Her gaze went from Philippe to Lady Elizabeth and landed on James.

James grunted. "Lot of rot. I don't believe in all that superstitious claptrap."

"Rightly so." Philippe preened his moustache. "That is why you have Philippe to think of these things and to insure your wedding, nay your future, is not marred by"—he waved his cigarette in the air and dropped ashes on the floor—"*superstitious claptrap.*"

"Look here, I think we may have been a little hasty when we asked you to come out here. After all, we're not having a grand wedding. It's just going to be a small wedding with a few friends and family. I hardly think we'll need a wedding planner to help us. I think—"

"I think what His Grace is trying to say is we hope you won't feel insulted by being called to assist with a small family wedding." Lady Daphne glanced over her shoulder at James and gave him a look that caused him to sigh.

"Of course not. Philippe is happy to assist where he can. All of the great families of England, they reach out to Philippe. Large or small." He waved his hand and picked up a silver lighter from a side table. "It is all the same. Elegance and culture are what matters. That is what Philippe will do." He stood very tall and clicked his heels. "You leave everything to Philippe." He bowed.

"Thank you, Philippe." Daphne smiled.

Thompkins entered the room quietly and rolled a tea cart to Lady Elizabeth.

"Thank you, Thompkins," Lady Elizabeth said.

James rolled his eyes and muttered, "Thank God."

The smell of food wafted from the kitchen to my office and my stomach grumbled. I heard Frank's voice and knew lunch had arrived. I hoped he'd brought enough for me too as I pressed "save."

I followed my nose to the kitchen. Lexi and Angelo were perched on stools at the bar with bowls of soup and grilled cheese sandwiches. Lexi slurped soup while hidden behind her book. Angelo kicked his feet against the bar while he bounced and told Frank about his new coloring book.

"That smells delicious." I sniffed. "Is that corn chowder?"

Frank smiled. "Chicken corn chowder and I brought plenty."

"Thank God." I grinned as I recalled I'd just written that same line.

Frank looked puzzled.

"Sorry. I was writing."

"Can I talk to you for a minute?"

"Sure." I glanced at the soup on the counter but hurried back into my bedroom. The quicker we talked, the quicker I'd get to eat.

Frank followed me to the bedroom and closed the door after himself. "I lifted the fingerprints from the glasses and sent them to a friend."

He didn't mention the friend's name or where he worked and I didn't ask.

I'd known Frank Patterson long enough to know there were a number of things in his past that he couldn't and wouldn't discuss. "Did they find out anything?"

"It was a long shot, but I had a feeling this wasn't the first time Lexi had gotten into trouble."

"Agreed, but she is a minor. Aren't her records sealed?"

Frank stared at me in a way that indicated things like rules for juvenile records wouldn't be a problem.

"Never mind."

"Alexis Gelano, age twelve. Daughter of Maria and Luis Gelano, deceased. One sibling, Angelo Gelano, age four."

"What was she picked up for?"

"Stealing."

I sighed.

"She stole bread and peanut butter from a neighborhood grocery store."

"Aww . . . she was hungry."

"Most likely."

"So, where are they supposed to be staying? I talked to Stinky Pitt today and he checked with Child Protective Services and no children were reported missing."

"Probably because the last known address was in Chicago."

"Chicago? You have got to be kidding. How on earth did those two children make their way over ninety miles in the middle of winter from Chicago to Michigan?"

He shrugged. "Hitchhiked? Or they could have taken the South Shore Train for less than ten dollars."

I shuddered. "Did your friend have a name and address for the foster family?"

He reached inside his pocket and handed me a piece of paper, where he had written down the name.

I stared at the paper, but my vision was blurry and I couldn't read what was written.

Frank reached out and pulled me into his embrace. "They need to go back."

"I know, but they were starving last night and their clothes were horrible. Plus, they might be beating them."

"You don't know that. You don't know where they got the bruises. They might have gotten them on their way from Chicago."

"Stop it. I don't want to be logical."

Frank chuckled. Eventually, I pushed away and took a deep breath.

"Do you want me to call?"

I shook my head. "No. I'll do it, later."

Frank looked skeptical.

"Chicago is on central time, so they're an hour behind us. I'll wait until after the meeting tonight."

He nodded. "Okay, but I'm here if you need me."

We rejoined the others in the kitchen. Nana Jo, Dawson, Jillian, and Emma were all joking and laughing and eating chicken corn chowder. I turned and looked at Frank, who leaned close and whispered, "There's another quart in the freezer." He kissed me and waved goodbye as he hurried back to the restaurant.

Thankfully, the soup in the freezer hadn't had time to get hard. Ninety seconds in the microwave and I was a happy camper.

Once I was full, my brain started working again. "Aren't you two supposed to be planning a wedding?" I asked Jillian and Emma.

"We are." Jillian pulled a stack of bridal magazines from her backpack. "We're meeting your mom here to get her approval for some of the details."

Emma pulled out her phone and swiped until she found what she was looking for and then held up the phone for me to see. There was a lovely dress of deep burgundy. It was a body-hugging velvet dress with a retro style. The neckline and the dress were straight and it went to mid-calf. It was beautiful and very modest.

"Nice," I said.

Emma smiled and then swiped her phone to reveal the back. The dress, which was extremely modest from the front, had a white scarf that started at the shoulders on the back and followed a deep V that ended in a bow right at the top of the model's butt.

I raised an eyebrow. "Wow."

"Too much?" Emma asked anxiously.

"That depends on who will be wearing it."

"You," Emma said timidly.

Nana Jo leaned over and looked at the picture. "Yowzer. That's a beautiful dress and it'll show off your assets to their best advantage."

"I'm not sure I want my assets shown off."

"I'll bet Frank will love that dress." Nana Jo grinned.

"I'm sure you're right, but I don't think he has the right legs for it," I joked.

Nana Jo swatted my butt. "You know what I mean. He will be proud to escort you in that little beauty."

Jillian looked anxious. "Please say you like it, because it was on sale and . . . well, we already ordered it. We had to order it today to make sure it gets here on time."

"Look, the girls are under a time crunch, so it's either that or the pink piñata dress."

"I love it."

"I thought that'd sway you." Nana Jo winked.

I knew I'd been bamboozled, but I was okay with that. It really was a beautiful dress and it certainly looked better than any of the ones I'd tried on at the bridal shop. It was a little more revealing than my usual style, but it was a special occasion.

Lexi had joined us at the table.

"Emma and Jillian, this is Lexi. She and her brother, Angelo, are staying with me for a couple of days." I pretended not to notice the light that flashed in Lexi's eyes. I turned to her to complete the introductions. "Lexi, this is Jillian and Emma."

"Who's getting married?" She stared from one of the girls to the other.

Jillian laughed. "Don't look at us."

"My mom is getting married in less than two weeks."

"Wow. I've never been to a wedding before."

I swallowed the lump in my throat at the thought that she wouldn't be attending this one either. I looked around for Angelo and saw him curled up on the floor with Snickers on one side and Oreo on the other.

Nana Jo whispered, "I thought Emma and Jillian could help while we go downstairs for our meeting." She nodded at Lexi and Angelo.

I looked at my watch. It was almost two, the designated time we arranged to meet to discuss our findings. The tight timeline meant we needed to work quickly to get this resolved.

Nana Jo and I went downstairs. Irma, Dorothy, and Ruby Mae were in the back conference room waiting for me. There was what appeared to be small rectangles of cake on a plate on the table. I suspected it was one of Dawson's samples.

"Let's get this meeting started." Nana Jo opened her iPad. "Volunteers?"

I raised my hand. I relayed what I'd learned from Stinky Pitt.

"So, Stinky Pitt is going to back off and let us solve another murder for him?" Nana Jo looked down her nose. "How magnanimous of him."

"We're saving his bacon. He should be grateful, the little ba—"

"Irma!" we all yelled.

Irma coughed.

"I thought you were going to get someone to look into that coughing." Dorothy picked up the pitcher of water sitting in the middle of the table and poured a small amount into a glass and slid it across the table to Irma.

Irma took the water. "Thank you." She opened her purse and pulled out a bottle of whiskey and poured a good amount into the glass and drank.

Ruby Mae shook her head as she pulled a pale green fluffy item from her knitting bag.

"I don't think we should be too cocky. We may have just been lucky the other times. Besides, we really have our hands full. This time will be harder than all the others put together." I sighed.

"What do you mean?" Dorothy asked.

"Well, all the other times, we've known something about the person who was killed. They were locals. None of us know Lydia Lighthouse or Lydia Jones, according to her police file." I stared at the ladies.

"Poppycock! None of us knew Melody Hardwick." Nana Jo looked down her nose at me.

"We didn't know her, but Dawson did. Plus, she went to MISU," I said quietly.

"She was enrolled at MISU, but she didn't attend and no one on campus knew her." Nana Jo looked at me. "What's wrong with you?"

"You don't think Harold actually killed that woman, do you?" Ruby Mae asked.

I hesitated. "No. No, I don't."

"Good. Then what's bothering you?" Nana Jo asked.

I shrugged. "I don't know. I guess I'm just afraid. What if I fail? Mom will be devastated."

Nana Jo patted my hand. "You won't fail. Now, stop acting like this is your first rodeo and suck it up and let's get down to business."

"Josephine, give the girl a break," Dorothy said.

I stared at Nana Jo and then burst out laughing. "It's okay. Nana Jo's right. I can't afford to wallow in self-doubt. We'll just have to do the best we can."

"That's right." She patted my hand again. "That's all anyone can hope for. Now, let's get back to work."

"Well, I'll go next if no one else wants to go." Ruby Mae looked up from her knitting.

Everyone nodded their agreement.

So, she continued. "Well, I looked at that website Josephine told us about where the people gave reviews. One of the reviews was from Chattanooga, Tennessee. I didn't know the couple who got married, but my cousin Flora Belle has a granddaughter who works at the Aquarium. That's where the guy said the reception was held." She paused to finish a row of knitting. "So, I called Izola, that's Flora Belle's granddaughter, and she remembered that wedding. Apparently, Lydia Lighthouse came through that place like a maniac. She was like a madwoman the way she yelled at the staff. Everything had to be perfect. If a flower was slightly off, she was a raving lunatic."

"Well, we knew she wasn't nice," Nana Jo said with a bit of disappointment.

"Not nice? Izola said she spent hours begging and pleading with people not to quit. She had to pay triple salary to get people to work with her and spent the majority of her time running interference to keep Lydia from going off on people." Ruby Mae looked up. "But, the biggest thing Izola told me was how the caterers, florist, and photographers complained because she didn't pay them what she promised." Ruby Mae looked around. "Well, you know if she did that in Chattanooga, she probably did it in other cities too."

The others nodded.

"Well done, Ruby Mae," I said.

"Yes. You're absolutely right, Ruby Mae." Nana Jo typed. "I'll bet she did the same thing to the people here."

"She certainly did to the florist." Dorothy took a bite of cake and wiped her mouth.

"I paid a visit to Felicity Abrams of Felicity's Florals." Dorothy ate another piece of cake. "You know this is good stuff." She chewed. "Felicity was really standoffish. At first, she didn't want to say anything against Lydia, but I told her the woman was dead now, what difference could it possibly make?" She ate more cake.

"Dorothy Clark, if you don't stop eating that cake and tell me what you found out, I'm going to scream." Nana Jo glared.

Dorothy stuck out her tongue. "All right. Felicity said Lydia threatened her."

"Threatened her? With what?" I asked.

"She told Felicity if she didn't give her a discount on the flowers, she would make sure she was blackballed in the wedding planning community."

"Could she do that?" I asked.

Dorothy nodded. "Apparently she could. Lydia Lighthouse was a rude, arrogant, mean-spirited woman, but she knew the right people. Apparently, one word from Lydia Lighthouse could ruin a business."

"That's what I found out too." Irma took a sip from her glass and belched. "Sorry, were you done?"

Dorothy nodded. "I am now." She slid her cake away.

"Teddy is this really nice accountant I met at the casino." Irma took a compact out of her purse and reapplied her blood-red lipstick. "He didn't know Lydia Lighthouse, but he did know that caterer, Rudy Blakemore." She finished her lipstick and patted her beehive hairpiece to make sure not a hair was out of place. Satisfied with her appearance, she put away her compact. "Apparently, he overheard Rudy telling his partner he was glad someone did away with Lydia Lighthouse because she was dragging him into the poorhouse."

"Well, well, well." Nana Jo smiled. "Nice work, Irma. Did he say anything else?"

She shook her head. "No. That's all he heard, but I told him to see what else he could find out." She smiled. "He's picking me up for dinner tonight, and I'll see what else I can get out of him." She coughed.

"That just leaves me." Nana Jo swiped a few screens on her iPad. "Freddie's son, Mark, got some of the same information Stinky Pitt gave to Sam. Lydia Lighthouse was probably strangled. I asked him to find out if the killer would have to be really strong or if it could have been done by a woman."

"Good question. That will help narrow the suspects." I smiled.

"Well, don't get excited." Nana Jo shook her head. "Unfortunately, because the killer used a scarf, it could have been a man or a woman."

"Darn!" I said.

"However, we should find out more tonight."

Something about the way she said *we* and the way she avoided eye contact made me suspicious. "We?"

"Yes. We're having dinner tonight at the Avenue," she said.

"Who do you mean we?" I asked.

"We, as in Grace, Harold, Jenna, Tony, you, and me." She hesitated. "Margaret and Oscar.

I stared at her. "When exactly were you planning to tell me?"

She sighed. "Look, I don't want to go to dinner with that stuck-up snob any more than you do, but if we're going to find out who killed that woman so your mother can get married, then we need to talk to the one person who knew her."

I glared, but she was right. I was only thinking about myself. This time was harder than any of the other times we had to investigate people. If I took time to analyze my feelings, I might acknowledge it was because this time my mom was involved. I loved my mother, but she had a strange power. Within a few hours in her presence, I wasn't an adult anymore. I quickly morphed from a confident, independent modern woman into a timid, uncertain, guilt-ridden marshmallow. If I failed, I would have to live with the knowledge that I had ruined my mother's life and all chances for her happiness. No pressure there.

Our meeting broke up with plans to meet again tomorrow. Nana Jo and I went upstairs to dress for round two of Meet the Robertsons. Emma, Jillian, and Lexi were still at the dining

room table looking through bridal magazines. There were pictures they'd ripped out covering the entire surface of the table.

Angelo was sitting on a barstool.

"What are we going to do about dinner for them?" I whispered to Nana Jo as I glanced around the room.

She smiled and walked into the middle of the room. "Sam
and I have to go. Who wants pizza?"

Every hand went up, including mine. Nana Jo glared at me
and I lowered my hand. She reached into her purse and pulled
out three twenty-dollar bills and placed them on the counter
in the kitchen near Dawson, who was practicing his piping
skills by creating designs on cardboard.

"Pepperoni. Pepperoni. Pepperoni." Angelo bounced up
and down.

"Vegetable or cheese?" Jillian shrugged. "I'm not picky."

"Not picky, just no meat." Dawson looked at Emma.
"What about you?"

"Forget that, I want the works." Emma ripped a picture
from a magazine and added it to a pile.

"Me too. I like everything." Lexi had Snickers on her lap
and was flipping through magazines with one hand and stroking
the poodle with the other.

"Good. One pepperoni, one veggie, and two with everything except the kitchen sink." Dawson picked up his phone
and was placing the order before we left the room.

I wasn't really in the mood for a fancy dinner at the Avenue, but I reminded myself it wasn't about me. I needed to
get information, and this would help. I hesitated about what to
wear. I had two new outfits. One was a cocktail dress I was saving for a date with Frank. The cocktail dress would be appropriate for the setting. However, I knew Frank had to work and
wouldn't be joining us, and I selfishly wanted him to see me in
the dress. So, I opted for a black pencil skirt with boots and a

nice top. I gave myself a good look from all angles in the floor-length mirror in my bedroom.

I picked up the jeans I'd worn earlier and a piece of paper floated onto the floor. When I picked it up, I saw it was the paper Frank gave me earlier with the name and telephone number of the foster family. I picked up the note, took a deep breath, and took out my phone and quickly dialed the number before I lost my nerve.

"Hello?"

"Hello, may I speak to Mr. or Mrs. Hooper?"

"Mrs. Hooper speaking."

"I was wondering if . . . do you have a foster daughter named Alexis Gelano?"

She released a heavy sigh. "What's she done now?"

"I was just—"

"I'm not responsible. Whatever she's done, I'm not responsible. My sister works as a paralegal and I've been assured whatever trouble she's done, you can't hold me responsible."

"I'm not trying to hold anyone responsible. I was . . . well, I was wondering if I could speak to her."

"She's not here."

"Where is she?"

There was a pause. "Look, who did you say you were?"

"I'm just . . . trying to find her. That's all. What about her brother, Angelo, is he there?"

"No. He's not here either. Look, who are you and why are you wanting to speak to them?"

"My name is Samantha Washington. I was hoping Lexi might be interested in an afterschool program. Perhaps you could tell me when you expect her?"

"I dunno when she'll be in, but she's too young for any programs."

"Could you call—"

She hung up.

I held the phone for a few seconds and heard a noise behind me. I turned. My door was slightly ajar and Snickers snuck in. I grabbed my handbag and Snickers and I joined the others in the main room.

Nana Jo was dressed in a lovely emerald-green dress and heels.

"You look lovely," I said.

"Thank you." She smiled. "You clean up pretty well yourself."

The pizza arrived and Dawson grabbed the money from the counter and ran downstairs.

Angelo jumped up and down. "Yay! Pepperoni. Pepperoni. Pepperoni."

Nana Jo and I said our goodbyes and hurried downstairs.

The drive from downtown North Harbor to downtown South Harbor was short. Despite a continuous blanket of snow that had fallen throughout the entire day, the roads weren't bad.

I pulled up to the front to let Nana Jo out, and a young man in bright red livery rushed out to valet park the car.

I rolled down the window. "That's okay, I can park myself. I just want to let my grandmother out."

"Just let him park the car," Nana Jo said as she got out of the car. "I want to talk to you."

I wasn't accustomed to valet parking or dinners at fancy restaurants that had valet parking, but I grabbed my purse and got out. I took the ticket the young man gave me and hurried inside.

I stopped at the grand staircase just inside the building. "What's up?"

"I know you're worried about not solving this murder and disappointing your mother, but I want you to know I have faith in you—" She held up a hand to stop me from interrupt-

ing. "I have faith in you and I know your mother does too. We
have a lot more faith in you than in Stinky Pitt." She pursed
her lips and frowned.

"I appreciate your faith, but—"

"Regardless of what happens, this isn't your fault. If by
some miracle you don't find the murderer, which I don't think
will happen, mind you, but if by some stretch of the imagination you lose your gray matter and suddenly become brain
dead and don't solve this murder, then we've got an ace up our
sleeve."

I raised an eyebrow. "Ace? What ace?"

She pointed.

I turned and my sister, Jenna, and her husband, Tony,
pulled up outside.

"Best attorney in the Midwest," Nana Jo said with pride.
"Your sister is a pit bull and she'll rip apart any evidence that
dingbat of a district attorney tries to throw at her."

My brother-in-law got out and walked around to escort
Jenna into the building.

"What are you two staring at?" Jenna asked. "Let's go. I'm
starving." She walked past us and went downstairs to the
restaurant.

Tony shrugged and followed his wife.

I looked at my grandmother. "Pit bull?"

She nodded. "Pit bull."

Harold and Mom were already downstairs when we arrived. The last to arrive were the couple with the shortest
commute. Margaret and Oscar strolled in right as the waiter
was showing us to our seats.

Harold had requested a table that was positioned in between a large picture window and the fireplace. The table offered excellent views of the icy winter wonderland that was

Lake Michigan in the dead of winter, with the heat and atmosphere of a warm, crackling fireplace. Margaret headed toward the seat closest to the fireplace, but Harold was quicker.

"Margaret, I'm sure you don't mind if Grace sits here closest to the fireplace." He pulled out the chair and helped Mom sit, not waiting to hear whether Margaret minded or not.

Margaret obviously minded, because she sulkily stood nearby.

"Margaret, why don't you take this seat near Sam and me," Nana Jo said with so much syrup in her voice I had to glance back to make sure who was talking. She winked and whispered, "I'm going to need insulin before the night is over."

Margaret plastered on a fake smile and sat down in the seat Nana Jo indicated.

I took the seat on one side, while Nana Jo sat on her other side. Tony and Jenna sat on either side of Oscar, and the stage was set.

I stole a glance at Nana Jo, who raised an eyebrow and then lifted her hand. "Waiter."

When the waiter arrived, Nana Jo ordered a Wild Turkey for herself. She turned to Margaret. "What would you like?"

Margaret smiled. "I'm not much of a drinker . . . I'll have what she's having." She pointed to Nana Jo.

I opened my mouth to warn her bourbon might not be the drink for someone who wasn't accustomed to it, but a look from Nana Jo stopped me.

"I'll have a Pellegrino." I decided I might need to keep my wits about me for whatever Nana Jo was cooking up.

The waiter took our drink orders and quickly returned.

Nana Jo raised her glass. "To Grace and Harold. May you both have a long, happy life together."

We all lifted our glasses. "To Grace and Harold."

Nana Jo tossed back her bourbon like someone doing shots.

Margaret stared at her and took a sip of her drink. From the scowl that followed, it was clear bourbon wasn't her favorite.

"It's best to just close your eyes and knock it back in one fell swoop." Nana Jo smiled at her.

I stared across the table at Jenna, who merely shrugged and sipped her sangria.

Margaret looked at Nana Jo and then put her head back and swallowed her bourbon. "Ugh. That burns."

"Isn't it wonderful." Nana Jo waved to the waiter. "Two more."

"Oh, no, not for me." Margaret shook her head.

"Perhaps something a little milder," Nana Jo offered. "A cosmopolitan."

"What's in it?" Margaret asked.

"It's just cranberry juice, lime, Cointreau or triple sec, and vodka." Nana Jo rattled off the ingredients like a bartender. "I think you'll like it."

Margaret nodded and the waiter was off in a flash.

We made small talk about the weather for several minutes until the waiter returned.

Again, Nana Jo tossed back her drink quickly. "Skoal."

This time Margaret was more cautious and sipped her Cosmo. "That's delicious." She sipped again.

"Drink up." Nana Jo encouraged Margaret and then motioned for the waiter to provide two more drinks for her and Margaret.

By the time the waiter brought Margaret's third drink, her eyes were bright and shining and what I thought was a permanent frown had been smoothed. Her lips hadn't yet made the upward turn into a smile, but the edges were smooth and friendlier.

"That's really nice of you," Margaret said as the waiter replaced her empty glass with a full one. "You say it's called a Cosmopolitan?" She sipped. "Was it named after the magazine?"

Nana Jo shrugged. "No idea."

Margaret giggled. "It's very pretty."

"Yes. It's lovely." Nana Jo smiled.

By the time we ordered dinner, the Ice Princess, Margaret Robertson, had melted. She wasn't as stiff and snobbish as the last time we'd dined together. In fact, by the time her dinner of grilled Scottish salmon with fingerling potato salad, Dijon dressing, Spanish olives, red onion, and frisée arrived, she was downright pleasant.

"Now, tell me exactly when you met Lydia Lighthouse," Nana Jo said.

Margaret furrowed her brow as though trying to remember something. Eventually, she laughed. "You know, I can't really remember." She leaned close to Nana Jo as though relaying a dire secret. "She really wasn't very nice."

"You don't say?" Nana Jo asked while signaling to the waiter to bring two more drinks.

I'd lost count of how many they'd had. I think it was five, but it might have been six. I had no doubt Nana Jo could handle her alcohol, but Margaret was an unknown. She didn't strike me as a big drinker. Add to the fact she hadn't eaten food yet and she'd mixed her drinks, with the Wild Turkey, numerous Cosmos, and the wine Harold ordered to accompany the meal, Margaret was well on her way to a hangover of massive proportions.

Margaret shook her head. "No. She was rude. I'm not surprised someone stabbed her in the back and strangled her." Margaret ate her salmon. "Why, this is really rather good." She leaned down the table and yelled to Mom, "Grace, did you try this salmon? It's delicious. I think you should have this at the wedding."

Mom looked at Margaret and forced herself to smile.

Margaret dug into the salmon and ate with a hearty appetite. "This has to be the best salmon I've ever had."

"Great." Nana Jo tried to steer the conversation away from

the salmon and back to Lydia Lighthouse. "You must have known Lydia for a long time, for her to come all the way from Virginia to Michigan for the wedding."

Margaret continued on eating. "Well, I've known her for years, but we were never what you might call close." She ate. "Didn't think I was good enough for her." She laughed. "Can you believe that?"

"Absolutely not," Nana Jo lied. "Why, you're a descendent of . . . who was it?"

Margaret nodded. "Exactly, and Lydia *claimed* she was a descendant of Stonewall Jackson, but you know what?" Margaret leaned close to Nana Jo.

"No, what?"

"I was having lunch at the club with Mimi Orwell." She leaned closer to Nana Jo and nearly fell. She put her elbow on the table and rested her chin in her hand to help steady herself. "Mimi is part of the UDC and she told me Lydia tried to join but had been rejected." She grinned at Nana Jo.

"Really? Rejected." Nana Jo tsked. "Scandalous."

Margaret went back to her salmon, and I mouthed, *What is the UDC?*

Nana Jo shrugged.

"What's the UDC?" I asked.

"United Daughters of the Confederacy," Margaret said. "It's a wonderful organization."

I stared at Margaret. "Like the Daughters of the Revolution?"

She nodded.

"So, all of the members are women who can trace their lineage to soldiers who fought for the Confederacy?"

Margaret must not have noticed the frost in my voice, which I didn't bother to hide.

She merely nodded. "Not just fought, but they had to have

fought honorably." She ate her potato salad. "So many men took the oath of allegiance but broke their vow and either abandoned their post or defected to the Northern cause."

I put down my silverware. "That's disgusting."

Margaret mistook my meaning. "Isn't it? When you've sworn an oath, it's binding for life. It's sacred, like marriage." Something must have finally gotten through to Margaret that perhaps she should temper her comments because she suddenly stopped talking and stared into space.

"Are you okay?" Nana Jo asked when Margaret didn't move.

She turned to stare at Nana Jo and there were large tears in her eyes. "Oh God."

Despite my frustration with Margaret, I was concerned by the sudden change in emotions. "What's wrong?"

"Marriage vows are sacred."

"Yes, of course they are," Nana Jo agreed. "Now, why was Lydia rejected?"

Margaret didn't seem to be in any mood to talk about Lydia Lighthouse, the United Daughters of the Confederacy, or anything else. She burst into tears in the middle of dinner.

"Good grief." Nana Jo put down her fork. "I was so close," she muttered. "Sam, help me get Margaret up to their room."

Nana Jo and I helped Margaret to her feet, but she was no longer crying silently. By now, she was sobbing.

"Perhaps I should . . . um . . . well, you know?" Oscar said as we dragged his wife past his chair.

"Just give Sam your key." Nana Jo grabbed Margaret around the waist so she had her full weight.

I reached for the key Oscar held out and then helped to take my share of Margaret's weight.

Margaret's sobbing became more and more intense with each step. We'd just made it to the elevator when she let out a wail.

Nana Jo merely rolled her eyes and muttered, "Darned sissy. She only had six Cosmos."

The elevator door closed and we rode up to the third floor with a woman who was crying hysterically.

I glared at Nana Jo and would have given her a reprimand, but I needed all of my strength to drag Margaret down the hallway to her room. When we got to the door, we propped her against the wall. I slid the card key into the lock and tried to hold the door open with my foot, but Margaret had slid down the wall and was now sitting on the floor.

"Crap," Nana Jo said as we tried to pick her up.

However, Margaret was now dead weight. We made several unsuccessful attempts to lift her off the floor and were both winded and tired.

"Good grief, she must weigh a lot more than she looks," Nana Jo replied as we stopped for a rest.

"I have no idea, but there's no way we're going to get her up by ourselves. We're going to have to get Tony and Harold to help us." I tried to get my breath. "Do you have your phone?"

Nana Jo shook her head. "I left my purse downstairs." She looked at me. "You?"

I shook my head. "I guess one of us is going to have to go downstairs and get help."

"Oh, no you don't. We're not giving up that easy."

I stared at my grandmother. "What are you talking about?"

"We're going to search her room once we get her inside."

"Oh, no *we* aren't."

"Don't be such a prude."

Margaret let out a loud belch and then started to laugh.

We stared at her.

"Well, what do you suggest?" Nana Jo put a hand on her hip.

I thought for a moment and then opened the door to the room and went inside. I opened the closet and found a blanket.

I grabbed it and went back into the hall. I put the blanket on the floor next to Margaret, who was no longer crying, laughing, or belching. She was snoring. Margaret Robertson was sitting on the floor in the hallway outside of her hotel room, sound asleep.

Nana Jo and I laid her down onto the blanket. Then I unlocked the door and slipped a slipper I'd found under it to hold it open. Then we grabbed the edges of the blanket and dragged Margaret into the room.

Once we had her inside, I pulled the slipper from under the door and it swung shut.

Nana Jo flopped down onto one of the two queen-sized beds in the room. "That was a lot of work." She fanned herself.

"You shouldn't have gotten her drunk."

"How else was I supposed to get her to open up and tell us about Lydia Lighthouse."

I sighed. "It didn't get us much." I stretched.

"I don't know. I think we got quite a bit."

"Well, you can tell me about it later." I looked at Margaret wrapped in a blanket, lying on the floor. "How do we get her off the floor and up onto the bed?"

"Why do we have to move her? Can't we just leave her?" Nana Jo asked.

I tilted my head and stared at her. "You have got to be joking. We can't just leave her on the floor."

"Why not?"

I stared at Margaret. "Because it's not the right thing to do."

Nana Jo huffed, but she got up and then spread her legs wide and crouched down onto one knee. Then she took several deep breaths. "All right, help me get her arms."

I helped to lift Margaret into a sitting position with her weight resting against my legs.

"Now what?"

"I'm going to count to three and then I'll stand up and pull her over my back onto the bed.

"Are you sure you can handle that? She's pretty heavy and you're o—"

"Call me old and you'll be the next person who gets tossed in this room."

My grandmother wasn't young, but she was also not frail. She had a brown belt in aikido and I'd seen her take down grown men on several occasions.

I nodded. "Okay."

"One. Two." Nana Jo grabbed hold of Margaret's arms. She took a deep breath. "Three." She gave a loud cry and then rose from her knee. She pulled Margaret while I used my knees and body to help push her up. As Nana Jo rose, she lifted Margaret off the ground and flipped her over her back onto the bed.

Margaret never woke but lay sprawled across one of the beds.

"Are you okay?" I gasped for breath and stared at my grandmother.

She nodded. "Yep. I've never tried that one before, but it wasn't so bad once I got my leverage."

We looked at Margaret.

"Now, are you going to help me search this room or what?" Nana Jo turned and began rifling through the drawers.

"What exactly do you expect to find in their hotel room? An extra pair of scarves?"

Nana Jo continued to search. "Anything that helps us know why Margaret hired someone she obviously didn't like very much to come and plan her brother-in-law's wedding."

I hated the idea of searching through someone else's belongings, but maybe Nana Jo was right. Margaret and Oscar were the only ones who knew Lydia Lighthouse. Maybe there was some reason why she did it. We searched through clothes and toiletries, but there was nothing out of the ordinary.

I was just about to give up when the telephone rang.

Nana Jo and I stood up and stared at each other. Then I reached over and picked up the receiver. "Hello."

It was Jenna. "Oscar and Harold are on their way up to the room, so if you two are doing anything you shouldn't, stop it!" She hung up.

"They're coming."

We tidied up. Nana Jo took a towel from the bathroom and wiped down the room.

"What are you doing?"

"Getting rid of fingerprints." She quickly wiped every drawer, knob, and handle. "I saw it on *Perry Mason*."

I waited anxiously by the door. When she was done, she tossed the towel on a pile in the bathroom, where we'd seen other dirty towels. We opened the door just as Oscar was about to knock.

"I was just about to knock." He smiled.

"No need." I handed him his card key. "We just managed to get Margaret onto the bed." I stepped aside and let Oscar and Harold enter. "Where's Jenna?"

"She and Tony are watching the purses downstairs with your mother," Harold said.

Oscar stood at the end of the bed and looked at his wife. "Sound asleep." He turned to face us. "Not sure how you both managed, but thank you."

"No problem at all." Nana Jo pushed me out of the room. "Well, we've got to be going. You take care," she shouted as we hurried down the hallway.

"What's the big hurry now?" I asked once we were safely in the elevator.

She pulled a small piece of paper, which was folded up, from behind her back.

"Where did you get that?" I gasped.

"Hidden in a box of feminine supplies in her toiletries in the bathroom."

"But, what is it and why did you take it?"

"It appears to be a marriage license." She read it. "Between Maggie Anne Tuttleford and Buford Jones."

"Who's Maggie Anne Tuttleford?"

"If I was a betting woman, which I am, I'd bet my life savings Maggie Anne Tuttleford and Margaret Robertson are one and the same."

I sighed. "So, what. Margaret was married before she married Oscar. Big deal."

The elevator descended.

"It's no big deal now, but it must have been a big deal to her if she went to all that trouble to hide it."

We walked out of the elevator and headed back to our table. "What made you look in her feminine supplies?"

Nana Jo snorted. "Woman that old doesn't need feminine supplies anymore."

"Fine, but how are you going to get it back in there? She's bound to notice it missing."

"Tomorrow we'll come over and pretend we made arrangements for lunch. Once we're up in the room, I'll ask to use the bathroom. People always think old ladies have weak bladders." Nana Jo marched back to the table.

I was glad she'd called herself old and not me.

Harold had already taken care of the bill. When we arrived, Tony had taken all of our tickets to the valet and was arranging to have our cars brought around. So, Nana Jo, Jenna, and I sat with Mom and waited.

"Did you find anything?" Jenna asked.

"How did you know we were searching?" I asked.

She gave me a look that said, *Are you joking?*

Nana Jo handed over the marriage license she'd pilfered.

"Margaret never mentioned anything about being married before, but I'll ask Harold." Jenna looked it over and then copied down the names before she handed it back. "I'll have my investigator look into it and try to find out who Maggie Anne Tuttleford and Buford Jones are."

Harold returned and we headed to the front. All of our cars were lined up at the front.

I hugged my mom before she got in the car.

"Thank you, Sam."

"For what?"

"For using your abilities to help Harold and for getting those wonderful girls to help with the wedding. They're both so energetic. It's nice to be around young people. It makes me feel young again." She smiled.

I hugged her again.

Tony pulled up and Jenna got into her car. "What time is the meeting tomorrow?"

"Noon at Frank's restaurant, but I think we're going to be meeting here instead."

She nodded. "Good. I'll meet you here."

My face must have registered surprise because Jenna laughed. "Close your mouth. I have information to report."

Before I could ask, Tony pulled off and they were gone.

The valet pulled my car up and Nana Jo and I got inside. As I pulled away, I looked at Nana Jo. "Tomorrow should be an interesting meeting."

Chapter 10

When I got home, Dawson was asleep on the sofa with Angelo.

"Where is everyone?" I asked.

"Jillian, Emma, and Lexi are in my apartment." He looked at Angelo stretched out on his chest. "This little guy wanted to stay with me." He slid from underneath, leaving Angelo on the sofa.

Nana Jo stood at the counter. There were several dollars and some coins.

"That's your change." Dawson walked up behind her.

"How many pizzas did you all eat?"

Dawson looked down. "That's why I wanted to be here when you got back." He looked serious. "I saw you take sixty dollars out of your purse."

Nana Jo nodded. "Yeah. I left three twenties."

"Well, when I went to pay, there were only two." He stared at her.

"Lexi?" I asked.

"Who else?" Nana Jo said.

I sighed. "I didn't think she was a thief, but . . . it had to be her." I shook my head.

"I'm sorry. I didn't want to say anything to her, especially without talking to you first," Dawson said.

I nodded. "Thank you." I suddenly felt very tired.

"Do you want my bed?" I offered.

He shook his head. "No. I've got the keys to Jillian's car. I'll go to campus and get some sleep. I'll be back first thing in the morning to take the girls back so they can shower and change."

He hugged us and then headed out.

I was tired and disappointed. I didn't know what I expected from Lexi and Angelo, but whatever it was, stealing wasn't a part of it. The very idea made me sad and discouraged.

Between the events at the restaurant and learning Lexi was a thief, I was tired, too tired to sleep. So, I sat down to write in the hopes I could settle my thoughts and calm my mind.

C᷎᷎᷎᷎᷎᷎᷎᷎᷎

"That peacock 'as been parading around 'ere as if 'e owns the place." Mrs. McDuffy marched into the servants' hall and slammed a feather duster onto the large oak table. "If 'e tramples snow and mud through that dining room one more time, I'll take this duster and shove it right up his ar—"

"Mrs. McDuffy!" Thompkins looked from the housekeeper to the maids, seated at the table, who were snickering as they polished silver, which was piled upon the table. "We must maintain decorum."

She huffed. "I can't stand the sly devil," Mrs. McDuffy said with venom. "Always slinking around where 'e's got no business."

"What do you mean?" Thompkins asked.

"Did you see the way he was eyeing the good silver?" she asked. "Like a dog looking at a bone."

"Well, perhaps he's taking inventory for the wedding supper." Thompkins looked at the housekeeper.

"Pshaw." The housekeeper rolled her eyes and folded her arms across her chest. "And it was only this mornin' that Gladys tells me she caught 'im sneakin' around in the library." She huffed. "And 'e says 'e's checkin' the room for overflow." She breathed heavily and her face grew red from anger. "You tell me why 'e'd need to be checkin' on anythin' in Lord William's library, that's what I want to know."

Thompkins tried not to let his concern show. "Well, I don't know—"

"Well, I do know and 'e's up to no good that one."

The butler would normally have reprimanded the housekeeper more, but he was also frustrated with the wedding planner's many changes and demands. Just as he prepared to lecture the housekeeper further, he was halted when raised voices drifted into the hall.

"I don't care what you're trying to do, and I don't give two pence about your bloody artistic temperament. I am not wearing that ridiculous outfit," Lord James Browning raged. "And, I'm warning you, Claiborne, if you don't stop manipulating Lady Daphne, I'll take that scarf and wring your ruddy neck."

"Your Grace, I have no idea what you're talking about," Philippe Claiborne sounded surprised and shocked, but the words lacked sincerity.

"Don't push me, Claiborne."

Footsteps marched down the hall, followed by laughter that held a cocky, arrogant tone as though declaring a win over an opponent.

The staff stayed perfectly still and listened. Another pair of footsteps descended the stairs. The servants waited to see who emerged. As the artistically dressed wedding planner turned the corner and entered the servants' hall, Flossie and Millie quickly rose and fled the room, leaving the senior staff to deal with the interloper. Gladys lingered in the corner and Frank, the footman, sharpened knives for the cook.

"Ah, Thompkins. Here's where you've gotten off to." Philippe Claiborne looked around the hall with a sneer. "The heart of the English Manor home, the servants' hall." He walked around the room and wiped a finger across a sideboard. Then he took out a handkerchief and wiped his hands.

Mrs. McDuffy huffed and turned bright red. She looked like a kettle about to blow steam.

The butler quickly stepped forward, coughed discretely, and bowed stiffly. "You wished to speak to me, sir?"

"I want to talk to you about the seating plan for the wedding supper." He flicked ashes from his cigarette onto the floor and then placed his cigarette and holder onto the table.

The burning embers of the cigarette were close to the feather duster and the already polished flatware. The housekeeper huffed, picked up the duster, brushed the ashes off the table, and moved the polished silver farther away.

Philippe Claiborne, oblivious to the housekeeper's ire, merely nodded. "Now, I want to move the wedding supper from the dining room into the front parlor. There's more light in that room and it will

photograph much nicer than that dark-paneled dining room with the heavy brocade drapes and that
massive mahogany table. So dark and old-fashioned."
He picked up his cigarette and took a puff, then blew
the smoke into the butler's face. "It's just so nine-
teenth century."

The butler stared for several seconds and then
blinked. "Excuse me?"

"What part didn't you understand?" Claiborne
smoked.

Thompkins coughed. "Do I understand that you
want to switch all of the furniture from the dining
room with the furniture in the parlor? All of the furniture."

"Yes. That's exactly what I'm saying."

Mrs. McDuffy looked shocked. "But that dining
room table is two hundred years old. It's massive. I
don't know if it'll even fit through the ruddy parlor
door."

Thompkins was too astonished to reprimand the
housekeeper and merely stared.

"Well, I suppose you'll figure it out, and be quick
about it. I have a lot to do." He looked around the hall
and spotted Mrs. Anderson as she entered the room.
"Perfect. You're the cook. Just the person I wanted to
talk to."

Thompkins and Mrs. McDuffy exchanged glances.
For a split second, the butler was shaken. However,
he quickly tried to intervene. "Perhaps it would be
best if we waited for her ladyship before discussing
the menu."

"Nonsense. I've been commissioned to make this

wedding a success. We haven't got time to waste."
He turned to Mrs. Anderson. "This menu is completely wrong. The entire thing will need to be re-
done." He pulled another paper from his pocket and
handed it to the cook.

Gladys gasped and hurried out of the room.

The cook's face grew red as she glanced at the
paper. "Two hundred squab? One hundred pounds of
caviar? Two hundred pheasant?" She stared. "You
must be out of your bleeding mind. How am I supposed to prepare all of this in two weeks, along with
all of the cakes and puddings?"

"Not really my problem, is it?" Philippe stared at
the cook. "However, if you're too old to do your job
properly, then perhaps it's time you stepped aside
and made room for someone else."

The blood drained from the cook's face and she
went from nearly purple with rage to a ghostly white
in an instant. "Why . . . you . . . how dare you . . . I
never . . . I—"

Philippe Claiborne stared at the cook. "I've dealt
with hundreds of old servants like you." He looked
around from the cook to Mrs. McDuffy to Thompkins
and then back at the cook. "Ancient relics who have
served the family for years but who are too old to
keep up with modern times and changes—hangers-
on. The family is too soft-hearted to tell you the
truth. It's time you move on and make way for someone younger and more capable."

Lady Elizabeth entered the servants' hall. "That's
enough."

Philippe Claiborne turned and plastered a smile
onto his face. "Your ladyship. I didn't hear you come in."

"I daresay you didn't or you wouldn't have had the audacity to speak in that manner." Lady Elizabeth's eyes flashed and her voice was iron. "In the future, you will run any comments or requests through me." She paused. "Do I make myself clear?"

Philippe Claiborne inclined his head slightly. "Perfectly."

Gladys peeked around the corner.

Lady Elizabeth looked around the room. "Please continue with your duties." She forced a smile onto her face.

The servants bowed respectfully.

Lady Elizabeth turned back to Philippe Claiborne. "I think we should finish our discussion upstairs." She turned and walked out.

Philippe Claiborne inclined his head slightly and turned and glared at the servants. Then he followed her ladyship upstairs.

After a few seconds, the tension vanished and the atmosphere became less charged. Mrs. McDuffy released a breath. "Lawd, if looks could kill, that fancy peacock would be dead. I've never seen 'er ladyship so angry in all my years."

A bowl crashed to the ground. Mrs. McDuffy and Thompkins turned and caught a glimpse of one of the twins, Josiah or Johan as they scurried from their hiding place in an alcove. The boys liked to spend time in the servants' hall watching and listening. Neither Thompkins nor the housekeeper minded, especially since the boys didn't speak or understand much English. However, they were intelligent lads and the butler wondered if maybe they understood more than they were letting on.

Thompkins stared down. His hands were shaking and he had crumpled the paper with the seating changes into a ball. He flexed and unflexed his hands to release the tension.

The next morning, Lady Elizabeth sent word for Frank to take the car into town to pick up Joseph Mueller, Thompkins' son-in-law, from the train station. Frank left the gamekeeper's cottage he shared with his dad and headed to the back hall to get the car keys. He whistled as he hurried through the cold winter morning. At the back door, he nearly tripped over a bundle someone had left near the back gate.

The footman reached down to move the bundle and realized what he had mistaken for a discarded bundle of clothes was the body of Philippe Claiborne. He recognized the knife sticking out of the man's back as one of the knives he'd sharpened the previous evening.

He reached out a hand to remove the incriminating knife but was halted at the sound of the back door opening.

Thompkins came outside and stared at the footman and then down at the dead man for several seconds.

Neither man spoke.

After a long pause, Thompkins stood straight. "I'll alert Lord William and her ladyship. You'd better stand guard over the body until I return." He turned to go back into the house but turned and looked at the footman. "You will most likely need to pick up the detective from Scotland Yard, Detective Inspector Covington."

"HELP!"

Both men looked around to see where the call for help came from when another call came.

"Help, I need help."

Both men followed the voice around the side of the house. When they arrived, a man stumbled out from behind a bush.

"Mr. Waddington, what are you doing here?" Thompkins asked. Under normal conditions, the butler would never have dreamed of questioning a guest in this manner, but with one person dead, these were definitely not normal conditions.

Percy Waddington had only recently arrived for the wedding. He was in his forties, but he looked ten years older. Once, slender and deemed handsome by many, he had now run to fat and his hairline had receded to the middle of his head.

The butler stared at the man. He was pale and one of his arms was covered in blood. If Percy Waddington intended to answer the question, Thompkins would never know. The bleeding man took one step forward and his eyes rolled back into his head.

Frank arrived in time to catch the bleeding man before he crumpled to the ground. "What the bloody hell is going on?"

Thompkins, stiff and proper, stared at the bleeding man. "I have no idea, but you'd better get him inside. I'll call Dr. Haygood." The butler rushed as quickly as he could, while still maintaining his demeanor, to the back door. He glanced at the body of Philippe Claiborne, which was still crumpled on the floor, and halted. He stared at the body for several seconds. Suddenly lightheaded, the butler swayed and had to hold on to the door to steady himself. He stared at the body and mumbled to himself, "The knife. Someone has stolen the knife."

Chapter 11

The next morning, I was tired from a late night of writing and from worry about Lexi and Angelo. When I eventually went to sleep, I tossed and turned for what felt like hours. My mind waffled between calling their foster parents and sending them home and calling the Chicago Child Protective Services and reporting the bruises I'd seen to calling the local police and charging them with theft.

When I finally woke up, I smelled coffee and heard voices in the kitchen. I got up, showered, and dressed. I went into the kitchen. Lexi, Emma, and Jillian had prepared breakfast and the kitchen looked as though a small tornado had blown through.

"Don't worry about the mess. We're going to take care of everything," Emma announced as I turned the corner and went to the coffeepot to pour myself a cup.

"I'm not worried." I inhaled the aroma and looked around. "What's that wonderful smell?"

"Dawson mixed batter for waffles before he left last night and left it in the fridge. All we had to do was fire up your waffle iron this morning." Jillian held out her arm in Vanna White fashion. "So, it's Belgium waffles for those of you who don't have to watch your waistlines."

Emma plopped one of the large waffles onto her plate. "Great. All the more for me." She poured a generous amount of syrup onto the waffle.

I wondered how she could eat so much and still maintain her tiny figure.

Lexi also had a large waffle, but, unlike Emma, she merely picked at hers.

Nana Jo brought a bouncing Angelo out of the bathroom. He quickly ran to the counter and demanded waffles.

"Look here, you little dictator, you can stop ordering people around like some kind of emperor. If you want waffles, then you can ask nicely." Nana Jo's words were spoken softly, but there was an authority behind them, which she'd honed over the years as a teacher.

This time was no different. Angelo poked out his lip but stood very still. "May I please have a waffle?" He climbed onto the barstool.

"Yes, you may." Nana Jo smiled and placed a plate containing a quarter of a waffle on his plate.

"But I want a whole one like Lexi."

"You eat that and I'll give you more." Nana Jo poured syrup on the waffle and Angelo was mesmerized by the amber-colored liquid. He stuck a finger into the puddle of maple goodness and licked it.

I ate one of the waffles and savored the delicious vanilla and maple fluffy concoction.

Dawson arrived while we were eating. He handed off the keys to Jillian and as soon as Jillian and Emma finished their breakfast and loaded the dishwasher, they were off to campus to shower and change, promising to return at lunchtime.

That left Dawson, Nana Jo, Lexi, Angelo, and me. I sipped

my coffee and looked at Nana Jo. If she didn't bring up the missing money, I would.

"My hands are sticky." Angelo licked his fingers.

Nana Jo rose, but Dawson volunteered. "Let me help you." He lifted Angelo up over one shoulder and took the squealing child to the bathroom.

We sat in silence for several seconds and then Lexi stood. She pulled a wrinkled twenty-dollar bill from her pocket and walked over and handed it to Nana Jo. "This is yours."

Nana Jo took the money. "Why'd you take it?"

Lexi refused to make eye contact and shrugged.

Nana Jo lifted her chin and looked in her eyes. "That's not good enough. I want you to tell me why you stole money from me."

Tears streamed down her face. "I heard her on the phone." She pointed at me. "She's going to send us back to Chicago to the Hoopers. I was going to run away again. I took the money to help pay for bus fare to New York."

"Why New York?" I questioned whether the book she was reading was a good idea. *From the Mixed-Up Files of Mrs. Basil E. Frankweiler* was about a young girl who ran away from home with her little brother and stayed in the Metropolitan Museum of Art.

She shrugged. "I dunno. It's big and maybe nobody would find me."

"Why don't you want to go back to the Hoopers?" Nana Jo asked.

She hesitated. "Because they're mean. They beat me and . . . I don't like Mr. Hooper."

Dawson and Angelo came out of the bathroom.

"Dawson, could you and Angelo do me a favor and take Snickers and Oreo outside please?"

Dawson must have noticed the atmosphere in the room

was charged. He nodded, hoisted Angelo onto his shoulders, and grabbed some dog biscuits out of the jar and then headed downstairs.

When they were downstairs, Nana Jo turned to Lexi. "You're going to need to tell us what happened, and we need the truth."

Lexi lifted her chin.

I steeled myself to hear the rest of her tale.

"He drinks." She licked her lips. "He's fine as long as he ain't had nothing to drink. When he drinks, then he gets mean. I used to share a room with Veronica and Taylor. Veronica is the oldest. She's fifteen. Taylor's eight. He don't like it if you talk back. Veronica used to talk back a lot. One night, he came in the room and he had been drinking." She paused for several moments. We waited for her to continue. "He was yelling at Veronica because she didn't wash the dishes before she went to bed. He had a leather strap and he started hitting her over and over and over." She stopped and tears ran down her face.

"Take your time," Nana Jo said softly.

"I tried to make him stop because he was hurting her, and Taylor was scared and she was crying. He kept yelling for her to shut up, but he just kept on hitting her." She took a deep breath.

"What happened to Veronica?" I asked.

She shrugged. "I dunno. She was just lying on the floor. There was a lot of blood all over the place."

"Did the police come?"

She nodded. "They took Mr. Hooper away, but before they got there, he said to keep my mouth shut. He said if I said anything, he'd beat me and Angelo."

"Where was Mrs. Hooper when this was going on?" I asked.

She shrugged. "She works nights. She's gone a lot because Mr. Hooper gets drunk and loses his job and then she has to work more. Sometimes they fight about him drinking so much, but then he hits her and she cries a lot."

"Did he ever touch you in a bad way?" Nana Jo asked.

She shook her head. "He just hits me and Angelo." She pulled up her sleeve and showed the bruises I'd seen before. Then she lifted her shirt and turned around. Bruises covered her back.

I covered my mouth to prevent the gasp from escaping. I took several deep breaths and regained my composure. "Did you tell anyone? Your caseworker or a teacher?"

She shook her head. "He said if we told, he'd make sure we paid for it."

One thing had been puzzling me. "Lexi, when did you learn to speak Italian?"

"My mom and dad used to speak it before they died." She shrugged. "I dunno. Angelo and I use it like a secret code. No one knows what we're saying."

I turned Lexi so she faced me. "Lexi, I called Mrs. Hooper because I thought she might be worried about you. Right now, she is responsible for you and Angelo. I need to talk to your caseworker and find out what the right thing is to do, legally."

"Why can't we just stay here with you?" Her eyes pleaded. "We won't be no trouble and I'm sorry I took the money. I just can't go back there."

"I know you won't be *any* trouble, but we have to follow the rules." I stared into her eyes. "I'll do everything in my power to make sure you don't have to go back to Mr. Hooper, but I'm going to need you to trust me."

She stared hard into my eyes as though she were looking into my very soul. Eventually she nodded. "Okay."

I hugged her and heard sniffing from behind me. I looked around and saw Nana Jo wiping her eyes.

Nana Jo held up the twenty dollars. "Stealing is wrong, but maybe you would like to earn some money."

Lexi nodded.

"I'll take her downstairs to meet Christopher and Zaq and put her to work shelving books, gift wrapping presents, and making sure the treats are replenished until Emma and Jillian return." Nana Jo led her away.

On the drive to the retirement village to pick up the girls for lunch, I asked, "What are we going to do?"

"Well, we can't send her back to that abusive creep. Although, I'd like five minutes alone with him." She glared. "In the meantime, we're going to have to ask Jenna for advice."

I picked up the girls and drove to the Avenue. I dropped them off at the front of the hotel and declined valet parking. I needed a moment or two to myself. I drove around behind the hotel and parked but sat for several moments with the motor running.

My husband, Leon, and I were never blessed with children. Over the years, I'd convinced myself I was better off without them. However, the truth was, I had wanted children. When my nephews were young, I doted on them. As they grew up, they spent less and less time with me. Opening the bookstore had changed things and they spent breaks and weekends at the store and it was nice to have young people around. Lexi and Angelo were not, however, my children. Nor were they relatives. It angered me that people like the Hoopers, who had charge over children, misused their authority and abused them. The very idea made me cry. I cried for the children Leon and I never had. I cried for Lexi and Angelo and I cried for Veronica, wherever she was.

Someone tapped on my window and I jumped. I looked and saw my sister, Jenna, looking in the car.

I got a tissue and wiped my eyes, blew my nose, turned off the engine, and got out. "You scared me."

"What's wrong with you?"

I sighed and told her about Lexi and Angelo as we walked up to the hotel. By the time we were inside, I'd just about finished.

She asked for the information Frank had given me and promised she would look into it. She also promised to call Mrs. Masterson from Child Protective Services.

"Do you think I'll have to send them back?"

She shrugged. "They'll have to investigate the allegations of abuse, but, in the meantime, I can ask that they stay with you until the investigation is over." She hesitated. "If that's what you want."

I was so pleasantly surprised I grabbed her and gave her a big hug. "Thank you."

"Sure thing." Jenna wasn't much of a hugger, but she endured it.

We found the girls at a large table in the dining room. Nana Jo came from the elevator.

"Where's Margaret?" I asked.

"Sick as a dog. Apparently, she has a monster-sized hangover. I barely got her out of the bathroom long enough for me to return the marriage certificate."

"Did you return it?" I asked.

"Of course." Nana Jo sat down at the table.

We waited until we'd finished lunch before starting our meeting.

Nana Jo started by telling the girls about the marriage license she'd found in Margaret's room.

Jenna looked at her watch. "Look, I have to get back to work soon. So, is it all right if I go next?"

Everyone nodded.

"I asked our firm's investigator to look into that marriage license and also into Lydia Lighthouse's background. He discovered something rather interesting.

"Margaret Jones was born Maggie Anne Tuttleford. When she was fifteen, she married Bufford Jones, brother to Lydia Jones."

"So, Margaret and Lydia were in-laws," Dorothy said. "What's the big deal? Divorce used to be a big deal, but now, it's common."

Jenna shook her head. "He couldn't find any record of a divorce."

"Widowed?" I suggested.

Jenna shook her head again. "Nope. Bufford Jones is alive and well and living it up in the Polk County Jail."

"Really? What did he do?" I asked.

"Blackmail, extortion, and fraud. He's a con man."

"Well, well, well. So, Mrs. Prim and Proper Margaret Robertson was married to a common criminal." Nana Jo huffed. "How dare she insinuate my daughter isn't good enough to marry Harold Robertson." Nana Jo fumed.

My sister and I exchanged glances. Nana Jo had missed the obvious. I itched to tell her, but it was Jenna's news, so I turned to my sister. "You tell her."

"Tell me what?"

"Maggie Anne Tuttleford Jones never got divorced. So, her marriage to Oscar Robertson isn't legal. She is, in fact, a bigamist."

"Hot dam—"

"Irma!"

Nana Jo smiled. "Well, isn't this an interesting development."

"I thought you'd like it." Jenna smiled but then looked at her watch. "Sorry, but I have to get back to work." She left money on the table for her bill and then hurried away.

We chatted about the bombshell Jenna dropped for several seconds, but then Nana Jo got us back on track. "All right, who wants to go next?"

Irma raised her hand. "I had dinner last night with my friend, the accountant." She coughed. "Teddy took quite a bit of convincing." Irma smiled and preened herself. "But, I managed to get some information out of him." She coughed. "Teddy thinks Rudy Blakemore might have been blackmailed."

"What makes him think that?" I asked.

"Rudy's restaurant was doing well, but he suddenly withdrew a really large amount of money." Irma took a lipstick from her purse and applied it.

"How much is a large amount?"

"Seventy-five thousand dollars." She waited for the shock wave to roll over everyone before continuing. "When Teddy asked why he needed the money, *in cash*, he wouldn't explain why or what he intended to do with it." She picked up a knife and checked her teeth for lipstick stains before putting it down. "However, the day *after* Lydia Lighthouse was murdered, Rudy was ecstatic and deposited all of the money back into his account." She looked around the table. "Sure looks like the little bas—"

"Irma!"

She coughed. "Sorry. It looks like . . . he was getting ready to pay someone off but was suddenly let off the hook." She coughed and took a swig from the flask she kept in her purse. "That's all I got, but I'll keep working on Teddy." She smiled.

Nana Jo rolled her eyes. "Who wants to go next?"

Ruby Mae raised her hand. "I might as well go." She pulled out a bright pink baby blanket. "One of my grandsons Andrew used to do ice sculptures." She turned to look at Nana Jo and me. "Y'all remember he did one for Christopher and Zaq's high school graduation party?"

We nodded.

"And he said he'd be happy to do an ice bowl for Grace and Harold's wedding. Don't let me forget to tell Emma and Jillian."

"Thank you," I said.

Ruby Mae nodded. "Least I can do." She paused and then picked up her knitting. "Well, I asked Andrew if he knew that Maxwell Dubois person." She paused to count stitches. "Turns out he knows him well. They've been in several competitions and well, there just aren't that many African American ice sculptors in North Harbor, Michigan." She looked around. "We're on a tight timeline, so I asked him to hurry and talk to him and see what he could find out." She put the knitting down. "Turns out, Maxwell Dubois picked up and left town very suddenly on Sunday night. No one has seen or heard from him. Andrew called me right before y'all got to the retirement village to say he heard from a mutual friend that Max was back in town." She updated the row counter on the end of her knitting needle. "He's going over to his place and will give me a call as soon as he gets some information."

"Seems odd he didn't mention anything when we ran into him Sunday about leaving town." Nana Jo typed on her iPad.

"Maybe he had a death in the family," I said.

Ruby Mae shrugged. "Beat's me, but I'll let y'all know tonight after I talk to Andrew."

I stared. "Tonight?"

"Oops." Ruby Mae smiled.

I stared at Nana Jo. "What's happening tonight?"

"I thought we might need to let off a little steam and since we missed our girls' night out, we were thinking . . ."

I sighed. "But, we have Mom and Harold's wedding plus a murder to solve."

"Well, we may be able to combine business with pleasure." Dorothy sat up and smiled. "Were you done, Ruby Mae?"

She nodded.

"I've been looking for information on Felicity Abrams, and a friend told me Felicity Abrams likes to gamble. There's a blackjack tournament at the Four Feathers tonight. My friend felt confident Felicity would be there."

"So, you see, we would be going, primarily, for information," Nana Jo said.

I looked around the table and stopped at Irma. "I thought you had a date tonight."

"I told Teddy I'd meet him at the Four Feathers. I'll ride up with you all, but if things go as I plan, I won't need a ride home."

Nana Jo rolled her eyes.

I knew when I was beat. "Okay, I'll pick you up at . . ."

"Seven," Nana Jo said.

We paid our bills and went to the lobby to get our coats.

"I'll bring the car around." I headed toward the door, but Nana Jo stopped me before I could leave.

"Isn't that Stinky Pitt talking to Lydia's assistant, April Jones?" She pointed toward the reception desk in the main lobby.

Standing at the counter was April Jones, with a large suitcase next to her.

"Looks like she's checking out," Dorothy said.

"I wonder what they're talking about." I started to walk toward the counter but was stopped when Nana Jo tugged on my coat.

"Wait. I just got a great idea."

Something about the look in my grandmother's eyes told me I wasn't going to like her "great idea." When I heard the idea, I was right.

"You want to do what?" I stared at her as though she'd lost her mind.

"You heard me. I want to search Lydia's room."

"How exactly do you plan to do that? We're at a hotel. I'm sure the police have already searched her room."

She looked at me. "Really? You honestly think Stinky Pitt thought to search her room?"

I huffed. Detective Pitt wasn't the brightest light in the harbor and, while my head wanted to argue the point, my heart told me he probably hadn't searched the room. I needed to approach this from a different angle. "How exactly do you propose to get into Lydia Lighthouse's room? I mean, it's not like the front desk is going to just give you a key."

Ruby Mae pulled a cell phone from her purse and started searching for something. "My great-niece, Mable, used to work in housekeeping." She stopped searching. "Here it is." She pushed a button and started to talk. When she was finished, she had a big smile on her face. "All you have to do is figure out which room it is and Mable will meet us at the door."

I shook my head and sighed. "What if you get caught?"

"That's where you come in. You need to keep Stinky Pitt and April occupied." She swatted my butt. "Now, get over there."

I sighed. Finding that marriage license last night had obviously given my grandmother a taste for a life of crime.

I marched over to the counter and smiled. "Detective Pitt, fancy meeting you here."

He didn't look happy to see me. "Mrs. Washington, what are you doing? Why are you here?"

"We were just having lunch." I pointed to Nana Jo and the girls.

He looked at my grandmother.

"Hello, Stinky—ah . . . I mean, Detective Pitt." She waved.

Detective Pitt's face colored. It looked as though his jaw clenched, and a small vein on the side of his head pulsed. "Mrs. Thomas." He nodded to Nana Jo. Then he turned to the girls and nodded. "Ladies."

"Hello, April. Can you excuse us for a minute?" I pulled the detective away from April. Nana Jo and the girls followed.

"Are you about to interview April Jones?" I asked with as much excitement and enthusiasm as I could muster.

"I was trying to before you and your gray-haired busybodies interrupted me."

"Sleuthing Seniors." Irma patted her beehive.

"What?" The detective looked genuinely confused.

"That's the name of our book club," Dorothy said. "The Sleuthing Seniors."

"I thought we should go with something a little sexier, like Seniors and Mysteries, so our acronym would be—"

"Never mind the acronym." Nana Jo glared. "We're just here minding our own business." Nana Jo smiled, but I think the effect was lost on Detective Pitt.

"Well, see you don't interfere." Detective Pitt stood straight but still only reached Nana Jo's chin.

"Yeah, well, I was wondering if you would mind if I watched." I smiled brightly and leaned close to the detective. "I'd love to watch a professional in action. I'm sure you could teach us something about interrogating a suspect." I laid it on thick. "That is what you're about to do, isn't it?" I looked over my shoulder at April, who was standing at the counter.

"I was about to interrogate her before you came up."

"Would you mind terribly if I watched? I'll be quiet and I promise not to interrupt. Besides, it might be good to have someone else present if you're going to be alone in a hotel room with a young woman." I gave the detective a knowing glance. "I mean, you wouldn't want her to accuse you of anything . . . untoward."

Nana Jo choked down a laugh. "Sorry. I got something stuck in my throat."

Detective Pitt rubbed the back of his neck. "Well, I had thought of taking her down to the precinct, but . . ."

"You don't think she might feel . . . inhibited down at the police station?" I asked.

"I don't suppose it could hurt anything if you watched." He pointed at me. "But, you be quiet and don't interrupt."

I nodded. "Of course. I will be as quiet as a church mouse." Before he could change his mind, I turned and motioned for April to join us.

She looked even more timid than before, but she came forward. "You want me?"

"Detective Pitt needs to ask you a few questions. I'm sure you'd feel much more comfortable in your hotel room, rather than the police station," I said hurriedly.

Her eyes got big and she gasped. "I don't want to go to the police station," she whispered.

Detective Pitt turned to some chairs in the lobby. I could see the wheels in his head turning and knew he intended to suggest they sit in the lobby. Dorothy and Ruby Mae flopped down on the two chairs. Irma sat on the sofa and patted the seat next to her and smiled at the detective. Apparently, I wasn't the only one who'd guessed the direction the detective's mind was going.

He sighed. "Perhaps your room would be better."

"You're in the room across from Margaret and Oscar, three fifteen, right?" I asked.

"No. I'm on the first floor," April said.

"I was sure Margaret said you and Lydia were in the room directly across the hall." I looked puzzled.

April shook her head. "No, Lydia never liked elevators. She always liked to stay on the first floor. We're on the first floor in adjoining rooms. I'm in one twenty-three and Lydia had one twenty-five."

April, Detective Pitt, and I walked down the corridor. As we turned the corner, I saw Ruby Mae on her phone and the girls were all up and ready to search Lydia's room.

When we got to the door, I let April and Detective Pitt enter first, stopping to fix my boot. As I stood up, Nana Jo looked around the corner so she could see which of the two rooms we were entering.

Inside, the room was barren of all personal belongings. However, April rolled her suitcase in and placed it behind the door.

Detective Pitt stared at the suitcase. "Going somewhere?"

"I'm going home."

"We're investigating a murder, the murder of your employer. You can't just leave town."

"Well, I can't afford to stay here." April folded her arms and flopped down on the bed.

"I'm sure my mom will be happy to let you stay in her guest room," I said, even though I wasn't sure how Mom would feel about April staying. After all, she might have been involved with Lydia in fleecing her. Not to mention the fact that she could also be a suspect in a murder investigation.

Fortunately, April declined my offer. "Thank you, but I'll figure out something."

Detective Pitt asked April common questions. "Who do you think would want to kill Lydia Lighthouse?" "Can you recall anything she might have said that might help us find her murderer?" Etc. etc. Based on the way he asked the questions and April's response, he was obviously rehashing the same questions he'd already asked. I tried to focus in the hopes she might reveal something in her body language, but I was distracted when a loud crash came from the room next door.

"What was that?" Detective Pitt asked.

"It's coming from Lydia's room." April stood and walked toward the connecting door.

I tried to think of something to prevent them from opening the door, but my brain froze.

Suddenly, the doorknob was opened and a large African

American woman with a short afro, dressed in a maid's uniform, opened the door. "Excuse me, folks, I was just cleaning and dropped something." She smiled.

Detective Pitt relaxed.

"I hope I didn't scare y'all too badly?" Mable smiled again.

"No. Not at all." Detective Pitt waved her off.

"Well, I'll just lock this door so I don't bother y'all." She closed the connecting door and we heard the lock slide into place.

I held my breath and waited. When April returned to her seat, I released the breath and relaxed.

Detective Pitt kept at it for about thirty more minutes. I couldn't tell if he made any progress or had learned anything new. April was as much of a mouse at the beginning of the interview as she was at the end. There was only one moment when I noticed any real change in her demeanor and that was when she was asked about specific individuals. In fact, when she was asked about Rudy Blakemore, I noticed a flush come over her and she seemed more awkward than before. Obviously, the mouse had a bit of a crush on the caterer.

April looked at her watch. "Detective Pitt, I've answered your questions and I'm tired. I need to—"

"Would it be okay if I asked you a few questions?" I looked as kindly at April as I could.

When Detective Pitt didn't object, April sighed and sat back down.

"I was just wondering how Lydia selected the subcontractors she used? I mean, you aren't from North Harbor, so how did she find caterers and florists?" I smiled and prayed I sounded like an inquisitive potential bride.

"Well, the wedding planning community is pretty small. You attend bridal expos and conferences and circulate within that community. Over time, you meet the same people at different shows and you make connections." She colored as she gazed out the window. After a few seconds, she must have realized she was daydreaming. "Also, you get referrals from other wedding planners in the area that you trust."

"Is that how Lydia knew who to call?"

She nodded. "We met Rudy . . . I mean, Mr. Blakemore, at a show in Chicago and then again in Atlanta, so it was fortuitous and only natural we would use him when we were asked to plan a wedding here." She fidgeted and blushed like a schoolgirl. She had it bad for Rudy Blakemore.

"One other question," I hurriedly asked when once again it looked as though April was going to get up. "Were you aware Lydia was blackmailing her subcontractors into lowering their rates while charging the clients full price and skimming the money off the top?"

"What!" Detective Pitt said.

The blood rushed from April's face and she was instantly pale. She swayed and fell back onto the bed.

I immediately rushed to her side. I patted her face. "April, are you okay?"

"What the devil did you do to her?" Detective Pitt panicked. He paced nervously while I tried to revive the mouse.

"Stop pacing and make yourself useful," I ordered. "Go into the bathroom and get a glass of water and a damp cloth."

I pulled my cell phone out of my pocket and quickly texted Nana Jo that April fainted and to come immediately.

She must have been waiting in the hallway, because, within seconds, she was knocking on the hotel door.

Detective Pitt came out of the bathroom and stared at me. "Open the door. It's Nana Jo."

"What do we need that busybody for? We need a doctor or a nurse."

"Nana Jo grew up on a farm and she learned about herbs and things. Plus, she used to work with the Red Cross during the war."

Apparently, the Red Cross changed Stinky Pitt's mind. He quickly turned and opened the door.

I don't think I'd ever seen Detective Pitt so glad to see my grandmother.

Nana Jo rushed into the room and immediately took charge. She pulled up April's eyelids and checked her pupils. She shook her vigorously while lightly slapping her face. "April, are you on medication?" She turned to me. "Get some pillows and elevate her feet so they're above her heart."

I took the pillows from both beds and put them under her legs.

Nana Jo pulled a small vial from purse and took the lid off and waved it under April's nose.

The vial did the trick and April came around.

I sighed and looked at Detective Pitt, who was standing behind Nana Jo.

When he saw April move, he said, "Thank God," and drank the glass of water he'd brought for April.

April tried to sit up, but Nana Jo stopped her. "Hold on. You fainted. Just lie still."

"I'm fine," April said weakly. "Could I just have some water? I haven't eaten today."

Nana Jo stared at the mouse. "Well, then, our first order of business is to get some food into you." Nana Jo picked up the phone and ordered a grilled cheese sandwich and chicken soup from room service. When she replaced the receiver, she turned to April. "How far along are you?"

I didn't think April could get any paler, but she did.

Nana Jo turned to Detective Pitt. "I'm going to need you to go to find a vending machine and get an orange juice and bring it back."

Detective Pitt headed to the door. At the door, he turned around, walked back to the bed, gave Nana Jo the compress, and then left mumbling, "Orange juice."

"And don't come back without it!" Nana Jo yelled before the door closed.

When Detective Pitt had gone, Nana Jo turned back to April. "He needed something to do. He was getting on my nerves." She smiled. "Now, why don't you tell me what's going on."

April looked frightened. "How could you tell? Does it show?" She looked down at her stomach.

Nana Jo shook her head and smiled kindly. "When you've lived as long as I have, you recognize the signs." She smiled and patted April in the motherly way she had. "Now, what I don't understand is why the secret. You're an adult and, well . . . if you want to have a baby, you can have one."

April stared at Nana Jo as though she'd suddenly realized the earth was round. "You're right. I am an adult and no one can stop me if I want to have a baby."

Nana Jo nodded. "Did Lydia try to stop you?"

April looked shocked, but it quickly passed. "She didn't know, but I knew she wouldn't approve." She rolled her eyes. "If you worked for Lydia Lighthouse, you had to maintain the image of respectability and class." She shook her head. "Having a baby out of wedlock wouldn't have been acceptable." She rubbed her belly. "I really want this baby. I was an orphan and grew up in foster care, and I certainly don't want that for my child."

"So, you could have left and found another job someplace else. Lydia Lighthouse isn't the only wedding planner on the planet," I said.

April laughed. "You couldn't tell her that. Lydia Lighthouse was *THE* epitome of class and dignity. She would have fired me and made sure no one ever hired me," she said softly. "She could be very vindictive when she wanted to."

"Quickly, before Detective Pitt returns, why did you faint when I asked if you knew Lydia was blackmailing her subcontractors and stealing from her clients? You knew, didn't you?"

April nodded. "I knew and I was afraid."

"Afraid of what?" I asked.

She hesitated but then shook her head. "I don't know. I was afraid of what she would do to me and . . ."

"And, to the baby's father?" Nana Jo asked.

April nodded.

"Is he married?" I asked.

April looked shocked and quickly shook her head. "No. No, Ru—he isn't married."

Detective Pitt returned with the orange juice and April's color also returned. We stayed until room service arrived and Nana Jo made sure she ate every bite. By the time we left, April looked less like a mouse than I'd ever seen her. She had color in her cheeks and her eyes looked bright.

Nana Jo ordered bed rest and promised to check in on her.

When we left, I noticed, for the first time, one of Nana Jo's pant legs was wet. "What happened to your leg?"

A slight flush crept up her neck, but she merely growled. "I'll tell you later."

On the car ride home, I learned what caused the loud crash while the girls were searching Lydia's room and also why my grandmother's pants and one foot was wet. Once Mable let them into the room, they decided to divide and conquer. Each of them focused on searching a different area while Mable was the lookout by the door. Having achieved success by locating Margaret's hidden marriage license in her toiletries bag in the bathroom, Nana Jo decided to focus her efforts on the bathroom. Lydia Lighthouse's toiletries were sitting atop a shelf over the toilet. Despite Nana Jo's height, which was five ten, she couldn't see everything atop the three shelves. So, she climbed up on the toilet seat to get a better look. The crash was the collapse of the shelves. Nana Jo lost her footing and one of her legs slid into the toilet.

When I finally finished laughing, I asked why she didn't lower the seat before she climbed up.

"I did close the lid." She admitted grudgingly. "The lid cracked and broke. I lost my balance and my foot fell into the bowl."

I was still laughing when I pulled into the garage behind the building. Nana Jo, normally good-natured and able to laugh at her own foibles, didn't see the humor in the situation and marched inside to change her clothes.

Back at the store, Christopher and Zaq had things running smoothly and my head was spinning. So, I went upstairs. Dawson was practicing making roses and leaves on a baking sheet while Angelo was knocked out on the sofa with Snickers and Oreo.

"Where's Lexi?"

Dawson continued making leaves. "She's gone with Emma, Jillian, and your mom to check out the South Harbor Yacht Club. Irma's grandson pulled some strings and they're going to have the reception there so Frank doesn't have to shut his restaurant down completely." He finished his row of leaves and stood and stretched. "I didn't think you'd mind."

"Of course not." I rubbed my head. "I've got a splitting headache. I'm going to lie down."

He nodded and went back to making leaves.

I downed about four aspirin and lay down. My head felt like it was on a carousel. Around and around words, phrases, and images spun in my mind. Lydia Lighthouse siphoning money from couples and blackmailing caterers. Lydia Lighthouse's and April's faces swirled and swirled until I, thankfully, fell into a sound sleep.

When I awoke, my head felt better. Noises indicated Angelo was awake and playing in the main living room. I'd have to figure out what to do about them, but, for now, I was going to wait until I heard back from Jenna.

Even though the headache was gone, I couldn't get April's, Lydia's, and Margaret's faces out of my mind. I had no idea what it meant. Writing always helped me to make sense of my thoughts, so I sat at my laptop.

~

"Blasted bad timing, getting himself knocked off now." Lord William filled his pipe, dropping a good amount of tobacco on the sofa.

"What about poor Percy? Will he be okay?" Penelope asked from her seat on the sofa. Her face looked pale and she seemed genuinely shaken up by the events.

"Dr. Haygood says he'll be fine," Lady Elizabeth said. "Thankfully, his wounds appear to be superficial. Apparently, he surprised the murderer and he lashed out at him."

"Well, that's good news, at least." Lord William chomped on the stem of his pipe. "More of that blasted Halifax Slasher. Police need to do more."

Daphne looked pale. "What are we going to do? The wedding is less than a fortnight away, and now, the wedding planner is dead and the police will be here questioning people and ruining everything."

James smoked in front of the parlor fireplace. He stared off into space. Although physically present, his mind seemed to definitely not be on current events.

"I thought the police said the Halifax Slasher was a hoax." Lady Penelope lounged on the sofa. Normally, she would have been full of pent-up energy and pacing the room. Instead, she sat quietly with her head back.

"Somebody needs to tell that to Philippe Claiborne

and Percy Waddington." Lord William chomped. "Dirty blighter is venturing out, expanding his territory."

"What are we going to do?" Daphne looked around. "Don't any of you care?"

"Of course we care, dear," Lady Elizabeth reassured her niece. "Detective Inspector Covington from Scotland Yard should be here at any moment."

Thompkins opened the study door. "Detective Inspector Covington." He stepped aside, and the tall, gangly detective entered the room.

Detective Inspector Covington removed his hat and ran his hands through his thick, curly hair. "Good afternoon."

"Detective, so glad you could make it." Lady Elizabeth warmly greeted the detective they met when he investigated the first murder the Marshes encountered when one of Daphne's suitors, an American named Charles Parker, was killed. They developed a friendship when he investigated the other murders the Marsh family encountered. After a number of months, and several murders later, the family viewed Detective Inspector Peter Covington as a family friend.

"Peter, thank goodness you're here to clear this whole mess up," Lady Daphne said.

The detective smiled. "Glad to come, but I figured you lot would have solved the murder already."

His friendly joke fell rather flat and he looked uncertainly around. "What's going on? Thompkins showed me the body. I've got men collecting evidence. The doctor has sedated Percy Waddington, so we can't talk to him yet, but I want to know what's really going on."

Lady Elizabeth sighed. "Well, you'd better sit down while we explain."

Thompkins entered the room and pushed a tea

cart to Lady Elizabeth and then discreetly and quietly left the room.

Lady Elizabeth poured and, while everyone sipped their tea, they each explained what they knew about Philippe Claiborne. When they'd finished, they merely sat and stared at the detective.

"So, Philippe Claiborne had only been here a few days and none of you knew him before he came?"

They all nodded.

"In the span of less than three days, Claiborne managed to insult Lady Daphne, the housekeeper, the cook, and the butler and argued with Lord James and Lady Elizabeth. He was a fast worker."

Lady Elizabeth pulled out her knitting and shook her head. "I don't know of anyone who's made me so angry in quite some time." She knitted. "I was fully prepared to sack him, except . . ."

Detective Inspector Covington paused from the notes he was taking and looked at Lady Elizabeth. "Except?"

James tossed his cigarette into the fireplace and pounded his fist on the mantle. "Confounded, man, can't you see what she's trying to avoid saying."

Detective Inspector Covington looked into Lord James's eyes. "Perhaps you can clarify for me."

"Lady Elizabeth knows I didn't get on with Philippe Claiborne, and she's afraid I murdered the man, but she's too kindhearted to accuse her niece's fiancé."

Daphne gasped.

Lady Elizabeth shook her head. "Actually, the idea you might have killed him never crossed my mind."

Everyone stared at Lady Elizabeth.

James turned to stare into her eyes. "Why not?"

She finished the row she was knitting before answering. "It's not your style." She turned her knitting. "You're much smarter than that. If you'd murdered someone, I don't think you'd have been foolish enough to leave the body by the back door where it would be discovered so promptly. I doubt seriously if you'd have used one of our knives, and you certainly wouldn't have taken the knife away after you'd killed him." She smiled. "I'm sure you would have supplied your own weapon." She paused for a few moments. "No, you're much too smart for this murder."

James Browning stared at Lady Elizabeth for several moments and then burst out laughing. When he was done, he bowed. "I'm glad you think so highly of my skills."

"If it wasn't the duke, may I ask who you do suspect murdered the man?" The detective stared at Lady Elizabeth.

She shook her head. "I don't know. Thompkins said he was stabbed in the back with a knife. He was such an odious and unlikeable man. I fear the list of people who would have liked to kill him might be rather a long one."

"Well, the coroner hasn't determined the exact cause of death yet, but it looks like he was stabbed and strangled, but we'll hold the strangling part back from the public." The detective stared around the room. "Technically, I shouldn't have told anyone, but . . . well, I think you're all trustworthy."

"Thank you for trusting us." Lady Elizabeth inclined her head toward the detective. "The fact that some of the wedding guests have already started to arrive makes things worse."

Lady Daphne rose from her seat by the window and walked to the sofa and sat next to her aunt. "Aunt Elizabeth, this is horrible. It's cast a dark shadow on the wedding. Please, you've got to figure out who killed that man."

James paced. "Maybe we should postpone the wedding until after—"

"Oh, no you don't. We're not postponing anything. We're getting married by Christmas Eve." Daphne's eyes flashed and her face looked flushed. "I'm not going to be stuck here while you go off to Italy."

James turned to his friend Victor, who sat silently by the window. "Victor, what do you think?"

Victor looked up from his private musings. "I'm sorry, old boy, I'm afraid my mind was on other things." He glanced furtively at his wife, Lady Penelope.

Lady Elizabeth followed Victor's gaze and looked at her niece, Lady Penelope. "Penelope, dear, are you sure you're feeling all right?"

"Yes, of course. I'm just rather tired." She stood. "I think I'll go upstairs and lie down." She walked out of the room.

"You agree with me that we should postpone the wedding, right?" the duke pleaded with his friend.

Victor shrugged. "I suppose so."

Detective Inspector Covington turned to Lady Elizabeth. "What can you tell me about the house-guests?"

Lady Elizabeth paused in her knitting. "Well, Percy Waddington, Major Andrew Davies, and Sir Wilbur Hampton all arrived in the past couple of days."

Thompkins knocked quietly and opened the door. "Lady Alistair Browning."

Lady Alistair Browning, a tall, stylish, well-bred woman swept past the butler into the parlor. Tall and slender, Helene Browning wore a smart suit of navy blue with a matching cape trimmed in fur and a small pillbox hat with a veil. Silk stockings and suede oxfords rounded out the look. The small head of her Chihuahua, Bitsy, poked out from the muff.

The Marshes' Cavalier King Charles Spaniel, Cuddles, lounged at the feet of his master, Lord William. When Lady Alistair entered, Cuddles lifted his head and sniffed the air. He glanced at her ladyship and Bitsy.

Bitsy growled and yapped in Cuddles's direction.

Cuddles stared for a few seconds, then stood, turned around in a circle, and lay down in a ball with his back to the yapping dog.

Thompkins watched the scene and then released a sigh, perhaps remembering the last time he'd met Bitsy. Noting no incident, he turned and withdrew.

"Mother." James Browning hurried over to kiss his mother on the cheek. "I wasn't expecting you until right before the wedding."

"I didn't think I'd be able to get away, but I suddenly thought I should be here to assist with the preparations."

Lady Daphne hugged her soon-to-be mother-in-law warmly. "Lady Alistair."

"Please call me Helene, dear." She smiled and then looked up and noticed Detective Inspector Covington. "Oh dear, please don't tell me there's been another murder."

"There's been another murder . . . hmm," I said even though there was no one to hear. "I don't know if I like that, but—"

My computer dinged and flashed a notification. I had new mail.

I switched to email and noticed that in addition to emails about sales from two of my favorite stores, I'd also received an email from my new agent, Pamela Porter at Big Apple Literary Agency. For some ridiculous reason, my pulse sped up and I suddenly felt nervous and out of breath.

I opened the email. It contained a welcome letter, an electronic copy of our signed contract, and suggestions for me to start working on marketing my brand. I wasn't sure what that meant or what my brand was. Her suggestions included setting up various social media accounts, including an author website.

I stared at the email and wondered what I could possibly include on an author website. However, before I allowed the panic to overtake me, I took a few deep breaths and decided to enlist the help of my nephews. Christopher was a marketing major and Zaq was studying computers. Between the two of them, I was sure they could explain to me what my author brand was and help set up the social media sites.

There was a knock on my door.

"Come in."

Emma stuck her head in. "I hate to bother you, but I was just so excited." She opened the door wider and held up a box. "It's here."

"What's here?"

"Your dress. Can you try it on?"

I took the box. "That was fast."

"We paid extra for rush delivery. That way, if you didn't like it or it looked awful on, we would have time to return it and go with something else." She smiled and stepped out, closing the door behind her.

Inside the box was the burgundy retro dress she'd shown

me just the day before. It was neatly folded and, when I took it out of the packaging, it was surprisingly less wrinkled than I expected.

I took off my jeans and sweatshirt and slipped the dress over my head. At five feet three and curvy, I was concerned the dress wouldn't fit and would emphasize every bump, bulge, and dimple. Mostly, I was worried I'd look ridiculous. However, the dress fit like a glove. I glanced at myself from all angles in the full-length mirror.

"Are you going to come out? We're dying to see how it fits!" Emma yelled.

I opened the door and walked out into the main living area.

I wasn't expecting the crowd that awaited me. Not only were Emma, Jillian, Mom, and Nana Jo there, but also Dawson, Angelo, Lexi, Jenna, and Frank. I stopped abruptly at the sight of the large crowd.

There were oohs, aahs, and a blush-inciting whistle from Frank.

"You look amazing, honey." Mom wiped tears out of her eyes.

I looked at my sister and saw she, too, had a large box. "You should try yours on too. Do you have the same dress?"

She shrugged. "No idea. I left the decision up to the girls. I trust their taste."

Jillian and Emma smiled.

Jenna got up and went into my bedroom. Within a short period of time, she came out in a beautiful dress that was the exact same shade of deep burgundy velvet; however, her dress was strapless with a sweetheart neckline and a slit that went up the side of the dress and showcased her legs, which were quite shapely.

"You look great." I stared as my sister twirled to applause and compliments. "Do you like it?"

She nodded. "Definitely." She smiled at both girls.

"Well, now you two look great. I'll have to find something equally stunning for the mother of the bride." Nana Jo smiled.

Jillian smiled shyly and then pulled another box from behind her back. "Actually, while we were shopping, we found another dress that looked like it would be perfect and so we . . ." She held the box out to Nana Jo.

Nana Jo's surprise quickly turned to joy and she snatched the box and quickly hurried to her room. She came back in a dark gray sequined lace column dress with three-quarter sleeves and a V back. There was a slit that went up the side of the dress, and Nana Jo looked amazing.

"Awesome. I love it." She kissed both Jillian and Emma.

"Whew." Emma breathed a sigh of relief. "I was so nervous."

"You look great, Nana Jo," Christopher said.

"All of you look great," Zaq said.

I caught Frank's eye and he winked, which made me feel shy. "What about the bride?" I asked.

"OMG we found the most amazing suit for your mom." Emma pulled out her cell and swiped until she found the picture and then held it up for us to see. The picture was a beautiful off-white suit. It was simple, but what made the outfit was the brocade overcoat. The suit was elegant. My mom's petite frame would look great.

"That's a beautiful suit." I glanced at my mom and saw genuine joy on her face.

"The girls were wonderful." She patted Jillian and Emma on the arms. "It's a lovely suit and I know it's something I will want to wear more than once, and it won't look like a traditional wedding dress." She smiled. "I will feel like a bride every time I put it on."

"Well, all the women are fixed, now, what about the men?" Nana Jo stared at her great-grandsons.

"All set," Christopher said. "Mom bought us black suits."

"They'll wear burgundy and gray ties."

Angelo jumped around and clapped. "Yay! What about me?"

I reached down and picked him up. "Do you want a suit?"

"Yay!" He clapped his hands.

"We'll have to see what we can do." I looked at my watch. "We better get out of these clothes. We've got to pick up the girls." I glanced around at Angelo and Lexi. "Although, I forgot . . ."

"We don't need a babysitter. We can stay by ourselves." Lexi turned away so her back was to me as she put her book up in front of her face.

"We thought we'd make popcorn and watch movies on television." Jillian looked at me. "If that's okay with you?"

"Of course."

She smiled. "All of my favorite Christmas movies are on tonight. *White Christmas, Holiday Inn, Miracle on 34th Street, Meet Me in St. Louis,* and *Scrooge.* I love Christmas movies."

"How about I provide dinner?" Frank asked.

Zaq looked at his watch. "I'd love to, but the movies start soon and I don't think we'll have time."

Frank waved that away. "No problem." He pulled out his cell and called in an order. "I'll have dinner delivered so you can eat and watch your movies."

"That'll be nice," Emma said. "Thank you."

"Least I can do." Frank kissed me. "We still on for dinner tomorrow?"

I nodded. We kissed again and he left.

Jenna, Nana Jo, and I changed out of our wedding attire. I was going to the casino with the girls, so I chose my outfit carefully. I wanted to look nice, but the Four Feathers Casino was extremely smoky. Consequently, my clothes and skin tended to reek of smoke after a few hours. So, I changed into old jeans and a sweatshirt that I could toss in the wash as soon as I got home. No dry-clean only sweaters for me tonight. When I was done, I took a last glance at myself in the mirror and headed into the main living area.

There was a crowd in front of the television eating roast beef sandwiches and watching *Miracle on 34th Street*. They barely looked up when we left.

Nana Jo and I drove to the retirement village and picked up the girls, and I made the thirty-minute drive to the casino.

"I know it's not an official meeting, but I heard back from Andrew about the ice sculptor, Maxwell Dubois, and I want to tell y'all what I know before I forget," Ruby Mae said.

Nana Jo looked over her shoulder at Ruby Mae. "Go right ahead."

"Andrew said Max Dubois didn't want to talk at first, but he convinced him nothing would be made public unless it absolutely had to. Max is a nice man, but he got in trouble years ago when he lived in Virginia. He robbed a bank. The police found him, and he spent five years in prison. That's where he learned how to sculpt."

"Sounds like he served his time and paid for his crime. Where does Lydia Lighthouse come in?" Nana Jo asked.

"Lydia contacted him specifically because she knew his past. She told him she could either propel his career forward or she could make sure he never worked again."

"What a bit—"

"Irma!"

"Sorry." She coughed.

"This means Lydia Lighthouse was blackmailing both Maxwell Dubois and Rudy Blakemore," Dorothy said. "I wonder who else she was blackmailing. I'll talk to Felicity Abrams as soon as I see her."

The girls enjoyed going to the casino for entertainment and the Four Feathers was a nice establishment that would rival just about any casino in Las Vegas, or so I'd been told. Nights out that included a trip to the casino always started with dinner at the buffet. Ruby Mae had so many relatives we barely stepped inside the door before a great-niece, great-grandson, or third cousin twice removed came over to talk to her. These visits inevitably resulted in free buffet tickets for Ruby Mae and her friends. Tonight was no exception.

After dinner, we split up so each of us could engage in our vices. For Nana Jo, that meant poker. Dorothy went to the high-stakes room to play blackjack and see if she could find Felicity Abrams. Irma went to the bar to pick up men. Ruby Mae sat in a corner eating, talking, and knitting. For me, I liked penny slot machines to engage in mindless low-stakes gambling. Twenty dollars could go a long way on penny slots.

Tonight, I found a machine called Sun and Moon. Playing all lines cost me a whopping twenty cents and, after my first two spins, I hit the bonus round, which resulted in fifty free spins. Betting the minimum amount would never make me rich but wouldn't result in wiping me out early either. Slow and steady, that was how I liked to play.

While I played, I thought through what we'd learned about Lydia Lighthouse and tried to fit the pieces together. Lydia Lighthouse was a bully and a blackmailer. She blackmailed Max Dubois and Rudy Blakemore. Although, I wondered what she had on Rudy. She couldn't have learned he'd fathered April's baby or April wouldn't have been hiding it. Nor would she still have been working for Lydia, if she could be believed.

Lydia Lighthouse was stealing from her customers. She charged more for services than they cost and then bullied or blackmailed the vendors into reducing their rates and pocketed the difference. She bullied her assistant, April.

Chances were good she was blackmailing Margaret. Lydia must have known Margaret was married—still married to Bufford Jones. We needed to look more closely at Margaret.

She could have killed Lydia. She could have—my mind boggled. "Jones, how could I have missed that?" I asked the lady sitting next to me. Thankfully, she must have thought I was talking about my machine. She merely shrugged and continued playing.

When my games finished, I cashed out and went to the lobby to wait. I needed to mull over the idea floating in my head.

At the front of the casino there were two massive fireplaces on either side of the door with sitting areas. Ruby Mae was knitting by the fireplace. There was a young girl in a white chef's outfit sitting nearby. The two of them looked comfortable, and I didn't want to disrupt, so I moved to the opposite side of the hall, in front of the other fireplace, and sat to think.

Writing always helped my thought processes. I hadn't brought my laptop, but I had started putting a notebook in my purse. That way, when ideas came or when I found myself waiting, I could still get some writing done.

Lady Alistair was quickly brought up to speed on the murder.

"Philippe Claiborne?" She stirred her tea absentmindedly. "Why does that name sound familiar?"

"Did you know him?" Lady Elizabeth asked.

She sat quiet for a few minutes and then shook her head. "I don't think so, but that name does sound very familiar. I think I know *of* him, but, for the life of me, I can't remember why."

Detective Inspector Covington flipped through his notes. "Let's see. You've got Percy Waddington, Major Davies, and Sir Wilbur Hampton?"

"That's it!" Lady Alistair placed her teacup on the table. "That's where I heard the name Philippe Claiborne." She turned to Lady Elizabeth. "You must remember the scandal it caused." She looked around the room. "It was . . . at least three . . . no . . . four years ago now, but now that I think about it, I think you had gone abroad, hadn't you?" She looked at Lady Elizabeth.

"Mother, I love you, but if you don't get on with the story, I'm going to throttle you," James said.

"Yes, of course. Now, where was I?" She paused. "Yes. It wasn't until you said all of the names together that I remembered. You see, Sir Wilbur Hampton was engaged to marry Percy Waddington's younger sister." She picked up her teacup and stirred the tea. "Yes, that was it. Percy Waddington is an art dealer and hired a young man he'd gone to school with to help plan the wedding."

"Let me guess, Philippe Claiborne?" Detective Inspector Covington asked.

She smiled. "Yes. Well, no one really knows all of the details, but whatever happened, Sir Wilbur called off the wedding at the last minute and refused to marry the girl."

Lady Elizabeth nodded. "I do recall some scandal. It would have been four years ago, in 1934. We had been abroad most of the year. William's cousin, Albert, died in that mountaineering accident in February." She turned to her husband. "Remember, dear?"

Lord William nodded. "Of course. Albert and I were good friends." He puffed on his pipe. "King of Belgium, but a good sort. Grew up in the Palace of the Count of Flanders. Wasn't supposed to be king, you know. His uncle's son died and then Albert's older brother died young. That left Albert second in line for the throne, behind his uncle." Lord William smoked. "Concerned about the working class, I remember. He used to get in trouble for dressing up like common citizens and sneaking out of the palace to see about the living conditions." He puffed. "Good chap."

"Yes, dear. I always liked Albert too." Lady Elizabeth pulled out her knitting. "We stayed in Belgium for a while after the funeral to see Leopold's coronation, then we came back in November for the wedding. My cousin, Alice, married Henry, the Duke of Gloucester."

"It happened when you were in Belgium," Lady Alistair continued. "Mary Waddington was distraught and Percy was furious." She leaned forward. "They say she had a nervous breakdown and had to go to Australia and stay with relatives to recover." She looked knowingly at Lady Elizabeth.

"Oh dear, I see." Lady Elizabeth knitted. "Isn't that the same time Lady Catherine's tiara was stolen?"

Lady Alistair nodded. "I believe so, plus . . . the other incident."

Detective Inspector Covington looked from Lady Elizabeth to Lady Alistair. When neither rushed to explain he grew impatient. "Perhaps one of you could explain what any of this has to do with Philippe Claiborne?"

"I'm sorry." Lady Elizabeth smiled at the detective. "Well, I believe what Lady Alistair is implying is that it was believed Mary must have gotten . . . in the family way and had to be rushed out of the country to save herself and her family from disgrace." She looked at Lady Alistair. "Is that right?"

Lady Alistair nodded. "Of course, no one knows for certain, except Mary and the young man; however, there was a maid that was also dismissed from service and she claimed Philippe Claiborne fathered her child."

"Why the dirty blighter." Lord William huffed.

"Claiborne didn't marry the girl?" Victor asked innocently.

Lady Alistair shook her head. "No. If I recall correctly, he denied the child was his." She took a sip of tea. "Of course, Sir Wilbur had very little choice in the matter. He had to dismiss the girl."

Penelope's cheeks flushed and she rose and paced. "I don't see what you mean he had no choice in the matter. Of course he had a choice." She marched across the room. "That poor girl was dismissed, most likely without references. She and her baby wouldn't stand a chance."

"Calm yourself, dear." Lady Elizabeth halted her knitting to stare at her niece. "It's an unfortunate situation, but let's not forget why we're here."

Detective Inspector Covington leaned forward. "Thank you, Lady Elizabeth. We're here to figure out who murdered Philippe Claiborne. Now, can we get back to—"

"I don't think I care who murdered him," Penelope said.

"You can't mean that?" Victor stared at his wife with concern registered all over his face.

"I most certainly do. He was a vile man with no re-
gard for life and his own responsibility, and I don't really
care if we ever find who murdered him."

Daphne gasped. "But if we don't find the murderer, people will think . . . they might believe . . ."
She stared at James.

Penelope turned and looked at the strain on her
sister's face. "Oh dear, I'm sorry." She sighed. "I certainly don't want anyone here to be arrested for the
murder." She sighed. "I'm just tired." She sat back
down. "Please forgive me. Of course, I'll do what I
can to make sure we catch whoever killed him."

"Now that's settled, could we get back to the problem at hand?" Detective Inspector Covington sighed.

Lady Elizabeth took one last glance at Penelope
and then picked up her knitting. "Well, I think we'll
have to divide and conquer to figure out what we
can, and we'll need to do it quickly." She turned to
Penelope. "Penelope, there's so much going on at
the moment between the murder investigation, the
wedding, and the children from the Kindertransport.
Would you mind taking the lead in seeing that the
children are taken care of until we can arrange for a
governess? How's your German?"

Penelope sighed. "Pretty bad."

"Well, I'm sure it'll do." She smiled at her niece.
"Plus, Joseph Mueller, Thompkins's son-in-law, has
come and is helping us understand Jewish culture.
I'm sure he'll be more than happy to help."

Lady Penelope nodded.

"Great." She turned to Lady Alistair. "I hate to im-
pose on a guest, but—"

"I'm hardly a guest." She smiled. "Soon, I'll be a member of the family and I'd love to help."

"Wonderful. You're such an excellent hostess, I was wondering if you would be willing to help with the guests and final wedding details."

Lady Alistair beamed. "I'd love to help." She hesitated and turned to Daphne. "That is if it's okay with you, dear. I wouldn't want to interfere."

Lady Daphne smiled and hurried to Lady Alistair and gave her a big hug.

"Wonderful. Now, Victor, do you think you could tackle Percy Waddington? See what you can find out."

Victor nodded, although his brow was still furrowed as he continued to glance at his wife.

Lady Elizabeth turned to her husband. "If I remember correctly, Major Davies is a member of your club, isn't he?"

"Used to be." Lord William spoke around his pipe. "But I'll see what I can find out from him."

Lady Elizabeth smiled. "James, I don't know that you'll have much time for investigating, but I have a little job for you."

James nodded. "I will gladly help." He looked at Detective Inspector Covington. "Provided I'm not under arrest."

Lady Alistair gasped and nearly dropped her teacup. "Arrested?"

James looked around the room and settled his gaze on the detective. "Everyone knows I got into several arguments with Claiborne."

Lady Elizabeth put down her knitting. "James, dear, I think if Detective Inspector Covington were to arrest everyone who had an argument with Philippe

Claiborne, he might find that would include me and most of the servants."

"You got into an argument with Claiborne?" Detective Inspector Covington stared openmouthed.

She nodded. "Yes. I'll tell you all about it, but first, would anyone care for more tea?"

Chapter 12

"Earth to Sam!" Nana Jo yelled.

"Sorry." I pulled myself away from the twentieth century. "I was writing."

"Guess who I just saw?" Nana Jo smiled like the cat who ate all the cream.

"Felicity Abrams?"

She shook her head. "Nope." She smiled. "Harold's brother, Oscar."

"Really?" I shrugged. "Maybe he's bored just sitting at the hotel all day and all night. Was Margaret with him?"

She shook her head. "Nope, but I asked one of Ruby Mae's relatives, who works here, Marvin, I think he said his name was, and he said Oscar's been here every day all day and he's dropped a *lot* of money."

I raised an eyebrow. "Really? Well . . . I guess, when you're rich, it doesn't matter."

"True, but Marvin said Oscar has lost a lot of money and has been playing on credit."

I shook my head. "I wonder if Margaret knows."

"Who knows." She shook her head.

Irma, Dorothy, and Ruby Mae joined us, and Nana Jo filled them in.

"Do you think he could have killed Lydia?" Dorothy asked.

Nana Jo shook her head. "I don't think he really knew her, but it won't hurt to ask. I'll mention it to Harold. Maybe he can find out."

Dorothy yawned. "I'm tired. I must have gone all over this place looking for Felicity Abrams."

"Any luck?" I asked.

She shook her head. "Nope." She stretched. "Oh, well. Time to settle up and go home."

"Settling up" for us involved splitting our winnings. The girls decided they would share all of their winnings equally. This pretty much insured no one went home broke. Generally, if one of us had a losing night, someone else would be winning. Normally, Ruby Mae, Irma, and I played the least, twenty to fifty dollars. Dorothy and Nana Jo were usually the big spenders and, therefore, the biggest winners. However, I had a fortunate night about a month ago, which resulted in a big hit. After taxes, we each went home with about eight thousand dollars. So, I didn't feel badly that my contribution tonight wasn't that much. Irma's date never showed up, but she chatted up someone she met at the bar. Dorothy and Nana Jo had modest wins. We all had a free meal from the buffet, thanks to Ruby Mae's connections, and each went home with twenty-two dollars more than we came with. Plus, I had a few more pages done on my manuscript.

The ride home was uneventful. We agreed to meet for lunch tomorrow at Frank's restaurant. Then Nana Jo and I headed back to the house.

When we went upstairs, the crowd was still there, in front of the television. As I passed through the room, I saw the Christmas marathon was still playing.

"Looks like Bing Crosby isn't the only one dreaming about a white Christmas," Nana Jo said softly.

I looked at the crowd of bodies in my living room. Each and every one of them was sound asleep, including the poodles.

We turned off the television and tiptoed into our rooms and left them all where we'd found them.

The next morning, I called Jenna and asked if she could meet me for breakfast. She sounded suspicious, but when I mentioned the name of her favorite breakfast spot and offered to pay, she agreed.

My sister wasn't a food snob, but she had certain standards that she expected, regardless of where she ate. Standards were a good thing to have, but mine weren't as high for fast food as they were for four- and five-star restaurants. Jenna didn't care. She expected the server at the drive-thru, who was making minimum wage, to provide the exact same level of customer service as a trained waiter at a five-star restaurant. So, meals out with my sister were often an experience.

Her favorite restaurant was a small hoity-toity quasi-French café that served Belgian waffles, her favorite breakfast food. The food was tasty, but I usually balked at spending five dollars for a cup of coffee.

I arrived first; punctuality wasn't my sister's strong point. However, I didn't have to wait long before her car pulled into the parking lot. Jenna sat in the car talking, I assumed on the phone, for several minutes. Then she got out and joined me in the restaurant. The fact that the waitress brought a cup of hot tea to the table, when she saw Jenna sit down, spoke volumes.

"Come here often?" I joked.

Jenna smiled and sipped her hot tea. "Ah . . . perfect. They know how to make a good cup of tea and so, yes, I do come here often." She sipped her tea. "Most places use the same carafe for tea and hot water, but it totally ruins the taste of the tea."

"Whatever you say." I sipped my expensive coffee and tried to detect something that would differentiate it from the coffee I paid a dollar for at the fast-food drive-thru, but my palette must not be sophisticated enough for that. It all tasted the same to me.

The waitress came and took my order. She looked at Jenna. "Your usual?"

Jenna nodded.

"You have a usual?"

She stared at me. "Did you invite me to breakfast to mock my dining habits or did you have a purpose?"

I told her what I'd learned from Lexi.

She listened and took a few notes until her food arrived. Then she took a deep breath and tackled the mac daddy of Belgian waffles.

We ate in relative silence for several moments.

Then Jenna said, "I reached out to Child Protective Services in Chicago to notify them of Lexi and Angelo's whereabouts. She said it might be a few days before they could send anyone to pick them up, due to the holidays."

"But, I don't—"

"I figured you weren't trying to get rid of them, so I told her they could stay until after the holidays and then we'd take them back to Chicago."

I breathed a sigh of relief. "Thank you."

"So, what do you want?"

"What makes you think I want something? Maybe I just want to have breakfast with my favorite sister."

"I'm your only sister."

"Okay. I was wondering if you could have your investigator check on something."

"What?"

I told her about my suspicion that April was Margaret's illegitimate daughter.

"I suppose it's possible, but why would she hide it?"

I shrugged. "Beats me. Maybe she didn't think Oscar Robertson would accept a package deal."

Jenna promised to have her investigator delve into it. She took a glance at her watch and then grabbed her bag. "I've got to run. I'm due in court in less than thirty minutes." She hurried to the door but halted before she left. "Thanks for breakfast." She waved and quickly headed out to her car.

I sat and drank the last of my coffee and then paid the bill.

I decided to pay a call on Detective Stinky Pitt. I hoped maybe the coroner's report would be ready and he might have more information.

Detective Pitt met me and escorted me back to his closet of an office. Inside the claustrophobic space, he closed the door. "Whaddya want?"

"I just wondered if the coroner's report was ready?"

He frowned but slid a file in my direction.

I read and looked up at the detective. "That can't be right."

He leaned back in his chair and smiled.

"According to this, Lydia Lighthouse was drugged, stabbed, and strangled." I stared.

He rocked in his chair. "That's confidential. We aren't releasing any of that to the media, so watch your mouth." He pointed.

"Why?"

"The real killer will know details no one else knows." He smiled arrogantly. "It's the way the professionals do things."

I tried not to roll my eyes, but it took a major effort.

Detective Pitt didn't have any other information and thankfully, I didn't have to stay long. The closet was small and poorly ventilated, so odors had no way of escaping and hung in the air like a sweaty locker room. When I found myself breathing through my mouth rather than my nose, I knew it was time to exit. So, I made my excuses and left.

On the way back to the house, I passed by what was left of North Harbor's shopping mall. The large complex was mostly empty, with only a few anchor stores still in business. It was a sad sign of North Harbor's economic demise. Just past the mall was a shopping plaza with a pet store, which reminded me Snickers and Oreo were running low on dog food. I glanced at my watch; even though it was early, the stores were all open to maximize the Christmas season spending wave. I hesitated about a half second and then swung my car into the parking lot. I hurried inside for dog food. I came out with dog food, treats, and new Christmas sweaters, because . . . well, it was Christmas. I was just about to head back when I saw a *Buy One Get One* sign in the window of a discount retailer. Now that Lexi and Angelo were going to spend the holidays with me, they'd need Christmas presents. Two hours later, I emerged with two cartloads of gifts.

I let the sales associate load the back of my SUV and tried not to think about how much I'd just spent on two kids I barely knew. Somehow, the money didn't bother me. It was Christmas and I always liked to give a bit more during the holiday season. Leon and I never had much, but we recognized we were blessed. So, during the Christmas season, we usually upped our charitable donations. At the school where I worked, we adopted a family for Christmas. So, if I looked at my purchases in that light, I didn't feel quite so bad. Besides, very few of the items were frivolous. I'd spent the most on clothes. Underwear and warm clothes were things they could use immediately. However, now that they were staying through the holidays, that also meant they'd be around for the wedding. So, I found a lovely burgundy dress that would look great on Lexi. Suits for small boys were scarce. But, I did find a nice pair of dark pants and a dress shirt. I considered it providence when I saw there was a burgundy vest. It might be a little big for him, but Nana Jo could take it in.

I pulled into the garage and spent a few minutes sorting through the bags. I tried to figure out what I'd wrap for Christmas and what they needed for today. Most of what I'd bought was clothing. It had been quite some time since I'd last bought toys. Maybe I'd spend some time talking to Angelo and try to find out what he'd like.

"Need some help?"

I dropped the dog food. "You scared me."

"Sorry." Dawson bent down and lifted the dog food onto his shoulder and then relieved me of my other packages. "Let me help you."

There were definite advantages to having a fit football player staying in your garage apartment.

He not only carried all of the bags inside, but also up the flight of stairs.

"Anything else?" He wasn't even breathing hard.

"No, but thank you."

He jogged back downstairs and continued on whatever had driven him into the garage in the first place.

I looked around. Angelo was watching cartoons on the television. Lexi was reading another book. *The Murder of Roger Ackroyd.* It was one of my favorite Agatha Christie books. She'd finished her other book and I'd told her she was welcome to read anything that could be classified as a cozy mystery. Agatha Christie was the queen of the cozy mystery, so she would be safe. I wasn't an advocate of limiting what anyone read. As a child, I read a great number of books that where above my reading level. My parents didn't sensor what I read, so I started reading murder mysteries and romance novels at a young age. However, after a while, I found the puzzle of the murder more appealing than the Happily Ever After of the romances and that was what stuck. I enjoyed other genres, but my heart belonged to mysteries. Reading books opened up an entire new world for me. I smiled as I thought about my bookstore and about the possibility of seeing my own book on one of those shelves. Buying the building and opening a bookstore gave me something to occupy my mind after Leon died. Writing filled a lot of lonely nights. That love for books had opened my eyes to a completely new world. I hoped Lexi would find something similar. Maybe she wouldn't open a bookstore or become an author, but, if nothing else, it would expose her to life outside of her foster family.

"Why are you staring at me with that goofy grin on your face?" Lexi stared at me.

"Oh, nothing." I tried to wipe the goofy grin off my face, but I was sure it was reluctant to leave. "Hey, I bought you guys some clothes."

"Yay!" Angelo jumped up and down. "Lemme see. Lemme see."

Lexi put down her book and walked over to the bags. "Really?"

I dumped the bags on the sofa.

Lexi picked up the burgundy dress and held it up.

"I thought you could wear it to the wedding." I tried to read her face to see if she liked it.

"We're going to the wedding?" She looked up and her eyes had tears. "I thought you'd be sending us back."

"My sister talked to your caseworker and she arranged for you both to stay during the holiday season." I hadn't considered the fact that maybe they wouldn't want to stay. Now, I was unsure. "That is, if you want to stay."

Lexi ran to me and threw her arms around me.

I hugged her tightly and tried not to cry. Angelo jumped up and down and joined in the hug so the three of us were hugging.

"What's going on?" Nana Jo asked. "Can I get in on some of this hugging action?"

Angelo ran and flung himself into her arms.

Nana Jo braced herself and caught him and gave him a fierce bear hug. "You give really good hugs." She looked at me. "Now, why are we hugging?"

"Sam says we can stay to the holly days," Angelo said.

Nana Jo looked at me.

I smiled. "Jenna worked it out with the caseworker."

Lexi wiped her eyes with her sleeve and picked up her dress. "And, we get to go to the wedding." She held up the dress.

"Maybe you should try it on." Nana Jo smiled.

Lexi grabbed her clothes. "We'll have a fashion show."

Angelo wasn't as inhibited and allowed me to change his clothes in the living room. The pants fit but were a little long. Nana Jo got some pins and promised to take them up. The vest was big, but she pinned it too.

"I forgot about dress shoes," I said.

Nana Jo removed the clothes, careful of the pins. "I'll get the dress shoes." She looked at Angelo. "Do you want to go shopping and buy some new shoes?"

"Yay! Shoes!" Angelo jumped in a circle.

I smiled. His enthusiasm reminded me of Oreo in his puppy days. Now, he barely glanced at Angelo.

The other clothes were casual things he could wear every day, sweatpants, T-shirts, socks, and underwear. No need to alter those things. If they were too big, he would soon grow into them.

Lexi came out in her burgundy dress, which fit her perfectly. She strutted like a model down a runway, with one arm on her hip. She stopped and posed several times before turning around and strutting out.

We applauded.

She tried on all of the outfits and walked with exaggerated steps and flair each time. Dawson joined the show and whistled and clapped, which caused Lexi to blush as she rushed away to change outfits.

"Hey, Jillian is performing in the *Nutcracker* at MISU tonight. She told me to ask if it would be okay if Lexi came along." He paused. "If she wants to."

Angelo bounced up and down. "What about me?"

I looked from Dawson to Angelo. "I think you might be a little young for the *Nutcracker*."

He poked out his lip. "I'm not too young for nuts. I like cracking nuts."

"I thought we had a date to go shopping?" Nana Jo poked out her lip. "We can get ice cream if you're good."

Angelo's face quickly changed to utter elation and he jumped up and down. "Ice cream. Ice cream. Yay!"

Lexi was ecstatic over the idea of going to her first ballet performance. She then spent thirty minutes debating what to wear. Ultimately, she decided on a plaid skirt and sweater I bought at the last minute. It was dressier than the other items, and I wasn't sure if she would ever have an occasion to wear it. I'd even bought a pair of cowboy boots that were on clearance and just happened to be in her size.

When the fashion show was over, Lexi and Angelo went downstairs to pilfer some of the Christmas cookies Dawson had baked earlier.

I'd spent so little time in the bookstore lately that I found myself missing the energy as well as the routine. Nana Jo and I went downstairs and worked the afternoon shift to give the twins a much-needed break.

Lexi was a big help shelving books and made herself useful sweeping, dusting, and helping out wherever needed.

By the end of the day, we were all tired.

I looked at my watch. "I've got to get showered. I have a date tonight."

Nana Jo's boyfriend, Freddie, picked them up early. Having spent hours at the shopping center earlier, I was grateful to pass along the shoe shopping.

Next was Lexi, who dressed quickly but then ran into fits about how to fix her hair for the ballet. She obsessed and lamented for so long that she finally agreed to a single ponytail at the nape of her neck with a bow made from a ribbon belt to one of my dresses. She looked sophisticated, but still twelve.

She was beaming when Dawson came up to get her.

At last, the house was empty, except for the poodles, who appeared to be exhausted from all of the activity and were laying in a dog bed, staring at me. Clearly, keeping up with two extra guests was arduous.

A glance at the time and I realized I needed to get a move on. I took a quick shower and hurriedly dressed for my date.

Frank Patterson, not surprisingly, was a bit of a food snob. He liked good cuisine. Normally, when we went out to eat, we hit restaurants with great ambiance, impeccable service, and outstanding wine cellars. However, when he asked where I wanted to go, I mentioned a place which wasn't known for any of those things. Dittos called their cuisine Asian Fusion. I wasn't sure what that meant, but it was delicious and I had a taste for it. Not surprisingly, Frank had never been to Dittos, but he was willing to give it a try. Even though I was a native and Frank had only moved to North Harbor two years ago, it was rare that I got to introduce him to a new culinary experience.

Dittos was a small restaurant in South Harbor that was a combination self-serve buffet and stir fry. When we sat down at the tiny bistro table, the server took our beverage order and handed us wooden sticks with the table number stamped on it and an ink pen. We were instructed to write our names on the stick and then go up to the first buffet area and fill a bowl with vegetables. The next stop was the sauce station, where we ladled our sauce of choice onto the vegetables. The sauces ran from a mild peanut sauce to something called Diablo, which topped out the spice rating of five. There were small cups for sampling and Frank spent a lot of time trying the various sauces and experimenting with combinations. Once he'd gotten his sauce mixture just right, we moved on to the next stop, the meat station. Here, we got a smaller bowl and filled it with whatever meat we wanted. Our options included duck, beef, pork, and chicken. The final station consisted of various colored plastic sticks, which instructed the cook to add shrimp, scallops, or flat bread to the order. When we were done, we put our wooden sticks in the bowls and left them at the end of the bar for the chef to cook on a giant Mongolian flattop grill. Frank was engrossed in watching the chef fry our food and even went up and asked questions.

When the food was done, our server delivered the bowls with a bowl of rice, which we shared. I watched Frank's face as he tasted the creation and felt elated by the look of pure joy that crossed his face.

"This is fantastic. I can't believe I haven't been here before."

"I'm glad you like it. I think my favorite thing about eating here is that as many times as I've been here, I never feel like it gets monotonous because I can never remember what sauces I used the last time, so it's different every time."

He looked at my plate with a longing that made me smile.

"Would you like to taste mine?"

I shoved my bowl closer and he tasted it.

"That's great." He pushed his bowl in my direction. "Would you like to taste mine?"

"No thank you." I shook my head. "I avoid the sauces with ratings above a two and saw you ladling that Diablo sauce on yours."

We savored our food. Dittos was too small of a restaurant for lingering, so, when we were done, we left. South Harbor was decked out for the holidays, and we spent a few minutes admiring the decorations when a horse-drawn carriage went by. Frank flagged down the driver and we took a carriage ride through the cobblestoned streets of South Harbor. Snuggled together under a blanket, with a thermos of hot chocolate provided by the driver, we admired the light displays along the bluffs overlooking the Lake Michigan shoreline. It was a very romantic experience. When the carriage driver brought us back, we stopped across the street from Dittos at the River Bend Chocolate Factory. I was stuffed, but a cup of coffee sounded lovely.

"That was a lovely evening." I sipped my coffee. "Thank you."

"Thank you for introducing me to Dittos."

We hadn't seen much of each other lately, so we sat and got caught up. Frank updated me on his plans for the food for the reception. Even though the location was moved, Frank was still catering the food. I updated him on the investigation.

"So, you think Margaret is April's mother?" he asked.

I shrugged. "Maybe. I don't know. Jones is a common name. It could just be a coincidence."

He frowned. "I don't believe in coincidences usually, but Jones is very common."

"I know. We really need to talk to Margaret. Maybe we can ask her."

"You're just going to come out and ask her if April is her daughter?"

I shrugged. "I don't know. What I need to find out is if Lydia was blackmailing her."

"I might be able to help you with that."

I must have looked puzzled, because Frank smiled. "I can ask my sources to check bank accounts and look for deposits. If Margaret withdrew a large sum of money and Lydia deposited that same amount shortly afterward, it would show a pattern."

"You can do that?"

He grinned. "Let's just say I know a guy."

"That would be great." I hesitated.

"What?"

"Well, since your guy is already checking, maybe he could check for Rudy Blackmore, Felicity Abrams, and Maxwell Dubois." I smiled.

Frank shook his head. "In for a penny, in for a pound."

I also shared what I'd learned about Lexi and Angelo and that Jenna had arranged for them to stay through the holidays.

"Then what?"

I shrugged. "No idea. I'm not excited about the idea of them going back to the Hoopers. Jenna reported the accusation of abuse and is looking into what happened to Lexi's friend, Veronica, but"—I shook my head—"she thinks the girl will deny the abuse. But at least they'll have to investigate it. So"—I shrugged—"we'll see."

Frank reached over and took my hand. "I'm sure you want to keep them, but you can't take in every stray kid you find hiding out in your bathroom or in my back storage room." He squeezed my hand gently.

"I know. I just wish I could help."

"You are helping."

We talked until the smell of chocolate was so overwhelming I could no longer resist its allure. I purchased two pounds of chocolate-covered raisins and two giant chocolate-caramel cashew turtles.

Frank stared at me with a puzzled expression and finally asked, "What's with the chocolate-covered raisins? I thought you only liked chocolate with nuts?"

I smiled. "I do. These are for Nana Jo and the kids. This is how I keep myself from eating all of the Halloween candy. I only buy candy I don't particularly like." I held up the cashew turtles. "These are for me."

He laughed.

When I got home, Jillian was demonstrating various ballet positions, and Lexi was excitedly dancing around the room and regaling Nana Jo with the details of the *Nutcracker* while Angelo ran from one side of the room to the other in his brand-new shoes.

Dawson had changed back into sweats, and Nana Jo looked tuckered out.

I left the younger folks with the bag of chocolate-covered raisins and went into my bedroom with my smaller bag and a cup of hot tea.

Once I was comfortable, I pulled out my laptop and typed the notes I'd made earlier into the computer. My mom's wedding was one week away, and I still didn't know who killed Lydia Lighthouse. I tried not to think about my mom standing alone at the altar while Stinky Pitt escorted Harold out of the church. I needed to clear my mind so I could put the pieces together and figure out who killed her. Nana Jo had told me writing helped me free my subconscious to figure out the solution. I prayed she was right.

⌒⌒⌒

Everyone rose to leave the parlor.

"I wondered if I could have a word." Lady Elizabeth turned from Detective Inspector Covington to Lord James Browning.

Both men nodded and stayed back while the others left the room. When the last person filed out, Lady Elizabeth turned to the duke.

Lady Elizabeth set aside her knitting and looked at James. "We've never talked about what you do, and I'm sure you probably can't talk about it. However, I wondered if you might have a way to look into Philippe Claiborne's bank account."

James stared at Lady Elizabeth with a puzzled expression. "Possibly, but it would help if I knew what we were looking for."

She sighed. "I have my suspicions about Philippe Claiborne." She turned to the detective. "Which I think would involve the two of you."

"Yes, milady," Detective Inspector Covington said.

"I wondered if the two of you could look into Philippe Claiborne's background." She sighed and looked up. "Specifically, I'm interested in knowing if you"—she turned to the detective—"have a way to cross-check burglaries with events where Philippe Claiborne was involved."

Detective Inspector Covington looked shocked. "You think he was a thief?"

Lady Elizabeth shrugged. "I don't know what I think, but I remember hearing about the incident with Mary Waddington, and I also recall Lady Catherine du Long's diamond tiara was stolen around that same time." She picked up her knitting. "Mrs. McDuffy said she found Claiborne coming out of the library." She shook her head. "There's really no reason why he should have ever been in that room." She knitted a few stitches. "Thompkins said he'd been going through the silver." She paused. "I suppose he could have been looking to see what was needed, but honestly, that's Thompkins's responsibility."

James flexed his hand into a fist and jutted out his chin. "Why the swine. If I'd known, I'd have wrung his bloody neck."

"I think someone beat you to it, dear," Lady Elizabeth said.

Chapter 13

If writing helped my subconscious mind, it certainly hadn't made the leap over to my conscious. My next option was sleep.

The next morning, I still hadn't solved the murder, but I awoke with a plan. I missed time in the bookstore, so I fed my soul by spending a few hours surrounded by books and talking mysteries to customers. Since opening the bookstore, I hadn't had as much time to read, but many of these authors were like old friends.

Dawson baked, decorated, and kept an eye on Angelo, who was engrossed in cartoons. Lexi lounged and read. Nana Jo left early. She said she had research to do. I wasn't sure if her research involved her current boyfriend, Freddie, whose son was a Michigan State Trooper, or if her research involved a trip to see her old boyfriend, who was a reference librarian. Regardless, she would get information and be ready to share.

Time in the bookstore went by quickly and, within a short period of time, I felt more like myself. The girls and I had agreed to meet for lunch at Frank's restaurant. I hadn't done any sleuthing, but the beginnings of an idea had started to take shape.

At noon, I walked the short distance to Frank's restaurant. He was busy behind the bar, as usual, but took time to wink as he mixed drinks and helped customers. The girls had taken a shuttle from the retirement village to downtown. I agreed to make sure they all made it home safely.

Nana Jo was the last to arrive and she flew in like a winter squall, with her scarf flapping behind her as she trudged toward our table. She flopped down in a chair. "Brrr . . . it's cold out there."

The waitress came by to get drink orders and Nana Jo ordered a hot cup of coffee. Before she could return, Frank came to the table with a carafe of coffee and a pitcher of ice water. He put the pitcher of ice water with lemons on the table in front of me.

"Somebody's getting special treatment," Dorothy teased.

Frank smiled and held up the carafe of coffee.

"Bless you!" Nana Jo held up her coffee mug. When her cup was full, she took a long drink and then pulled out her iPad. "Let's get started." She took off her coat.

"You're in a hurry," Irma said.

"Must have found out something," Ruby Mae said.

"As it turns out, I did find out some information, but I can wait my turn if someone else wants to go first." Nana Jo looked around.

We all looked at each other and either shook our head or shrugged in response.

"Great. Then, I'll start." Nana Jo swiped on her iPad screen a few times. "I had lunch with Freddie. His son, Mark, had been on vacation, so he hadn't been able to get much information before. Now, Mark's back and he ran the names of our suspects through the police database. It turns out Bufford Jones isn't the only person we know who has spent time in the Polk County Jail."

"Really?" I asked.

"Rudy Blakemore, Maxwell Dubois, and Rubin Abrams, husband to Felicity Abrams, all served time in the Polk County Jail." Nana Jo looked up from her screen.

"Why were they in jail?" I asked.

Nana Jo looked at her device again. "Let me see. Rudy served time for failure to pay child support."

"Poor April." I shook my head. She can't catch a break.

Nana Jo shrugged. "Well, the poor girl is so homely, she was probably happy to have anyone show her some attention. Maxwell Dubois served time for bank robbery and later for possession of marijuana."

"They say it does wonders for glaucoma," Ruby Mae said.

"Rubin Abrams is married to Felicity. He's the only one still locked up. He was convicted of murder."

"Who did he kill?" Dorothy asked.

"His business partner, Gerald Lighthouse."

"Lighthouse?" I realized my mouth was open and quickly closed it. "Any relation to Lydia?" I frowned. "But, wait. How can it be? Lydia's real name wasn't Lighthouse, it was Jones."

Nana Jo nodded. "Common law husband. They never actually got married."

"Maybe that's why she became a wedding planner, because she never had one," Irma said.

"Maybe." Nana Jo shrugged.

"So, Rudy Blakemore, Maxwell Dubois, and Felicity Abrams all have ties to Polk County Jail, where Lydia's brother is incarcerated."

"Yep." Nana Jo nodded. "So, any one of them could have a strong motive for killing her."

"You mean, if they didn't want their records exposed," Dorothy said.

"Nowadays, employers run background checks on everyone." Ruby Mae pulled her knitting out of her bag. "I know my daughter, Stephanie, has such a hard time with her cleaning company. You know, if you're going to give people access to your home, you can't be too careful."

"That's all I've got." Nana Jo looked up. "Who wants to go next?"

Ruby Mae raised her hand. "I'll go." She put down her knitting. "My grandson Andrew talked to Maxwell Dubois. He couldn't have killed Lydia Lighthouse." She picked up her knitting. "Maxwell Dubois has an iron-tight alibi."

"How iron tight?" I asked.

"He was in jail." She knitted. "He claims he had a drug problem a few years ago but got cleaned up."

"Probably when he was in jail the second time." Dorothy looked from Ruby Mae to Nana Jo.

Ruby Mae shrugged. "I guess so. Anyway, he claims he was clean and minding his own business and then Lydia came demanding he basically do the ice sculpture for practically nothing or she would blackball him and make sure he never worked again."

"How?" I asked.

"A lot of people don't like hiring ex-cons," Ruby Mae said.

"That seems to have been her modus operandi." Nana Jo typed.

"I don't know what that means, but if you mean that's how she rolled, then you'd be right," Ruby Mae said. "So, he got scared and fell off the wagon."

"So, he got high?" Irma asked.

Ruby Mae nodded. "He got lit up. Went walking around River Bend butt naked."

"If he was high, maybe he killed her in a drug-induced fit," Dorothy said.

Ruby Mae shook her head. "Naw, I asked the same thing. He was picked up early Sunday night and spent the night in jail." She finished the row she was knitting and updated the row counter on the end of her needle. "Apparently, his wife threatened to leave him if he didn't get help, so he went to a clinic in Chicago. That's why no one knew where he was."

"I'm glad he got help. I guess we're crossing him off the list of suspects?" Nana Jo looked around.

We all nodded.

"Okay, nice work, Ruby Mae. Now, who's next?"

Dorothy raised her hand. "I may as well go. I went to Felicity Abrams's florist shop, and it was closed. She has a note on the window that she's going to be out of town due to a death in the family." Dorothy frowned and slumped in her seat.

"It might not be true," Nana Jo said encouragingly.

Dorothy shook her head. "It's true. My sister had her number and called to ask if there was anything she could do." Dorothy sighed. "Felicity's cousin died and she went to Detroit for the funeral."

"She left after Lydia was killed, so she could still be a suspect." I tried to encourage her.

Dorothy shook her head. "Unfortunately, she was in her shop the entire night Lydia Lighthouse died. She already had a wedding and a Christmas party booked. She tried to back out of your mom's wedding, but Lydia wouldn't hear of it."

"But that makes her even more of a suspect. Maybe she killed Lydia so she could get out of doing Grace and Harold's wedding." Dorothy turned to Nana Jo and me. "Sorry."

I shrugged. "No apologies necessary."

"I can't imagine she would kill to avoid providing flowers for a wedding. However, I did talk to her assistant, Ian, and he swears they never left the shop." Dorothy drank her coffee.

"If she has an assistant, why did she have to close her shop?" I asked.

"He's a student at MISU and only works part-time," Dorothy said.

"Great job, Dorothy." Nana Jo looked encouragingly at her friend. "Thanks to you, we can eliminate Felicity as a suspect."

We halted our conversation while our waitress came and took our orders.

"I'll go next." Irma coughed. "I had a date with Marty and—"

"Who the heck is Marty?"

Irma grinned. "Just a guy I met when we were at the casino last."

Nana Jo shook her head. "I don't know how you keep them all straight."

"It's a gift." She smiled. "Anyway, Marty and I went to the Four Feathers." She leaned close and whispered, "He's a whale." She nodded. "He gets free food and drinks. He even gets to stay for free in the penthouse suite." She sat up straight and proud. "It's huge and there's even a butler and chef who prepares all of the food," she gloated.

"Sounds like a cheap date if he took you to the casino where he gets everything for free." Nana Jo rolled her eyes.

I kicked her under the table. "That sounds really nice."

Nana Jo rolled her eyes. "That's great. Now, what did you find out from Marty that is relevant to Lydia Lighthouse's murder?"

"Well, I didn't find anything out from *Marty*. Not anything I can share anyway." She smiled coyly. "But, Marty likes to gamble in the high-stakes room. So, I was in there sitting beside him." She leaned close and fluttered her eyelashes. "He says I bring him luck."

"If you don't get on with it, so help me God, I'll—"

I kicked her again.

She glared at me. "And if you don't stop kicking me, I'll put you over my knee and spank your bottom."

Unfortunately, Frank chose just that moment to stop by the

table. He heard Nana Jo's comment and immediately turned around and walked away.

"Smart man." Nana Jo turned to Irma. "Now, get on with it."

Irma straightened her back and held her head high. "When we went in the high-stakes room, Oscar Robertson was there. So, I asked one of the servers about him. He said Oscar has been at the casino practically every night and he's been losing *a lot*. I specifically asked about the night Lydia Lighthouse was murdered, and he checked the tab and he was definitely at the casino all night."

"Looks like Harold's brother might have a problem," Nana Jo said. "I don't think any of us ever seriously considered him a suspect, but it'll be good to wipe him off the list."

Frank whispered in my ear. "Can I see you a minute please?"

"Excuse me." I got up and followed him to the back.

When he turned to face me, he looked so serious, I got worried. "What's wrong?"

He took a deep breath. "I had a friend track Lydia Lighthouse's bank deposits and Margaret's withdrawals." He unfolded a sheet of paper and handed it to me. "Whenever Margaret withdrew large amounts of money, Lydia made large deposits within a day of the exact amount of Margaret's withdrawal."

"That proves she was paying Lydia blackmail. She must be the killer."

He held up both hands. "Hold on. It *might* prove Margaret was paying blackmail, but it doesn't prove she's a murderer."

"You're right. I can't jump to conclusions." I smiled. "Anything else?"

He nodded. "My friend said the deposits go back for years."

"Thank you." I folded the paper and smiled, but the smile froze on my face at the look in his eyes. "What's wrong?"

He sighed. "I had another friend do some checking on

Lexi and Angelo. I thought it was odd that she speaks Italian so well."

I raised an eyebrow. "Why? You speak Italian."

"I speak a lot of languages." He took a deep breath. "Their father was Enrico Gelano, a physicist, and their mother, Maria Gelano, was a chemist. They died in a car accident."

"I know that. Lexi told me."

"What she may not have known was that her parents were only here on temporary visas to work with scientists at Cornell. Her family in Italy was expecting them to return to Italy."

I felt as though someone had punched me in the stomach. "Family?"

He nodded. "Grandparents and cousins."

"Why didn't they ever try to find them?"

He grabbed my shoulders. "Apparently, they have been looking for them. They've been working with the embassy. The big problem was they thought they were in New York. No one knew they were in Chicago."

"Why didn't Lexi remember about her family? Angelo would have been too young to remember, but she should have remembered grandparents and other relatives."

He shook his head. "My friend thought it could have been trauma from the accident, but, whatever the reason, they'll have to be told. They've been going crazy hoping for word of some kind." He looked intently into my eyes. "You okay?"

I nodded.

"I know you've gotten attached."

I nodded. "I'll be okay. I knew I couldn't keep them forever, but I didn't know you'd find their family so quickly."

He pulled me close and hugged me.

I buried my head in his chest and cried. After a while, I forced myself to stop and pushed away from him.

He handed me a tissue.

"I don't know why I'm crying. It's a good thing, right?

They don't have to go back to the Hoopers. They'll be with their family."

"It is a good thing."

I sniffed and forced a smile. "Thank you for finding their family."

He hugged me again and then walked away.

I took a moment to collect myself before heading back to the table. Our waitress had brought our food and I tried to hide the fact I'd been crying by diving into my food, even though eating was the last thing on my mind. I should have known better than to think I could hide anything from my hawk-eyed grandmother.

"Sam, are you okay?" Nana Jo asked.

"I'm fine." I hurriedly took a bite of my BLT minus the T.

Irma pulled off her six-inch hooker-heel shoe and held it up. "If he hurt you, we can kick his a—"

"Irma!"

She burst into a coughing fit, took a look around, and then pulled a flask from her purse and took a swig. "Sorry."

It took me a few seconds before it dawned on me they blamed Frank for my red puffy eyes and general distress. "Oh, no. He's fine. He just told me some news . . . it's good news, really."

"Well, if this is how you react to good news, I don't want to see how you look after bad news." Nana Jo glared. "Now, either you tell me what's wrong or I'm going to take my peacemaker out and turn him from a tenor to a soprano."

"It's not Frank's fault. Honestly, he just found Lexi and Angelo's family, and it made me sad to think about them leaving."

"I thought their parents are dead," Nana Jo said.

"They are, but they have grandparents and cousins and other family who love them and care about them. They've been looking for them and working with the embassy."

"If they were working with the government, that's probably what took so long," Ruby Mae said. "Red tape."

Everyone nodded.

Nana Jo patted my hand. "I understand now." She took a napkin and wiped her eyes. "I've gotten attached to them too."

Frank came by the table. "Is everything okay?" He looked worried.

Nana Jo stood and gave him a hug.

He looked surprised but accepted the situation. I didn't have the heart to tell him how close he came to disaster just a few seconds earlier.

I shared the details about Margaret's bank withdrawals coinciding with Lydia's deposits.

"Well, that explains why she recommended Lydia for the wedding," Nana Jo said.

"Who's left?" Ruby Mae asked.

Nana Jo made a few swipes on her iPad. "Margaret, Rudy Blakemore, and April."

"Are you seriously considering April as a suspect?" Dorothy asked. "She seems like such a . . ."

"A mouse?" Nana Jo asked.

Dorothy nodded.

"I hadn't really considered her. She seems so meek and . . . mousy, but maybe she didn't like how Lydia treated her like a drudge."

"Or maybe she didn't like the way Lydia hit on her boyfriend," Nana Jo said. "I'd have drop-kicked anyone who did that to Freddie."

"What do you mean?"

Nana Jo looked up from her iPad. "Surely you saw how Lydia was flirting with Rudy and how she kept brushing up against him and stroking his arm."

Frank had once again chosen the wrong time to bring a

fresh pitcher of water to our table. As he straightened up, Nana Jo proceeded to stroke his arm and leaned against his body.

I didn't think anything could make Frank Patterson blush, but Nana Jo managed to do the impossible.

He looked like a frightened rabbit. "What's going on?"

I burst out laughing, but Nana Jo wasn't done. As he turned to leave, she swatted his butt like a football player after a big play.

Frank stopped, turned, and faced Nana Jo. "The least you could have done was buy me lunch first."

We laughed, along with the other waitstaff and some of the patrons.

When the laughter died down, we planned our next meeting.

I stopped at the bar to say goodbye before I left.

"I don't know what was going on, but tell me your grand-mother wasn't really hitting on me," Frank said.

I laughed. "She was demonstrating an important point in our investigation.

He nodded. "I was just checking."

On the short walk back to the bookstore, Nana Jo and I agreed to delay telling Lexi and Angelo about their family for a bit until Frank was absolutely positive about the details. I'd hate to raise their hopes and have it turn into nothing. His friend was going to contact the appropriate embassies. It might take time to get passports and arrange passage. I wanted to ask if they could stay until after the holidays, but I didn't want to be selfish. After all, the family had been looking for them and must be out of their minds. Instead, I hoped that bureaucratic red tape would buy me the extra time.

I worked in the store during the afternoon to give my mind something else to focus on. Thinking about Lexi and Angelo made me sad. Mentally, I knew they would have to leave some-day, but I felt sad realizing how very close that day was.

When the store closed, I went upstairs. Emma, Jillian, Dawson, and Zaq took Lexi and Angelo ice skating. Which meant I had a quiet house all to myself. I walked around for several moments, trying to remember what things were like before there were crayons and books laying all over the place. Snickers and Oreo were also getting a lot more attention as one of Angelo's favorite activities was chasing them around the back courtyard in the snow. I looked at my two poodles, who were lying in their dog beds fast asleep. I was at a loss for how to occupy my time and decided a trip to the British countryside might help me collect my thoughts.

Victor entered the library, where Percy Waddington was walking around admiring the art.

Percy turned when the door closed. "Oh, Victor. You startled me."

"Sorry. Admiring the art?"

Percy laughed. "Force of habit."

The men sat down and smoked in silence for several moments.

"How's your arm?"

Percy Waddington held up his bandaged arm and flexed it several times. "Seems to be healing well." He smiled. "But, I won't be taking the court at Wimbledon anytime soon."

Victor smiled at the joke. "I wanted to ask you about something."

"Certainly." Percy looked at Victor.

"How well did you know Philippe Claiborne?"

Percy smoked. "Not very well. We'd met at a few house parties, but certainly not well enough to want to stick a knife in his back and strangle him." He chuckled. "However, I do have a bit of a confession."

"A confession?"

Percy chuckled. "Don't look so frightened. I knew it was bound to come out sooner or later. It's just that, well, things haven't been going so well at the shop." He leaned forward. "In fact, things have been rather dire, actually."

"I'm very sorry to hear it."

"I wasn't exactly invited, you see. I ran into Major Davies and learned about the wedding and thought I'd just . . . well, you know, slip in with the others and bunk here for a bit while I get back on my feet."

"I see." Victor looked relieved. "I don't suppose anyone will care. What's one more person."

"Thanks." Percy smiled, and the two men smoked in silence.

Lord William and Major Davies sat in the library and enjoyed a glass of whiskey.

"Glad you could make it, old chap. Been a long time." Lord William raised his glass to his friend and took a sip.

"Ah, yes. Certainly." The major tossed back the drink quickly.

Lord William quickly refilled the major's glass. "Haven't seen you around the club." He stared at the major to gage his reaction.

"Darned shame that." Major Davies was a large man, who had once been muscular and attractive to the ladies. Now the muscles had gone to fat. His hair, once thick and curly, was wispy and patchy.

Lord William refilled the major's glass and replaced the top on the decanter.

"Had to drop out. Darned embarrassing that." He glanced at the decanter on the sideboard and sighed. He sipped rather than gulped his drink.

"What happened? If you don't mind me asking." Heat rose to Lord William's face. Personal questions were always difficult for the kindly duke, but Daphne's happiness was at stake, so he did his duty.

Major Davies paused and stared at the amber liquid in his glass for a long time before he spoke. "Bad financial investments. I met that cocky event-planning fellow, Claiborne, when my goddaughter got married several years ago. Seemed a good enough chap. Always at the right parties, invited to the best homes for weekends, you understand."

He turned to glance at Lord William, whose neck heated again. Whether due to guilt for inviting Philippe Claiborne to his home and exposing him to friends or for guilt over delving into private matters, he rose and placed the decanter on the table close to his friend's chair.

Major Davies smiled and gulped the remaining amber liquid from his glass. He then picked up the decanter and refilled his glass. He took a sip and sighed. "Well, he asked me to put in a word for him at the club and recommended some investments." The major shook his head. "Diamond mines in South Africa."

Lord William shook his head. "Risky business that."

Major Davies nodded. "Took every cent I had. Mines were worthless. Then, he did a bunk and disappeared from the club. Left word I would cover his debts." He laughed. "I could barely cover my own debts, let alone his." He swirled his whiskey. "Had to sell land to come up with the money to pay the blasted things off."

Lord William stared openmouthed. "I had no idea. I certainly wouldn't have had him at the house if I'd known."

The major sighed. "No reason you should know. The club hushed it up, and I went to live with a nephew in India for a bit. Gave me time to get back on my feet."

"Well, I'm terribly sorry, old chap."

Major Davies downed his drink. "I heard someone killed him. If I'd run into the arrogant little blackguard, I'd have killed him myself."

Chapter 14

It was Sunday, so any plans would need to wait until after church with Mom. I got up and dressed and was surprised to see Lexi and Angelo both dressed in their Sunday finest at the breakfast bar, eating pancakes.

I looked an unspoken question at Nana Jo, who was drinking coffee.

She shrugged. "Grace thought it would be nice if we all went to church as a family."

I got so excited I nearly spilled my coffee all over the counter. "Do you think that means Margaret and Oscar will be there too?"

She looked suspiciously at me. "Why are you suddenly so interested in worshipping with Margaret Robertson?"

I glanced over to make sure Angelo and Lexi weren't listening. Fortunately, Angelo was distracted by cartoons and Lexi had her nose buried in a book. Still, I leaned close to Nana Jo and whispered, "My interest developed this morning. I think we need to confront Margaret and ask her if April is her daughter and if Lydia Lighthouse was blackmailing her."

Nana Jo stared at me and raised an eyebrow. "What are you planning to do, drag her to the altar and accuse her of adultery, like Hester Prynne in *The Scarlet Letter*?"

"Actually, I thought maybe I'd just get her in a corner and ask."

"I guess that's one option."

I turned around and heard a loud *YELP* as I stepped on Snickers, who was, of course, underfoot. I reached down and picked her up. "I'm sorry, girl, but you can't get under my feet all the time."

She took a few moments of stroking and murmured apologies before she forgave me and gave my nose a lick. Only then did I know I was truly forgiven. I put Snickers down and got two biscuits from the doggie jar. I turned to Angelo. "Would you like to let Snickers and Oreo outside?" I handed him the biscuits and he ran screaming down the stairs while being chased by two poodles.

I looked at Nana Jo. "Are you sure taking him to church is a good idea? He has a lot of energy."

Nana Jo shrugged. "We'll take crayons and he'll be fine."

When Dawson arrived, we all piled into the car and headed over to the church. Normally, I picked my mom up for church. According to Nana Jo, she said she'd ride with Harold and meet us there. I wondered if this was a sign of the future. Once Mom and Harold were married, she would want to ride to church with her husband. I wasn't really sure how I felt about that. A few months ago, I dreaded the Sunday excursions with my mom. Church, brunch, and then time spent shopping, watching a movie, or some other activity complete with a guilt-ridden interlude of criticism about my appearance, life choices, or lack of refinement. Once she was married, things would change. As much as I dreaded the emotional roller coaster of Sunday outings with my mother, I knew there was a part of me that would miss it when it was gone. Change was never easy and I'd been through quite a bit of it in the last eighteen months. Nevertheless, I knew change was inevitable. Perhaps Sundays with Mom and Harold would be a pleasant experience, which didn't involve criticism or guilt.

My contemplations distracted me to the point that I nearly passed the church.

"Sam, where are you going?" Nana Jo asked.

I forced my brain out of the clouds and whipped across two lanes of traffic and pulled into the church parking lot. The early service wasn't as crowded as the main service would be, so finding a good parking space wasn't hard.

Angelo skipped between Nana Jo and Dawson and held their hands, while Lexi and I walked together. She seemed solemn.

"What's wrong?" I asked.

She shook her head. "Nothing. It's just so pretty here." She looked out at the snow-covered church with its brick exterior and stained glass windows.

"I love the windows. There are beautiful scenes of the nativity, the last supper, and the crucifixion." I leaned closer. "When I was a kid, a tornado blew through town and shattered one of the stained glass windows. The church commissioned a famous stained glass artist to replace it. My dad was one of the people who helped open the church for the installation and I watched." I leaned close. "The artist saw me staring at the window and came over and told me a secret."

She looked up surprised. "What secret?"

I looked around to make sure no one was listening. "He said he hid a picture in the glass, but you won't see it unless you look carefully."

"What's the picture?"

I shook my head. "You have to find it for yourself." I smiled.

We hurried inside and found the pew where Mom, Harold, Margaret, and Oscar were already seated.

I pointed out the window to Lexi and noticed her eyes barely left the window for the entire service.

When the service was over, I felt a tug on my sleeve. I looked down at Lexi.

"I don't see the picture. What is it?" she begged. "Please. I may not be back and have another chance to see it."

I leaned down. "Look at the very bottom right-hand corner of the window." I looked at her. "I don't know this for a fact, but I'm pretty sure there wasn't a dog at the crucifixion of Christ."

She stared and finally saw the picture of the small brown dog with his tongue hanging out. Her face lit up with excitement. "That's amazing. I never would have seen it if you hadn't pointed it out."

We left the church and headed for Tippecanoe Place. I wasn't thrilled about the drive to River Bend, simply for brunch. However, I hoped the atmosphere would put Margaret in a good mood so she would answer my questions. During the drive, Nana Jo and I decided it would also be a good chance to tackle the River Bend Mall and finish our Christmas shopping. Under normal circumstances, nothing could have compelled me to drive down Grape Road, the street that went by the mall. During Christmas, it would be a nightmare. However, the idea of picking up a few toys that would put a smile on Angelo's face was all it took to get me to comply.

Dawson called Christopher and Zaq earlier and had gotten their agreement to distract the kids so Nana Jo and I could shop. Since we had to drive to River Bend, we might as well make the most of it.

Tippecanoe Place was as crowded as always, but, just as in previous visits, Harold Robertson's name opened doors. In our case, his name opened a private dining room, which was quickly

set up to accommodate our party of thirteen. Thirteen—an unlucky number, at least that was what my mom announced
once everyone was counted.

The foyer of the mansion was crowded, making it difficult
to stand or sit together while we waited. In typical Harold fashion, he commandeered a chair for my mom. Margaret tapped
her foot impatiently and looked at Oscar as though she expected the same treatment. Oscar must have been accustomed
to the look because he was able to ignore it. Margaret must
have become accustomed to being ignored because she merely
rolled her eyes at her husband. She turned to the hostess,
snapped her fingers, and demanded a chair. However, before
the chair arrived, I spotted a newly vacated seat. I quickly sent
Lexi to sit and hold it.

"Margaret, here's a seat if you'd like to sit." I pointed to the
wingback chair where Lexi was currently perched.

Margaret hadn't defrosted much and merely inclined her
head like a queen acknowledging a peasant's obeisance. Unfortunately, she didn't get to enjoy her seat for long. Almost immediately after her butt hit the seat, the hostess came to let us
know our room was ready.

I had to hustle to keep up with Margaret as she mounted
the stairs and went to the room set aside for our brunch. I was
determined to stay close to her in an effort to be seated within
close proximity to facilitate conversation during brunch. Once
in the room, there was a moment of hesitation while we
looked at the table and got our bearings.

Harold placed Mom at the seat closest to the fireplace and
settled himself next to her. That determined the head of the
table. Margaret positioned herself opposite to Harold, and I
hurried to take the seat next to her. I might have been a little
overzealous in making sure I was seated next to Margaret, because I nearly pushed Nana Jo aside. Her raised eyebrow was

the only response, but she chose the seat on Margaret's other side.

When we were all settled and our drink orders were given, I wondered how to start the conversation with Margaret. How did you ask someone if they were being blackmailed?

Harold smiled. "It's so nice to have our entire family together."

Margaret grunted.

We all pretended we didn't hear her.

"Speaking of families, Grace was just telling me about her research." Harold stared lovingly at Mom. "Why don't you tell everyone what you've found, dear."

Mom blushed. "Well, I really have Margaret to thank for getting me started."

We stared at Margaret, who looked as surprised as the rest of us.

"I have no idea what you're talking about." Margaret took a sip of her mimosa.

I hoped there was enough alcohol in there to loosen her tongue sufficiently but wondered if I should order her something stronger.

"Oh, yes. You've spoken with so much pride about being able to trace your family all the way back to Robert E. Lee; I just wanted to know how far we could trace our family." Mom smiled. "So, I ordered some of those kits you see on television that will trace your genealogy and I sent it off."

"That's awesome, Granny," Christopher said.

"What did you find?" Zaq asked.

Mom fluttered her hand, but she pulled some papers from her purse. "I paid extra to get the results expedited, and it turns out we can trace our family tree all the way back to Thomas Jefferson."

"Really?" Nana Jo looked at Margaret. "I guess Thomas

Jefferson, one of the Founding Fathers of our nation, principal author of the Declaration of Independence, *and* the third president of the United States, trumps Robert E. Lee."

Margaret rolled her eyes and sipped her drink.

"The research is absolutely fascinating. I mean there's so much you can learn from DNA," Mom said.

I turned to Margaret. "I feel like there's so little we know about you." I hoped my voice sounded interesting. "Like, I don't even know where you're from. Do you have brothers and sisters, children?"

Something flashed across Margaret's face and, for a moment, I thought I saw fear in her eyes. However, the emotion vanished as quickly as it appeared.

"Why would you want to know?" she asked.

"Since we're going to be family, I think it would be good to get to know each other. I can start. I was married to my husband, Leon, for twenty-five years but he died about eighteen months ago. We were never blessed with children, but I've been very fortunate." I looked down the table at Dawson and across at my nephews, who were still talking about DNA and biology with Harold and my mom. A bit of their conversation drifted toward me. Dawson was talking about his biology class and how he'd learned about dominant and recessive genes. I had a flash and a moment of clarity.

"Good for you." Margaret took a sip from her glass. Obviously, she wasn't in a mood to share.

"Perhaps you were raised in a barn, but when someone asks a question, it's good manners to answer them." Nana Jo glared.

"I have no desire to get to know any of you people," Margaret sneered. "Don't think I haven't done my research. I know all about that juvenile delinquent and his alcoholic father that you've befriended and tried to pass off as a part of your family." She glanced at Lexi and Angelo. "Apparently, you've picked up two more orphans from God only knows where."

The room had gotten very quiet as all eyes turned to the fight brewing between Nana Jo and Margaret. I stole a glance at Dawson. His jaw clenched and a flush rose from his neck.

"How dare you?" I spoke softly and enunciated every syllable, a sure sign of my fury. "You, of all people, have no right to say one word about anyone's background."

The look of fear lingered longer this time. "What are you talking about?"

"I wonder what Robert E. Lee would have to say about Maggie Anne Tuttleford or should I say Maggie Anne Jones, because that's your name."

Margaret's face went from a bright red to ashen. "How do you know?"

"We know all about you and your real husband, Bufford Jones," I said.

"Real husband?" Oscar asked.

"That's right," Nana Jo said. "Real husband because Buford is alive and kicking, which means that Little Miss Fancy Pants is nothing more than a bigamist."

Margaret looked liked a scared, cornered rabbit. Her hand shook slightly as she took a drink from her glass. "You're both crazy."

"That's not all, is it?" I asked.

Margaret stared.

"Lydia knew. She knew you committed bigamy when you married Oscar because Bufford was . . . is her brother. Bufford Jones, who is currently incarcerated at the Polk County Jail."

Emotions of fear crossed her face.

"Lydia knew and she was blackmailing you."

Margaret put down her glass and tried to smile, but it looked more like a grimace. "You don't know anything."

"I know you've been withdrawing large amounts of money from your bank account for years. She's been bleeding you dry, which is why that sable you wear so proudly is nothing but a fake. You probably had to hock it to keep paying Lydia."

"You can't prove any of this," Margaret said.

"I know every time you made a withdrawal, Lydia made a deposit of the exact same amount." I looked at Margaret's face. "I also know Lydia was blackmailing you with more than just the fact that you're a bigamist."

Margaret's eyes narrowed. She stood up. "I don't have to take this."

"Sit down!" Nana Jo ordered. She reached for her purse, but it slipped onto the floor. Her gun fell out.

Both Margaret and Nana Jo lunged for the gun, but Margaret was quicker. She grabbed it before Nana Jo could get it. Then she grabbed Lexi around the neck and put the gun to her head.

We froze.

"One step and I'll blow her head off."

We stared at Margaret. The door opened and our server entered. She took one look at the gun, dropped the tray, and ran from the room.

"Back up. Up against the wall."

Everyone rose slowly and backed up against the wall. Everyone, except me. I was frozen to the spot. I tried to force my feet to move, but they wouldn't.

"You're a lot smarter than you look." Margaret sneered. "Lydia had been bleeding me dry for years. She took every cent I had to keep her mouth shut. I hocked all of my jewels, furs, everything to pay her off. But, this was supposed to be the end. I didn't have anything left to give." She shook her head. "So, I recommended her to my wealthy friends and family so she could bleed them dry." She laughed. "Marrying her brother Bufford was the biggest mistake of my life and I've paid for it over and over again." She chuckled. "Oh, yes, I have definitely paid for it."

I took one step forward.

Margaret pushed the gun into Lexie's head and I saw her gasp. "Don't try to be a hero. I've killed once, I won't hesitate to shoot all of you."

"Please." I willed my legs to move, but, try as I might, they wouldn't budge. "Please, don't hurt her. Take me instead."

"MOVE!" she yelled.

"I can't move. I can't. Please, take me. I'll be your hostage. I'll help you get out of here. I'll drive you to the airport. I'll give you my credit card." Tears streamed down my face.

"If you take the kid, we'll call the police as soon as you leave the room. Take me." Nana Jo took a step forward. "I'm an old woman and I'm sure it would give you a great deal of pleasure to shoot me."

"Now that's a tempting offer, but something tells me you're a lot tougher than you look." She slowly walked backward toward the door, with one arm around Lexi's neck and the other pointing the gun from me to Nana Jo. She was almost to the door. A few steps and she would be out of the room. I gauged the distance and knew there was no way I could get there before she had time to fire a shot. I looked at Nana Jo, who was slowly trying to inch her way toward Margaret.

Margaret turned slightly toward the door and, in that split second, my mom walked up to Margaret, reached back, and punched her in the face with a sharp right jab. The blow stunned Margaret and she teetered. Nana Jo rushed forward and wrestled the gun from her.

I grabbed Lexi and clutched her to my chest. When I turned again, Margaret lay in a heap on the floor, blood pouring from her nose.

I stared at my mom, who stared down at Margaret on the floor. "I hope she doesn't get blood on the carpet. I think that's an Aubusson rug. They're very expensive."

Chapter 15

The police arrived shortly thereafter, and we let them know Margaret was wanted for murder in North Harbor, Michigan. They took her away in an ambulance and notified Detective Pitt so he could start the paperwork for extraditing her to Michigan. Despite a bit of shock, Lexi and Angelo both seemed to be handling the trauma fairly well. I wasn't sure if they would suffer nightmares or if they really understood how dangerous the situation really was. Neither was anxious to go to the hospital, so Zaq, Christopher, and Dawson took them home.

Oscar looked dazed. We had to run through the details of what Margaret had done several times before it actually seemed to sink in. When he finally grasped the situation, his overriding emotion seemed to be relief. He kept looking from me to Nana Jo and repeating, "You mean we weren't legally married? I'm free?"

Mom sat quietly in her chair and drank strong tea with sugar, which Harold said was good for shock.

When I finished giving my statement to the police, I went to my mom and gave her a hug. "Are you okay?"

She nodded. "Of course, dear . . . it's just so . . . unlady-like." She shook her head. "Fighting in public is just so common. I'm terribly ashamed."

I kissed her. "I'm so proud. Who knew you had such a strong right hook?" I joked.

She tsked and shook her head.

Needless to say, there was no shopping done. In fact, by the time the police left and we headed back to Michigan, I was exhausted.

There was a note on the counter of my apartment that everyone had gone to Frank's for dinner. It was only then that I realized I hadn't eaten all day. I was physically and mentally exhausted and made a grilled cheese sandwich and went to bed.

Unfortunately, sleep was elusive. After tossing and turning for close to an hour, I decided to try another tactic and pulled out my laptop.

Thompkins started to enter the servants' hall, but was halted when he saw a disturbing sight, Mrs. McDuffy sitting at the large oak table softly crying into a handkerchief. He turned to leave, but the housekeeper stopped him.

"You might as well come in." She sniffed.

Thompkins turned slowly and entered the hall. "I didn't want to interrupt."

She waved away his protest. "You'll need to hear soon enough. May as well get it over with." She looked up. "It would make things easier if you'd sit down so I don't get a stiff neck looking up at you."

The butler sat tentatively but maintained his posture as he perched on the edge of his seat.

"Turns out that cocky peacock tried to get fresh with the maids." Mrs. McDuffy pursed her lips. "Tried it with Millie and Gladys both 'e did." She huffed. "Thankfully, they wasn't fooled by 'is fancy talk and bright clothes." She made a fist with her hands.

Thompkins stared. "I take it Flossie wasn't so lucky."

Mrs. McDuffy hit the table. "Filled 'er 'ead with all kinds of nonsense about meeting film stars and important people. Told 'er 'e could get 'er in the flicks. That's what done it." She shook her head. "Silly cow."

Thompkins took a deep breath and then coughed. "How is the girl?"

Mrs. McDuffy looked up. "Well, she's been crying 'er eyes out. Scared she's going to lose 'er position, and 'er young man." She leaned toward the butler and whispered conspiratorially, "The butcher's son Tom's been sweet on 'er for years. But she wouldn't 'ave 'im." She shook her head. "Dreams of 'ollywood and meeting film stars . . . I thought it was 'armless fun. After all, I had my fancies too when I was young."

The butler frowned. It was too taxing on his imagination to think of stout, sturdy Mrs. McDuffy fanaticizing about actors.

The housekeeper looked at the butler's face and laughed. "You can't imagine me dreaming about running away with a famous actor?" She chuckled. "I 'ad my fantasies all right. I was young once meself. Although, it wasn't the cinema in my day. All we 'ad was the stage, but I tell you, sir, 'enry Irving cut a fine figure as 'amlet." She shook her head and chuckled.

Thompkins coughed. "The girl will have to leave. Her conduct—"

"What about 'is conduct? It takes two to tangle."
Her nostrils flared and her face got red. "If I 'ad 'im
'ere, I'd box 'is ears and wring 'is scrawny neck." She
pounded the table with her fist.

Thompkins stared at the housekeeper. "Someone
has beaten you to it."

Mrs. McDuffy took a deep breath. "There's one
more thing I need to tell you."

The butler waited.

"Gladys was cleaning out the nursery and . . .
well, she found something."

"What was it?"

Mrs. McDuffy pulled a white large object wrapped
in a bloody cloth from her lap and placed it on the
table.

The butler stared.

"If I'm not mistaken, I'd say it was the murder
weapon."

Daphne and James sat side by side in the library
going through the seating chart. Daphne intently
studied the layout.

James was more interested in admiring the curve
of Daphne's neck. He bent close and kissed her neck.

Daphne giggled. "James, you're not taking this seriously."

"Oh, I am very serious." He nuzzled her neck.

"I'm talking about the seating chart, silly." Daphne
turned to her beloved. "The sooner we finish, the
sooner we can move on to other things."

James quickly straightened up. "Why didn't you
say so?" He looked intently at the chart. "What do
you need me to do?"

Daphne smiled. "I need you to make sure all of your guests are correctly placed."

James frowned and pointed to one of the squares. "Percy Waddington should be on your side. I didn't invite him."

Daphne looked puzzled. "You must have invited him. I certainly didn't invite him."

James stared from the layout to Daphne. "Are you sure?"

She nodded. "I know him, but he's not a close personal friend and I only invited close friends and family."

The Marsh family, along with a few members of their inner circle convened in the library, Lady Elizabeth knitted near the fireplace.

The butler entered with a tea cart and turned to leave.

"Thompkins, I think you should stay for this meeting." Lady Elizabeth put her knitting aside and began pouring tea.

He nodded and moved to a wall and stood tall and erect.

Lady Elizabeth distributed the tea. "Now, who wants to go first?"

Lord William sat in his favorite chair while Cuddles lounged at his feet. He shared the information he'd learned from his conversation with Major Davies. "Major Davies certainly had a reason to want Philippe Claiborne dead."

Detective Inspector Covington sat in an armchair and took notes. He looked around. "James . . . ah, I mean, His Grace isn't here, but we learned there was a burglary reported at nearly every home where

Philippe Claiborne staged some large soiree. No one thought to check the event planner." He shook his head. "The boys at the Met really dropped the ball on this one. However, to be fair, they've had their hands full, chasing their tails with the Halifax Slasher nonsense." He sighed and then went back to his notes. "We can't prove it was really Philippe Claiborne who pinched the items or if he was the front man who came in and cased the place for his confederates."

"Oh my." Lady Alistair fanned herself. "How terrible."

"Dirty blackguard." Lord William beat his fist against the arm of his chair, shaking it enough to wake Cuddles.

Detective Inspector Covington stared at Lady Elizabeth. "What put you on to him?"

Lady Elizabeth sipped her tea. "I think it was the way he walked around the room the first time we met. He looked at the paintings and picked up several of the objets d'art. I think that's why he used that flamboyant persona. It made his actions fit the character he'd created." She sipped her tea. "Plus, there was the comment Helene made that reminded us."

Lady Alistair looked puzzled. "Me?"

"Yes, dear, don't you recall? You reminded me the scandal occurred at the same time Lady Catherine's tiara was stolen. It made me wonder if perhaps that stolen tiara was really important."

"Well, I never . . . I mean really."

Lady Elizabeth nodded. "Must have been buried in your subconscious."

"Victor?" Lady Elizabeth asked.

Victor gazed into the fireplace. Upon hearing his name, he started. "I beg your pardon."

"Were you able to talk to Percy Waddington?"

Victor relayed his conversation. "Seems he's been in a bad way, financially, and thought he'd bum a free stay. Nothing much to it I'm afraid."

"That explains it, then." Daphne looked around. "I have no idea where James is, but when we were going over the seating chart, we realized neither of us invited Percy Waddington to the wedding." She shrugged. "It's rather sad. He must be in an awful state to just show up in the hopes of having a place to stay."

"Hmm . . . I suppose so." Lady Elizabeth put down her cup. "I think he's an art dealer, isn't he?"

Victor nodded. "Yes. He has a shop in Mayfair."

"Rather expensive area, Mayfair," Detective Inspector Covington said.

Victor looked surprised. "You think he made it all up?"

There was silence.

Detective Inspector Covington coughed. "If Philippe Claiborne was pinching art and jewels, he'd need a fence to unload the stuff."

Victor stared. "Surely not Percy."

Lady Elizabeth turned to the detective. "Did you tell anyone how Philippe Claiborne died?"

Detective Inspector Covington shook his head. "We like to hold back some of the details. We haven't released that yet."

"So, how did Percy Waddington know he'd been stabbed in the back?" She picked up her knitting.

"There's only one way he could have known that." Detective Inspector Covington wrote in his notepad.

"Could you have someone check into his shop in Mayfair?" she asked.

The detective nodded. "I'll have someone check it out."

Lady Elizabeth knitted. After a few moments she looked up. "Thompkins, perhaps you should share what you learned from Mrs. McDuffy."

The butler coughed discreetly but stepped forward and relayed the information about Flossie. "I've offered my resignation to her ladyship but would like to apologize formally to his lordship and to accept responsibility for this incident, which has happened on my watch."

"Nonsense, man. I won't hear of it." Lord William reassured the butler. "Times are very different and young girls are . . . well, not as careful as in years gone by."

"Young girls?" Lady Penelope sat up in her chair. "Why are the young girls to blame? If you ask me, its men like Philippe Claiborne who're to blame. They waltz into a house and fill a young girl's head with promises and then, after he's had his way, he tosses her aside like a piece of garbage." Her eyes flashed and her face flushed.

"I heartily agree," Lady Daphne chimed in. "Besides, I hardly think it fair Flossie should lose her job and be tossed out on the streets because of the likes of Philippe Claiborne."

Lady Elizabeth raised a hand. "No one is being tossed out of the house." She turned to the butler. "Thompkins, I appreciate your concern for the family's reputation, but as far as I'm concerned, it's over and no one will lose their job."

The butler bowed stiffly. He then told the family about the knife.

"Good Lord," Lord William said.

Detective Inspector Covington flipped his notebook. "I sent the weapon back to the yard for analysis. Amazing what they can find nowadays. Not just fingerprints, but hair and nails and all kinds of information. Those blokes in the crime lab can tell you just about everything by looking through their microscopes these days."

Lady Penelope looked distressed. "I don't understand. Surely you don't believe those children had anything to do with murdering Philippe Claiborne?"

Detective Inspector Covington shook his head. "No. I talked to the boys after Thompkins showed me the knife." He sighed. "Turns out one of the twins overheard the duke and Lady Elizabeth arguing with Claiborne." He flipped through his notebook. "Johan it was." He looked up. "He didn't want any of the family to be blamed, so he took the knife and hid it." He smiled. "Thought he was protecting them."

Penelope relaxed. "That's so sweet." She wiped tears away. "I know it was naughty for them to take the knife, and it had to be really scary for them to remove a knife from a dead body." She sniffed. "I hope you won't punish them." She stared at the detective sternly.

Detective Inspector Covington shook his head. "I explained to them"—he looked at Thompkins—"with the assistance of Thompkins's son-in-law, that he didn't need to worry."

"The poor boy probably doesn't know how things are handled in a civilized nation like England." Lord William chomped on his pipestem.

Lady Elizabeth knitted for several moments in quiet thought.

"What's bothering you?" Lord William asked. "I know that look in your eyes. You've figured out something."

Lady Elizabeth finished the row she was knitting. "I just think it's very unusual that of all the houses Percy Waddington could have chosen that he chooses us."

"What do you mean?" Detective Inspector Covington leaned forward.

"Don't you remember what Lady Alistair told us? When she mentioned the stolen tiara, she also mentioned Percy Waddington's sister, Mary?" She turned to Lady Alistair.

"Percy Waddington's sister, Mary, was supposed to marry Sir Wilbur Hampton, but he refused to marry her. It was a big scandal at the time." She sipped her tea. "They say the poor girl had a nervous breakdown. The family sent her off to stay with relatives in Australia. The last I heard, she's still there."

"I think I see what you're thinking." Lady Penelope leaned forward.

"How can we verify something like that?" Lady Daphne flushed.

"It would certainly provide a good motive." Lady Elizabeth turned to Detective Inspector Covington. "I suppose there would be records at Somerset House?"

Detective Inspector Covington nodded. "It'll take time."

"It would be in bad taste, but wouldn't it be faster if we just asked Sir Wilbur?" Lady Alistair asked.

Lady Elizabeth nodded. "Leave it to me."

Lord William looked around from his wife to his nieces. "Confounded, I wish someone would enlighten me." He pounded his fist on the arm of his chair.

Lady Elizabeth smiled. "I'll explain it to you later, dear."

Chapter 16

The next few days flew by. Between the Christmas rush at the bookstore, getting ready for the wedding, and preparing Lexi and Angelo to reunite with their Italian relatives, it was a busy time. Initially, Nana Jo and I had decided not to tell Lexi or Angelo about their relatives, but when Frank received word their family planned to travel to Michigan to spend time with them, we were forced to share.

Lexi took the information rather stoically. She didn't remember her relatives, which might have been a result of the car accident. She was grateful she wouldn't have to return to the Hoopers, but she was torn between leaving us and being with her family. Angelo was too young to be anything but excited.

It turned out getting passports for Lexi and Angelo wasn't as long of an ordeal as it typically could be in the United States. They were born in Italy, and the Italian government was able to expedite replacement passports. I had several calls from Italy. My side of the conversations were short, but since Frank, Lexi, and Angelo all spoke Italian, they served as translators.

I got a real Christmas tree for the first time in years. When Leon and I were first married, we always had a real Christmas tree. As the years went by, we stopped taking the time. I bought an artificial tree with lights attached that involved connecting four pieces and plugging it into an outlet. After Leon died, I didn't even bother taking the artificial tree out of the box and settled for a wreath on the front door to appease my family and stop all references to the Grinch and Scrooge. This year felt different. Something about having children in the house made me want to get a real Christmas tree and pull out all of my decorations.

One of the many presents wrapped and under the tree for Lexi and Angelo was a large suitcase. When I learned they would be leaving right after the wedding, I let Lexi open it. She used the suitcase like a chest of drawers and kept her clothes in it.

I barely saw Lexi, Jillian, or Emma as they rushed to get the Yacht Club decorated for the reception. Fortunately, April decided to help out. She said she felt guilty for Lydia's plans to bilk money from Harold. However, I suspected it might have been a desire to remain close to Rudy Blakemore. My feelings for April were complicated. She was aware of what Lydia did and, while she could have gone to the police, she chose not to. In the end, I decided to forgive and forget. It was the season for giving and forgiveness was one of the greatest gifts we had. It was true April was aware of Lydia's deceptions, but she was just as much of a victim as Lydia's clients. In the end, April proved herself to be an excellent organizer and we were all extremely grateful. So grateful, in fact, that Nana Jo invited her to the bachelorette party Nana Jo and the girls insisted on throwing for my mom at the Four Feathers. Not to be outdone, Frank and Tony arranged a similar gig for Harold.

A Hummer limousine as long as a city block picked up those of us who were over twenty-one, while the younger crowd had an overnight sleepover at the Avenue. Harold paid for the hotel rooms, pizza, movies, and games.

The ride to the casino was certainly entertaining. Champagne flowed freely. Irma opened the sunroof and stood on the seat so she could stick her head out of the top of the car. Unfortunately, it was freezing and she failed to account for the wind. So, when she stuck her head out, her beehive hairpiece nearly flew off. Had Nana Jo not pulled her down by the seat of her pants, she might have been extremely embarrassed.

I leaned close to my sister and whispered, "Hummer limousine rental, one hundred fifty dollars per hour. Bachelorette party at the Four Feathers, including three hotel rooms, free food, alcohol, and casino bucks, twelve hundred dollars. Watching Irma's hairpiece flapping in the wind while traveling seventy miles an hour on Interstate 94, priceless."

The look in my sister's eyes was a cross between a deer caught in the headlights and "I can't believe I just saw that."

I couldn't help laughing and she eventually joined in.

"Are they always like this?"

I wiped a tear from my eye. "This is nothing. You should see them once they're good and liquored up."

The fright in Jenna's eyes caused me to laugh harder. Over the past few months I had grown accustomed to Nana Jo and the girls and long ago shed any layers of sensitivity and embarrassment. Clearly, Jenna had a few layers left.

Endless food and alcohol, plus a desire to let your hair down and party, made the night at the casino a lot more exciting than our typical girls' nights to the Four Feathers. We dined together with the men but would be separating soon after.

In the private dining room, in one of the casino's restaurants, we all enjoyed watching a Japanese Hibachi chef slice, dice, and fillet an amazing meal. I found myself sitting next to April.

"How are you holding up?" I asked.

"Apart from the occasional morning sickness, I'm doing great." She smiled. "I wish I could drink something stronger than a Coke." She patted her tummy. "However, all things considered, I'm very happy."

"You look happy." I stared at her closely. I'd heard pregnant women had a glow, but I honestly hadn't met too many pregnant women I'd describe as glowing until now. I wasn't sure if her clear skin, bright eyes, and shining hair were due to the bun in her oven, freedom from Lydia's tyranny, or the fact she was, obviously, in love. Whatever the reason, April looked less like a mouse and more like a vibrant woman.

"I never realized how much working for Lydia took out of me. I feel like a heavy weight has been lifted from my shoulders." She looked up and smiled. "I know it sounds horrible, but I feel so relieved."

"That doesn't sound horrible at all. Will you be staying in North Harbor?"

April shrugged. "I don't know. Rudy's here and he wants me to stay." She smiled shyly. "I think it would be nice for him to be around for the baby. I don't really have any family, so it doesn't really matter where I live.

Mom was sitting nearby and I hadn't realized she heard our conversation. "Well, you have family here. Harold is working on convincing Oscar to move back to the area and he is your stepfather. I think you should stay and open a wedding planning business right here."

"What do you mean?" She stared openedmouthed. "Oscar is my step . . . father?" She stared from Mom to Oscar at the other end of the table.

Mom fluttered. "I'm so sorry, dear. I thought that detective told you?"

"Told me what?" April stared from me to Mom.

"Margaret Robertson was your biological mother. I thought you knew."

April looked pale and I grew concerned for her health. "Take a drink of water." I handed her a glass. "Detective Pitt was supposed to have told you."

She drank from her glass.

"Why that lazy flatfoot gives policemen a bad name," Nana Jo said.

"I'm so sorry you had to find out like this." Mom reached out a hand to April.

She stared at Mom but then shook her head as though shaking away the cobwebs. "He said they didn't know for sure . . . He thought it was either Lydia or Margaret, but he said I wouldn't know for sure until DNA results came back."

"Pshaw." Mom waved a hand as though whisking away the very notion. "Anyone with a brain could see Lydia couldn't possibly be your mother."

I stared at my mom. "How can you be so sure?"

Mom stared at me. "Weren't you paying attention the other day at Tippecanoe Place when we were talking about biology and genealogy?"

"I might have been distracted by the hostage situation and the gun Margaret was pointing at Lexi. Perhaps you could enlighten me?"

Mom shook her head. "Lydia had red hair and blue eyes. When we first met her, she mentioned that everyone in her family had red hair and blue eyes. She specifically mentioned her husband, her brother, and her parents." Mom stopped as though everything should be crystal clear now.

Still puzzled, I stared and shook my head.

"April has brown hair. Red hair and blue eyes are recessive genes. It would be rare for two redheaded, blue-eyed people to have a brown-haired, brown-eyed child. However, Margaret has dark hair. Margaret has to be her mother."

I stared at my mom, but this time in awe rather than surprise.

She continued, "So, April will pass along the red hair and blue eye genes she got from Bufford Jones, her father, to her baby. But unless your . . . ah . . . partner carries the same gene, then your child will most likely have dark hair and eyes, like you." Mom smiled. "Dark hair and eyes are dominant."

I was impressed. "You found all this out through that DNA test you sent?"

She smiled. "I researched it and Harold knows a lot about biology. He explained some of it, but really, it seems pretty easy to understand."

A flash of joy crossed April's face but quickly vanished and was replaced by sadness. "I always knew I was adopted. I lived with so many different foster families, I stopped counting." She looked at her belly. "You can't help wondering about your parents." She laughed. "When I was small, I used to imagine all kinds of tragic stories about what happened to them." She swallowed hard and sighed. "I never dreamed my parents would both turn out to be criminals. My mother was a bigamist and a murderer." She looked cautiously at Oscar, but he was too far away and not listening.

Mom reached over and patted April's hand. "You can't choose your biological parents, but that doesn't mean you will inherit their criminal behaviors. Now, you need to eat more leafy greens and milk. You're pregnant." She turned to Harold, who immediately sent a waiter to get a salad and a glass of milk.

April tried to protest, but I knew she was wasting her time. Harold had been given a task to complete and he would make sure it got done.

After dinner, the two groups split up along gender lines. There was a great deal of alcohol and dancing involved with the girls' group. I was prepared for a rowdy night with Nana Jo and the girls. However, I might never recover from the shock of seeing my mom and my grandmother dancing atop the bar. I looked at Jenna, who was staring with her mouth open.

"I may need therapy after this," she said.

The limo meant I didn't have to worry about being the designated driver, but I still wasn't interested in drinking. I guessed old habits died hard. Instead, I found a quiet corner, sat down, and pulled my notepad out of my bag.

Detective Inspector Covington paced in front of the fireplace in the library at Wickfield Lodge. He was dressed in the tuxedo he'd purchased for the first murder at Wickfield Lodge. He smiled as he looked at his reflection in the window.

Thompkins opened the door. "Percy Waddington," he announced and then turned and walked out, closing the door.

The detective glanced from Waddington to Lady Elizabeth. Receiving a slight nod, he took control. "It took a while to get the proof we needed, but we got it."

Percy Waddington looked from the detective to Lord William and Lady Elizabeth. "I don't know what you mean. Proof, what proof?"

Lord James Browning rushed into the room. He halted at the sight of the detective with Percy Waddington. "You haven't arrested him yet? The wedding starts in less than half an hour."

Percy Waddington stood. "Arrested?"

Detective Inspector Covington sighed. "I was getting to that."

"Getting to it? You'd better get on with it. I need this wrapped up before the wedding." He smoked and paced rapidly. "Get on with it."

Percy Waddington continued to look from the duke to the detective as though watching a tennis match. "Look, I don't know what this is about, but I think you've got the wrong man."

Lady Elizabeth, dressed in a beautiful long gown, rose from her chair and turned to the detective. "I think James is right. William has to get upstairs shortly, and it would be wonderful if we could get this wrapped up before the wedding."

"I was just about to—"

Thompkins opened the door again. "Constable Freeman."

The constable entered the room and stood by, unsure which direction to go.

Detective Inspector Covington took a step toward Percy Waddington. "Percy Waddington, I—"

Waddington tried to back away from the door. "I don't know what this is about."

Penny opened the door. "What's going on? James, Father Timmons is looking for you." She turned to her uncle. "And you'd better get upstairs before Daphne has a meltdown."

Lord William got up and hurried to the door. Before he left, he turned and looked at Detective Inspector Covington. "Get on with it, man."

Detective Inspector Covington huffed. "Percy Waddington, I—"

The door opened and Victor entered. "James, we've really got to get in the parlor or there'll be hell to pay."

"I'm trying." James turned to Percy Waddington.

"Look, I don't have time for this. We know you killed Philippe Claiborne. You were partners. He stole art and jewelry and you fenced it. Now, you can either go along with the constable nicely or I'll punch your lights out."

The blood drained from Waddington's face. "Why would I . . ."

"Claiborne seduced your sister and when he found out she was with child, he dumped her," Victor said.

"When Sir Wilbur found out, he refused to marry her. Your family shuffled her off to relatives in Australia," Lady Elizabeth added quickly.

"So, when you heard Philippe Claiborne was here, you made your way and stabbed him," James added. "You totally gave yourself away when we talked."

"I don't know what you're talking about." Waddington stood, trembling.

"You said you didn't know Philippe Claiborne well enough to stick a knife in his back and then strangle him," Victor said.

"The police withheld that information. They never revealed how Mr. Claiborne was killed," Lady Elizabeth said.

"So, the only way you could have known that he was stabbed and strangled was if you were the one who killed him." Victor pulled out his pocket watch.

"Now, go along with the nice constable or I'll break your scrawny neck." James stepped toward Percy Waddington. Although, Lord James Browning wasn't an extremely tall man, he was solid.

Percy Waddington looked from James to Victor to the two police.

Detective Inspector Covington held up a piece of paper. "I have proof."

Percy Waddington pulled a gun from inside his jacket and waved it from James to Victor as he inched backward toward the door. "Don't move. I'm going to walk out of here and—"

The door swung open suddenly.

Virginia Hall, a tall, dark-haired American spy, entered. Despite having only one leg, Virginia Hall was a top-notch agent and a crack shot. She reached down and pulled up the skirt of her dress, revealing a small caliber gun strapped to her wooden leg. She grabbed the gun, pointed her weapon, and fired at Percy Waddington. The gun fell from his hand.

Percy, dazed and clutching his bleeding hand, stared at the well-dressed, gun-toting American.

James looked from Virginia to Percy. "Oh, bugger it all. I don't have time for this." James reached back and slugged Percy Waddington in the nose with a sharp right hook.

Percy Waddington crumpled like a rag doll.

Victor turned to Virginia. "Glad you could make it."

"I wouldn't have missed it for the world." She smiled. "Now, you better get going or there'll be another body."

Detective Inspector Covington nodded. "You better go. We'll take care of this." He looked at Percy, still sprawled out on the floor.

Victor, Virginia, and James rushed out of the room just as the first strains of "The Wedding March" began to play.

Percy Waddington was quietly and discreetly removed from the premises. James and Daphne were married in the presences of friends, family, and loyal and dedicated servants. If guests wondered why the Marshes' traditional Christmas decorations also included a menorah, no one bothered to ask. The wedding dinner prepared by Mrs. Anderson was scrumptious and kosher friendly, thanks to Thompkins's son-in-law, Joseph Mueller.

Daphne was radiant. James wasn't the only one who gasped at first sight of her. The celebration went on late into the night. A few minutes before midnight, the couple slipped away for a few quiet moments on the terrace overlooking the hedge maze. Neither of them seemed to notice the cold weather as they snuggled together and watched the dawning of one of the most religious days of the year.

James turned to face his new bride. "Happy Christmas."

Daphne's face radiated pure love and happiness. "Happy Christmas to you too."

He pulled her close and kissed her passionately and intensely. When he finally released her, she snuggled into his chest.

"I'm so incredibly happy. I think the world is a wonderful place, and I'm so excited to start our new life together."

James was silent.

Daphne turned and looked at her husband.

James gazed into the night sky. After several moments, he said, "I feel like an absolute rotter to be so incredibly happy when I know there is so much pain and suffering in the world." He looked at Daphne. "There are going to be dark days ahead. All signs indicate we may be headed into another war soon." He looked away. "You realize if England needs me, I'll have to go. I shouldn't have—"

Daphne pressed her fingers gently over his lips. "I know."

James shook his head and tried to speak, but she halted him. "I know. I know you work for MI5. I know you have registered for war service. I know if there's a war, you'll likely be called to serve." She stared into his eyes. "I knew exactly what I was getting into when I agreed to marry you, and I'm so proud of you and proud to be your wife."

James pulled Daphne close and nearly crushed her as he kissed her ardently. "You're amazing."

She smiled. "No, I'm just a woman. Women have been supporting the British Empire in much the same way for centuries. We've supported our husbands, brothers, and fathers as they've gone off to war and fought incredible battles to keep the empire safe. I'll do the same." She frowned. "I can't say I'll enjoy it, but I know my duty too." She lifted her chin proudly. "Hail Britannia."

Hours later, when all of the guests were gone, Victor noticed Penelope outside on the terrace in the same spot James and Daphne had occupied earlier. He hurried outside and draped his jacket around his wife's arms. "You'll catch your death of cold out here."

Penelope continued to gaze into the night sky. "On a night like tonight, the stars are so bright. It's easy to imagine a star guiding shepherds and wise men to a stable."

Victor tore his gaze from his wife to the sky but immediately turned back to her. "Look, I've been

wanting to talk to you for some time now." He swallowed hard. "Now the wedding is over, I'm taking you
to the doctor. You've been sick and tired and . . .
well, I'm taking you to the doctor and that's that."

Penelope smiled and then turned and whispered
in her husband's ear.

Victor's face went from concern to elation in a
flash. "Are you sure?"

Penelope smiled. "I wasn't at first until Aunt
Elizabeth suggested it to me, but Dr. Haygood confirmed it."

Victor kissed his wife and spun her around but
quickly stopped. "Sorry, are you okay? Maybe you
should sit down."

Penelope laughed. "I'm fine."

Victor gazed into his wife's eyes. "When?"

Penelope patted her stomach. "Dr. Haygood says
we should expect the next Earl or Countess of Lochloren
midsummer."

Victor looked at his wife's stomach. "I can't believe it. I'm going to be a father. Why didn't you tell
me sooner? Does anyone else know?"

She shook her head. "At first, I didn't know myself. I wasn't positive. Once I knew, well, I decided to
wait until after the wedding. I didn't want anything to
overshadow Daphne and James's big day."

"Is that why you've spent so much time with the
children from the Kindertransport?" Victor asked
softly.

Penelope smiled. "I don't know. I feel so badly
that they've had things so hard."

"I thought you might want to keep them," he
said.

Penelope smiled. "When things settle down, I suspect Thompkins's daughter, Mary, and his son-in-law, Joseph Mueller, may want to take the children. They haven't had children of their own and they've been so helpful."

She pulled her husband's arms around her and looked up at the stars.

The two stood that way for some time. Eventually, Penny said, "I can't help thinking about another baby that was born on this date."

Victor squeezed her tightly. "Happy Christmas."

"Happy Christmas."

The next day, Harold and Grace were married in a small but elegant wedding. Ruby Mae's granddaughter sang and Tony accompanied her on the piano. It had been a long time since I'd heard my brother-in-law play. I'd nearly forgotten what a great musician he was. The happy couple went to the Yacht Club, which was beautifully decorated. Frank was busy making sure the food was hot and presented in the best possible light. The pièce de résistance was the wedding cake. A nervous, but extremely proud, Dawson created a work of art, complete with roses, pearls, flowers, leaves, and a fleur-de-lis border. The four tiers were each elegant and extremely beautiful. Mom took one look at the cake and burst into tears.

Dawson's face turned ashen. "You don't like it?"

Mom grabbed his face in her hands. "Not like it? I love it. It's the most beautiful cake I've ever seen." She kissed him. "It means all the more to me because you made it."

Dawson blushed.

The cake was as delicious as it was beautiful.

Lexi and Angelo were perfect angels and looked great in

their fancy clothes. I got misty-eyed thinking about how much I would miss them when they left. Their aunt and uncle, Jerri and Ryan Cachero, would be arriving early next week and their grandparents would be here soon afterward. I couldn't believe how quickly I got attached.

I looked around the room, amazed at my new extended family. From Harold and Mom to Nana Jo and the girls to Dawson, Jillian, Emma, and now Lexi and Angelo, my life was full of friendship and love. The clock struck midnight and we all raised a glass in salute.

This year, I said, with a full heart, "Merry Christmas and Happy New Year."

Connect with

Us

Visit us online at
KensingtonBooks.com
to read more from your favorite authors, see books
by series, view reading group guides, and more.

Join us on social media

for sneak peeks, chances to win books and prize packs,
and to share your thoughts with other readers.

facebook.com/kensingtonpublishing
twitter.com/kensingtonbooks

Tell us what you think!

To share your thoughts, submit a review,
or sign up for our eNewsletters, please visit:
KensingtonBooks.com/TellUs.